HIS RULE

THE RITE TRILOGY BOOK 1

A. ZAVARELLI
NATASHA KNIGHT

Copyright © 2022 by A. Zavarelli & Natasha Knight
All rights reserved.
No part of this book may be reproduced in any form or by any electronic or mechanical means, including information storage and retrieval systems, without written permission from the author, except for the use of brief quotations in a book review.

Cover by CoverLuv
Photograph by Wander Aguiar

1

MERCEDES

Blood.

Every time I close my eyes, I see it. That pungent metallic odor still burns my nostrils, and it's seeped so deep into my flesh, I can't wash it away. I know because I've been trying for well over thirty minutes. My skin burns as the spray from the shower pelts the areas I've rubbed raw, but I can't feel sorry for myself. This is the least of what I deserve.

My eyes are swollen, and it hurts to shed more tears, but I let them fall because this is the only time I have. I can't allow the world to see me vulnerable. Santiago can't witness me crumbling any more than he already has. The De La Rosa blood runs through my veins, and we are not weak. So I try again to burn the image of the lifeless corpse from my mind. I blink through my tears, hoping to wash away the memory of her battered and bloodied face.

It doesn't work.

She's everywhere. The entire car ride here, she haunted me. As Santiago's tires crunched over the gravel, all I could hear were the shards of broken glass beneath my blood-streaked heels. Every muscle in my body aches even though I made it out with little more than a gash on my cheek and some bruises that will inevitably fade. Time has a way of dealing with wounds, at least physically. But there is no cure for a broken spirit.

I can't forget the look in my brother's eyes when he saw me tonight. When he came to my rescue, the way he always has. I tried to explain it away, the way I always have. It was never intentional. I just needed to make things right. I was going to take that woman back to him so he could punish her for the things she'd done. But it didn't work out that way. My flimsily constructed plan blew up in my face, and by the end of the night, it was my hands stained with her blood. There was no pride in what I'd done. Santiago certainly wasn't proud.

He looked at me like I was a monster, and the worst part was, I couldn't deny it. That's what I've become, isn't it? It's why he brought me here, to the IVI compound instead of the safety of the manor. He doesn't want me tainting the halls of our family home with the misery that seems to follow me everywhere. Now, there's a voice in the back of my mind, whispering the fate I don't want to accept.

He's going to send me away.

As I step out of the shower, I try to muster up some denial, pacifying myself with paper-thin assurances. Santiago is the only family I've got left. He wouldn't hurt me. Not like this. Not when he knows the pain of losing everyone we've ever loved. Our grief tethers us together for life. Our blood is the same. Our loyalty is unshakable. It's the one truth I have to cling to.

I can be difficult. Intolerable at times. I won't deny that. But he loves me regardless. He protects me, and I'm certain he always will. I can accept his disappointment in me. I can find a way to bear his shame, which can't be worse than my own. But I will show him there's still something in me to love. Something worth salvaging. I just have to pull myself together and figure it out. The way I always do.

I release a few shuddering breaths and force my gaze to the reflection in the mirror. I don't recognize the person staring back at me. The woman with the long black hair and dark eyes may as well be a stranger. I feel detached from her. Empty. And it's a fucking relief.

That means numbness is setting in. As long as I can stay like this... unfeeling, I can survive.

Robotically, I brush my hair and dress in the

cheap sweats Santi bought me on the way here. They are a far cry from my usual clothing, but I don't care. I'm exhausted, and I need to face him. I need to show him that it's okay. I'll find a way to fix everything.

When I emerge from the bathroom, my brother stands by the window, his gaze unfocused as he peers through the glass. I know he feels my presence, and he certainly heard me open the door, but it takes him a few moments to turn and face me. His expression is guarded, his eyes equally anguished and frustrated. It sets me on edge, the tightness in my chest gripping my breath like a vise.

"Santi." My strangled voice forces his name out. "Why are we here?"

He swallows the words he doesn't want to say, and it hits me like a punch to the gut. Even so, I can't accept it. I have to believe there's a purpose for me being here other than what my instincts are screaming at me.

"Tell me everything," he orders in true De La Rosa fashion.

I make myself move, taking a seat on the bed, my hands twisting together in my lap. "I will. But I need you to promise you won't hate me. No matter what. I need to hear that from you."

"I can't promise you anything." He glares at me.

A quiet sob slips from my lips before I can stop it, and tears hover precariously on the edges of my eyes as I turn and try to wipe them away. So much for being numb. I swore I wasn't going to do this, but for the first time in my life, I really can't control it. I hate crying. I despise it. And more than anything, I hate that I allowed my brother to see such a display of emotion. If our father were here right now, he would have backhanded me into the next week for showing such cowardice.

"Now, Mercedes," Santiago clips out. "If you don't tell me now, you will decide for both of us. You will never hear from me again."

Horror washes over me as I glance up at him, blurting the words out before I can think about how pathetic it makes me look. "No, you can't do that!"

"You aren't in a position to argue anymore." He turns back toward the window, reaching for the curtain as he glances down into the courtyard again.

I'm terrified of what he might be looking for, but I'm even more terrified that he'll follow through on his threat. If my brother disowns me, I'll have nothing left.

"It wasn't supposed to happen this way," I cry out. "I never meant for any of this to happen. I was just so irritated with you, Santi. To see the way you looked at that Moreno girl. You were falling for her right before my eyes. I could see it, and it felt like such a betrayal."

He releases the curtain and turns to look at me, his pity unmistakable. He can see my jealousy for what it is, but I don't care. What did he expect? He betrayed our family when he married the enemy. He committed the most egregious crime he could by falling for her. And in the end, instead of following through on our plans as he had promised, he ousted me from the scheme entirely. Our revenge fell by the wayside, and now he's making his own little family with the blood we swore we'd extinguish from this earth.

"She was going to take you away from me," I snap. "I had to do something. I just wanted to make her hate you. So I hired that courtesan who used to work for IVI to lure you away at the gala and seduce you. Ivy was supposed to come out of the bathroom and see you together. That was it. Nobody was ever supposed to get hurt."

He's quiet as he paces across the room, refusing to look at me, and in my desperation for his understanding, I rush to get the rest out. I go on to explain how I knew it was a stupid idea, but I thought I could trust her. I could never have predicted that she was in bed with the enemy too. That mistake almost cost Santiago his life, and I was trying to make it right. That's why I went to the courtesan's apartment tonight. I just wanted to make it right, so he'd forgive me.

"How can I believe anything you tell me?" He turns and shakes his head. "How can I believe any of what you're telling me now is even true?"

"Because she told me so herself!" I bellow.

"When you were beating it out of her?"

The silence is deafening as I try to recover from that fatal blow, the reminder I don't need. He doesn't have to tell me what happened. I'll never forget.

"It wasn't like that," I whisper on a shaky breath. "I was fighting for my life. I didn't mean to kill her, but I had no choice. It was either her or me."

Santiago collapses into the chair by the door, and I can see that nothing I've said has managed to soften his anger. It eats at me, and I just wish he'd look at me for one second without complete revulsion. As I consider that it might never happen, a fresh wave of tears washes over me.

"Would you rather it was me? Is that it? Do you wish it were me who was dead on that floor?"

"What I would have rathered was that you never lied to me at all!" he roars. "You betrayed me. You schemed. You nearly fucking killed me. My own sister. Do you understand that?"

I suck in a sharp breath and stare at him pleadingly. "I would rather die than hurt you, brother. Please believe that, if nothing else."

His eyes move over me, his grief palpable. He feels as if he's lost me too. But instead of death, it was the darkness that stole me. I'm too far beyond redemption, and he's tired of trying to save me. I can feel it in my bones. It rattles my teeth, and for a second, the agony makes me wish I were actually dead. Perhaps that would have been the best outcome for everyone tonight. If I'd given up the fight and let her win, at least I wouldn't have had to witness this anguish from the one person who's always loved me, even at my worst. I wouldn't have to feel him giving up on me.

"Get in bed and try to get some sleep," he says quietly.

"What's going to happen now?" I argue.

"Now, you are going to get some sleep," he repeats. "And when you wake up, you will start fresh."

Hope breathes anew as I watch his posture relax with a sigh. I can see his resolve, his acceptance that we have no choice but to move forward and put this behind us. For a moment, a calm settles over me. Nothing is all right, and it won't be for a long time, but Santiago isn't giving up on me. Blood is the unbreakable bond that can't be severed. We've been through too much. We've come too far to abandon each other in a time like this.

That relief wraps me in a warm cocoon, and I don't dare utter another word. Santi is the head of our household, and in our world, that means his word is law. It doesn't matter that I'm twenty-five years old. It's his job to look after me, and he takes it very seriously. I haven't been taking it seriously enough. I've already tested him too many times, and I know we're on tenuous ground at best.

As I climb into bed and quietly secure myself beneath the covers, it's a small way of showing him that I can listen. I can abide by the rules of The Society and do what's expected of me. I can prove that I'm worthy again and find a way to move forward, even if I'm broken inside.

When I close my eyes, that moment of warmth expanding in my chest is blotted out by the darkness as the reminder of what I've done haunts me all over again. I see her face. I feel her blood dripping from my hands as I stumble back with the horrifying realization that I've killed someone. It torments me. It grabs me and doesn't let me go until eventually, by some miracle, exhaustion steals me away.

I wake with a jolt, my breath hissing between my teeth as fragments of the insidious nightmare try to drag me back to the hell that unfolded only hours ago. Or was it hours? As I bolt upright, fear crawls up my spine, tickling every one of my senses. How long have I been asleep? Was it all a dream? Could that even be possible?

My eyes adjust to the darkness, and I stare at the figures sitting across from each other in the shadows. Dread curdles the blood in my veins.

"Santi?" My voice fractures as I cling to the covers around me. "What's going on?"

He rises from his seat, his back rigid, and I want to believe I'm confused. I'm not awake at all, but still trapped in a nightmare somehow.

"You are dangerous," he says softly. "And you have proven that I can't trust you. Not in my home. Not in my life. And now, there is only one solution that can save you."

I'm shaking my head in denial as my eyes move to the other figure. The one sitting like a silent warden as he watches me in the dim light. Instinctively, I know who he is. I've known him for years. He's Santi's friend, and more importantly, he's tasked with the Rite of my care should anything ever happen to my brother. Lawson "Judge" Montgomery is an unyielding, razor-sharp beast of a man. He's as cold-hearted as they come, and he lets it be known in the harsh way he delivers his verdicts, both in the courtroom and outside of it. Nobody dares to question him. Nobody dares to challenge him. Few can even really look him in the eye, and I have to admit, I find myself among that crowd. He terrifies me in ways I can't admit to myself, but the idea of him stealing me away leaves my heart racing and my head pounding.

"No," I shriek, yanking the covers off me. "You can't send me away. You can't!"

"It's done." Santiago nods to Judge, and I scramble from the bed, trying to force my stiff limbs to cooperate.

Judge steps forward, and for one split second, our eyes lock, and I freeze. I'm too emotional to understand what's happening, but something in his gaze tells me it's going to be okay. He silently implores me to listen and not to make this difficult, and for a moment, I want to believe in that false comfort. I want to collapse into his arms, if for no other reason than I need someone to comfort me right now. Just for a minute. But I would have to be delusional to believe Judge could ever offer that to me. He didn't come here to soothe me. He came to capture me.

I bolt for Santiago, prepared to beg and plead for my life. I will do anything, say anything... but I don't even make it to him. Judge intercepts me, snatching me from the side and wrapping a steel arm around my waist, yanking me back against his huge frame.

An agonizing sound heaves from my lungs as I try to fight, but it's useless. Within seconds, he has my arms pinned behind my back and my body snug against his. I'm too exhausted to challenge him. I've already fought for my life once tonight. Now, all I can do is scream.

"Santi, please don't do this!"

"Go," Judge tells him. "I will handle this."

My brother looks at me one last time, and all I can see is his betrayal.

"You won't do this to me," I whisper. "I know you won't."

"It's already done." He tears his gaze away and doesn't glance back as he walks out the door.

"Shh," Judge murmurs against my ear as I let out

one last wail. "That's enough now. Just relax. Don't make this any worse, Mercedes. I don't want to hurt you."

It isn't his threat that makes my body collapse against him. It's my adrenaline crashing, something else taking over. It's so heavy, I can't move. I have nothing left to fight for. The one person I thought would always protect me just discarded me like I'm nothing. And surely, there is something more terrifying on the horizon in the clutches of this man, but right now, I can't see anything but the truth in front of me.

My life as I know it is over.

2

JUDGE

The door closes, the sound of it a demarcation of time. A forking of the road in all of our lives.

Mercedes watches the space where her brother stood for a long moment as if waiting for the door to reopen and for him to reappear. Not quite believing what's happened, she goes limp in my arms, an anguished sound coming from somewhere deep inside her.

I loosen my hold but don't release her. She looks up at me, her face streaked with tears, the delicate skin around her eyes puffy. A bruise is forming around the gash on her cheek, and damp hair sticks to her forehead.

"Let me go," she says, her voice like that of a wounded animal.

I release her wrists and take my arm from her middle.

She slips away, putting space between us, and her gaze moves to the exit behind me.

"Don't," I tell her.

She's quiet as she considers her options. A part of me hopes she'll try to run for it and go after her brother. He won't save her. What's done is done. But I'm not sure she's finished trying. Mercedes De La Rosa is a woman used to getting her way.

"What are you going to do?" she asks in a tone she reserves for staff. She wants to wound, but I know her too well. She may not realize that, but it's true. And I see this as her attempt to deflect attention from herself. She's vulnerable. And she doesn't like being vulnerable.

She folds her arms across her chest. Her gray sweats are a few inches short of her ankles, and her feet are bare. The matching top is too baggy. Not her usual attire. Not to mention a face free of makeup. She looks younger without it. I wonder if anyone would recognize her if I walked her out of here.

Not that it matters. She won't be leaving from the front door.

"I think you know," I say, taking a step toward her. The truth is, I want this. I want it too much. Santiago is my closest friend. The man I trust most in this world. And he trusts me. But would he give me custody of his sister if he knew just how much I wanted it?

I should have refused and told him to find someone else. Someone impartial. A better man may have. But the temptation of having Mercedes De La Rosa beneath my roof and under my control was too much to resist.

Besides, she was in no state to be refused. Neither of them were. I keep telling myself that.

She takes a step backward as I take another forward. She's known me all her life, but only ever as her big brother's confidante and friend. Apart from the time she stayed in my home while Santiago recovered at the hospital, we haven't spent much time together, and even then, I made sure to keep our interactions brief. Proper. What does she see when she looks at me now?

Her gaze flits over my shoulder to the door again, but I don't comment. If she wants to run, I'll allow it, but she won't get past me. Maybe she needs to learn that for herself. And the feel of her pressed against me moments ago, her slight weight in my arms? Well, I am a man. And we're all beasts, aren't we? Men and women alike? Animals. For all our refinement, money, and polite conversation, underneath it all, we are all just animals ruled by our baser needs. Our wants and desires.

"Are you going to put me in that cellar?" she spits, lips tight, arms hugging closer as she takes another step away until her back hits the wall. "Huh? String me up like you did her?"

Her. Ivy. She can't even say her name.

I close the space between us so I'm standing inches from her.

She tilts her head back to look up at me. At five-foot-ten, she's tall, taller when she's wearing her usual heels, but I still have about six inches on her. And even though her throat works to swallow and the pulse at her neck thrums in double time, she steels herself, gritting her jaw. Dark eyes like lasers burn into mine.

I raise my hand, and she winces.

I pause, eyebrow rising.

She presses her back to the wall and blinks.

Hair sticks to the gash on her cheek. I brush the strands away, feeling her shudder at my touch. My gaze falls to her lips. Her mouth is open, breathing shallow. And when I inhale, I smell shampoo and beneath it that acrid scent of fear.

She's afraid.

She's afraid of me.

It's how it should be. How it needs to be.

"Are you going to put me in that cellar or not? Answer me!" Lines crease the perfect skin of her forehead in her ill-fated attempt to take control of the situation.

Patience, I tell myself.

"Are you afraid of that?" I ask.

She presses her lips together and exhales through her nose. "I'm not afraid of anything."

"Not even me?"

Her eyes search mine, and she shakes her head. The little liar.

"Hm." I let the moment hang, listening to her short, trembling breaths. "No, Mercedes. You don't belong in that cellar."

She exhales with relief and closes her eyes, pressing the heels of her hands into them.

Did she really think I'd string her up like I did Ivy? Although perhaps I should. When Ivy was in my care, it was for this same reason. She was accused of being the woman who poisoned Santiago. An act Mercedes was at least partially responsible for. An act Mercedes had set her up to take the fall for.

I remember those days. How Mercedes asked what I'd do to Ivy. How she wanted to know every detail. Guilt, I realize now. That was guilt. But it was pride that never allowed her to come clean. To save Ivy from a fate she did not deserve.

And Mercedes will be punished for that.

"But you will go there if you earn it." She looks up at me again, small fists between us. I grin. "And I have a feeling you will earn it, little monster."

That does it. That burns the fire hot in her eyes. Good. Her light should not go out. Ever. And this is the work I'm tasked with. This is why Santiago entrusted his sister to me. Get her under control. Tame her. Teach her to bend but do not break her.

Mercedes shoves me as hard as she can, and when I give her an inch, she runs for it, lunging for the door.

I catch her easily, an arm around her middle lifting her off her feet. But it's a mistake because she spins, enraged, and drives her nails into my face, that wounded animal cornered and desperate, fighting for her freedom, her pride, her life.

I throw her onto the bed, then watch her bounce once and turn to scramble across it. Capturing her ankle, I tug her flat on her stomach, then set my knee on her lower back. I pin her down as I take her wrists, clutching them in one of my hands.

"Let me go! This is a mistake. Santi wouldn't do this to me! He wouldn't abandon me like this!"

"He didn't abandon you," I say, my tone calm. I reach for the black duffel I'd brought with me.

Mercedes struggles, but she must know it's pointless. Her strength is no match for mine. She turns her head to watch as I unzip the bag and take out the length of rope.

I straighten, the scratches on my face stinging. "This is the opposite of him abandoning you," I tell her as she begins her struggle anew at the sight of the rope.

"What are you doing?" she screams as I flip her

onto her back and bind her wrists, then haul her to her feet. "You can't do this to me!"

I look her over. Her hair is wild, the waistband of the too-big sweats askew from her struggle revealing an expanse of toned olive skin. I bend to take one more thing out of the duffel and hold it up for her to see.

She looks at the strip of black silk.

"Turn around, Mercedes."

She shifts her gaze from it to me. "Why?"

"Blindfold. I don't think you want me to walk you out through the courtyard."

She swallows.

"There's a secret passage, but you need to be blindfolded."

"I want to talk to my brother," she tries, the tone of her voice betraying her anxiety, her understanding of how powerless she is at this moment. But the decision has been made for her. And she will submit.

"In time. Do as I say and turn around. I'll take it off as soon as we're in the car."

Tears slip from her eyes. "Why are you doing this to me? You're supposed to be his friend."

"I am his friend. That's exactly why I'm doing this."

Silence.

More tears.

I watch, transfixed. She is so wounded. And so

fucking beautiful. I should have refused this task. The decent side of me knows this. Has known it all along. But the animal inside, it wants.

"Mercedes," I say. "You're tired. It's been a very long night. Turn around. Let's get this done and get you out of here."

"I want to go home."

"That's not happening. Not now."

"It was a mistake. I—"

"Turn around, Mercedes. I won't ask again."

She looks up at me, her lower lip trembling, stubborn pride warring against acceptance.

I set my hands on her arms and turn her, and she doesn't resist. It's the weight of the night. Of what she's done. I slide the silk cloth over her eyes. She whimpers as I secure it at the back of her head, then walk around to look at her, my little captive. Her head bowed. Delicate wrists bound by thick rope.

Something shifts inside me at the sight. Something dark awakening. Wanting.

Fuck.

I swallow it down and lift her in my arms. She yelps and struggles momentarily. I tighten my grip in warning, and she stills, stiffening, pressing against my chest as I move toward the passage that leads to the tunnels beneath. Santiago chose this room with that purpose in mind, I'm sure. Save his sister from further humiliation. Protect her.

She makes a sound as I carry her down the stone

stairs, tucking herself closer to me as her bare toes scrape the rough stone wall. And I know as I take my captive through the tunnels beneath the compound that tonight, the course of both of our lives has shifted. There will be no going back. Not for either of us.

3

JUDGE

She's quiet on the drive to the house. As promised, I remove the blindfold but leave the rope around her wrists. Not that she's going anywhere, but her lessons begin tonight. And I need to set expectations.

She keeps her gaze out the window as we drive the avenue of ancient, giant oaks toward the estate. She's told me before how beautiful she finds it. Magical was the word she'd once absently used.

From the alley of oaks, the house comes into view, a classic albeit mammoth plantation home that my family built and has owned over centuries. It's mine now. Since the passing of my grandfather, Carlisle Montgomery, half a year ago, I am the sole inheritor.

The mansion is beautiful. Elegant with balconies spanning all three floors supported by grand columns and ornate friezes in the Greek Revival style. The design is simple. Symmetry is the focus of the exterior, with a sweeping stone staircase leading to the front doors and large, evenly spaced windows with decorative shutters. Lights glow warm from within, hinting at the opulence that awaits.

It's a very different sight from the gothic style of De La Rosa Manor.

Raul, my driver, pulls to a stop. Mercedes turns to me. She can't hide the anticipation in her eyes. The anxiety of not knowing what comes next.

"Thank you, Raul," I say as I climb out and walk around to open Mercedes's door. I extend my hand to help her out, but she ignores it to lumber out on her own. She's off-balance with her wrists bound and stumbles into my chest. I catch her, then right her. Although perhaps I should let her fall. Begin to teach her that she needs this. Needs me.

She tugs free of me, putting space between us. "You don't need to keep me bound," she says, shifting her weight. The stones beneath her feet can't be comfortable. "I'm not going to run. I have nowhere to go."

"Perhaps I just like the look of you tied up."

She opens her mouth, then closes it, uncertain of my meaning.

I clear my throat. I need to be careful with her. Need to remember she's Santiago's little sister.

"Shall I carry you?" I ask.

"I'm perfectly capable of walking."

"Your feet."

"I'm fine."

"Suit yourself."

I gesture for her to go ahead. A shadow moves in the upstairs window. Mercedes sees it too and pauses. She looks over her shoulder at me. It's late. The staff should be in bed. But there will be one witness to her arrival.

"Go on," I tell her.

She does, her bare feet quiet on the stone stairs. I open the heavy front door to let her enter ahead of me.

Mercedes hesitates on the threshold. I wonder what she's thinking. What she's expecting.

She takes a deep breath and steps inside, studying the grand foyer as if it's the first time she's seen it. Mercedes isn't one to be impressed by money. God knows the De La Rosa family has plenty of it. But she appreciates the white marble floors and walls veined in shades of gray. All three floors are visible from here with a central staircase, also marble, to the second floor and two more modest staircases to the third.

She turns back to me. "My room," she says, her tone haughty. "I'm tired."

I smile. I almost thought to let her sleep tonight and begin tomorrow, considering what she's been through. But no.

"Same room as the last time you were my guest."

"Guest," she snorts. "Do you tie up all your guests?"

"Only those who need tying."

The mask of superiority falters. It's her defense. It's always been her defense.

Without another word she turns to climb the stairs. I keep one hand at her elbow in case she trips but I don't quite touch her. When we get to the second floor, however, movement at the end of the corridor has her stopping.

"What..." she starts, trailing off as Miriam, a housekeeper I inherited from my mother, clears her throat. She waits just outside Mercedes's bedroom door in her traditional matronly shapeless black dress with its white lace collar.

Miriam has been with my family for about six years. And I'm still not sure I like her. For as efficient as she is, she's neither kind nor warm-hearted which makes her perfect for the task at hand.

Mercedes looks at me. I know she was hoping her arrival would be more private, but that's not part of the plan.

"You remember Miriam?" I ask.

She nods tightly. Is she remembering how condescending she was toward the woman when she was last here? When I held my tongue considering the circumstances. Her brother on the verge of death.

"She's prepared your room," I tell her.

She forces her mouth into a smile, lifting her chin as she makes her way to her bedroom.

"Miss," Miriam says in greeting, nodding to Mercedes. "Sir."

I greet her. Mercedes doesn't. Instead, she enters the room, stopping just inside to take it in.

Just like last time, I chose the most comfortable bedroom for her. Second only to mine. It's spacious and luxurious in shades of dusty rose and creamy white. The room has large windows and French doors that lead onto the balcony with a view of the avenue of oaks she so loves.

She walks to the plush, king-sized bed draped with the finest duvet and more pillows than she'll need. She takes it all in as if for the first time. Then she looks at me, ignoring Miriam even as the woman enters and closes the door behind her.

"I'm tired," Mercedes says.

"Hold out your wrists. I'll untie them."

She does, and I undo her wrists. She makes a point of rubbing the reddened skin.

"Hungry?" I ask.

She shakes her head. In her eyes, I see the uncertainty she's trying to hide. She's wondering why Miriam is here.

"Just one more thing to do before you sleep," I tell her.

I note how vulnerable she looks again. How

small without her high heels, the armor of her designer clothes and made-up face. The signature crimson lipstick.

"What?" she asks coldly.

"Your clothes."

Her eyebrows practically disappear into her hairline. "Pardon?"

"Your clothes, Mercedes. I think it's best there are no reminders of this night. Tomorrow, like Santiago said, you will start anew."

She glances at the matronly woman standing nearby, the witness to her humiliation, then to me.

"Is this some sort of joke? Because it's not funny."

"No. No joke. Your clothes."

"My brother would not allow this!"

"Your brother initiated the Rite. You're mine. I will decide what is best for you. You will simply obey."

She snorts.

"Do you need help?"

"I want to talk to him. Get him on the phone. Now!"

She takes a step toward the door. I grab her arm before she can take another. She tries to shrug me off, but I turn her to face me fully and shift my hands to her shoulders. Her hands close over my forearms, and she stares up at me. Her long black hair hangs loose around her face and over her shoulders, revealing a softness I've only ever caught glimpses of. She hides herself well.

"Why are you here, Mercedes?"

Her jaw clenches. She knows exactly why she's here. What she's done. Her eyes dart over my shoulder, tears on the verge of falling, but she refuses to allow that. Instead, she narrows her gaze, glaring up at me. That softness from moments ago is gone.

"Why are you here?" I repeat.

After a long moment of weighted silence, she finally breaks the lock of our eyes and lowers her gaze. A fat tear drops onto the back of my hand. I watch it, and for a moment, I forget myself. Forget the point of this. The reason for it.

For a moment, I want to pull her to me and tell her it will be all right.

But Miriam clears her throat and catapults me back into the why of this.

"Answer me," I say and pause.

Mercedes turns angry eyes to mine. "Fuck. You."

My hands flex, fingers tightening on her arms. This woman will test me. I take a deep breath in and smile. Because this is exactly why she's here.

"You'll remain in this room until you can answer that question. Now," I start, releasing her and stepping away. "Do you need Miriam to help you undress?"

"No," she spits and clumsily tugs at the sweatshirt, getting it tangled in her hair as she pulls it off and throws it at me. It hits my chest, then drops to the floor.

I don't take my eyes from hers as she continues with the pants, bouncing on one foot, daggers cutting me through as she holds my gaze and strips them off, balls them up, and throws the ill-fitting pants at me too.

"Satisfied?" she asks, straightening to stand at her full height. Not covering herself.

Unable to stop my gaze from sweeping over her, I swallow, taking in all that skin, the scraps of lace barely covering full breasts, the slit of her sex. I push my hands into my pockets, clenching them into fists, nails digging into my palms. My jaw tightens as I remind myself who she is. Remind myself that this little monster needs me to remain in control. To not be undone by the sight of her nearly naked.

I drag my gaze slowly back up to hers and see that her hands, too, are clenched and her cheeks flushed with color.

"Continue," I say, my voice thick.

Her mouth opens, her short breaths audible as she gazes from me to Miriam and back. "I think it's enough. I think my brother—"

"Miriam," I say, neither moving nor taking my eyes from Mercedes.

Miriam moves into action, striding toward Mercedes in three quick steps. Mercedes gasps, clearly not expecting this, and when the older woman raises her arms to strip the rest of her clothes, Mercedes grips her wrists hard. She's stronger than I realized. But Miriam is as strong and as determined. It's why I chose her.

"Don't you fucking dare touch me! Get the hell away from me!"

There's a brief struggle. Mercedes shoves Miriam and runs, but Miriam is quick to steady herself and move toward her target.

Mercedes glances frantically around, her hand closing over the base of a heavy lamp. She falters then. I wonder if she's remembering the event that led her here, that has her in this predicament. The murder of the courtesan. The very violent scene she left behind.

She squeezes her eyes shut, and I put a hand up to halt Miriam as I watch her, the already puffy skin around her eyes growing wet. She's been crying. Hell. She looks like she's been crying forever.

With a violent shake of her head, she opens her eyes, glaring at me. "Call her off!"

"Continue, and I will," I tell her calmly, hardening myself against the wounded creature that calls to the protector inside me.

"I hate you," she says, a shudder to her voice as she releases the lamp and reaches behind her to unhook her bra and strips it off. She drops it to the floor, then pushes her panties down, kicking both away. "I fucking hate you."

She bares pretty, full breasts, nipples tight and her sex shaved to reveal the pretty slit. The latter makes me stop. Has any other man seen her like this? There was Jackson Van der Smit. Did he—?

I shake my head to stop myself. I don't know why I'm going down that road. She would have followed the rules. Breaking them would shame her brother and incur his wrath. Besides, that's not why she's here. But her nakedness, it strikes me. She's certainly not the first woman I've seen. Far from it. But here I am, unable to drag my gaze away.

"Sir?" Miriam interrupts.

"Get out," I tell her.

Self-control. Discipline. Two traits I've worked hard to perfect in myself. I draw a deep breath in. Exhale. Getting hard at the mere sight of her is anything but controlled. She'll be stripped bare more often than she'll like, and I can't get a fucking hard-on like some teenage boy every time I see her.

"Yes, sir." Miriam leaves. I wait until I hear the door close.

I've taken women into my home before and disciplined them. Something I've done quietly for certain members of The Society. Not a single one of them has affected me like Mercedes De La Rosa. And I haven't even started with her.

"Get into bed," I snap, needing her to cover herself. I walk to the adjoining bathroom, taking a moment there. Gripping the edge of the counter, I push a hand through my hair. What the fuck is wrong with me?

Rummaging through the cabinet beneath the sink, I find the first-aid kit. When I return, I find her sitting in the middle of the large bed, clutching the thick duvet to herself. Again, I think about how small she looks. How different to the girl I've watched grow into a woman. A formidable woman at that. Now, at this moment, she is something else entirely.

And the animal inside me stirs.

I clear my throat, and she looks up, although she doesn't quite meet my gaze. Her face is unreadable. She's good at that. Always has been. Probably had to be. I know a little of her upbringing. Although surely, her father would not have been as physical with her as he was with his sons.

I cross the room and sit on the edge of the bed.

She tugs the blankets closer, inching farther from me.

"Look at me."

Her jaw clenches.

I close my fingers over her chin and make her look. Her eyes are narrowed to slits when they meet mine. She won't be easy to bend. But I don't want her to be. I tilt her face up and brush the hair from her cheek. The gash is already closed up, the blood dried, and a bruise is taking shape. I'm surprised this is all she walked away with considering. Mercedes

His Rule 33

De La Rosa murdered a woman. She should have to stand before The Tribunal to answer for it. Any other member of The Society would. But Santiago will take care of that. And I will help him protect her.

I have a feeling, though, that her own guilt and the thought of losing her brother's love are more punishment than anything The Tribunal could dish out.

I clean the dried blood off her cheek and smear antibiotic ointment onto the cut, careful to be gentle. I feel her eyes on my face, and I take my time doing it. Once I'm finished, I set the ointment aside and pour a glass of water out of the crystal pitcher on the nightstand. I take the pill Miriam left on the small dish and hold both out to Mercedes.

She looks at the pill.

"To help you get a good night's rest."

"I'm fine," she says, turning her head away.

"It will help, Mercedes."

She looks again at the pill in my palm. She wants it. She wants the oblivion it will bring. And this once, I'll allow it. She reaches a tentative hand to pluck the pill from me and places it on her tongue, then takes the glass, sipping from it before handing it back.

I set it on the nightstand and get to my feet.

She lies down and turns away from me. Long dark hair spills over the white pillow, the duvet she is clutching tucked up to her chin, leaving most of her back exposed. I reach for the blanket to cover her fully, but something catches my eye. A mark. Something I've never seen because her back has never been fully bared to me. It's a scar. Many years old from the look of it. I glimpse the edge of another, deeper one, lower. It's hidden by the blanket.

I know what leaves this particular mark. I've seen it before.

When I touch the tips of my fingers to one, the skin around it tightens, and she stiffens. I stop. Now isn't the time. It's enough for one night. Especially this night. So I draw the blanket up to her shoulders and watch her burrow beneath the weighted duvet, small hands like fists holding on tight. Reaching for the switch, I turn off the light beside the bed and walk toward the door. I pause there and glance back at her. But when I hear her sniffle, I walk out of the room.

4

MERCEDES

I broke my cardinal rule. The one absolute law I have always abided by.

Never let anyone see my scars.

In my discomfited state of mind, I wasn't even considering it. It's probably the first time in my life I forgot those scars were there. Nobody was ever supposed to see them. Nobody ever has, apart from the one witness who won't utter a word.

But now Judge has. He knows, and it seems to tip the scales of inequity even further in his favor. I hate this. I hate him. I hate everyone right now. And even though I promised myself I wasn't going to cry anymore, that's exactly what I do when he leaves me alone in the silent abyss of my room. I cry at the loss of the only life I've ever known. I grieve for the woman I thought I was. And I grieve for the woman who almost killed my brother before I killed her. I don't know why. I didn't know her, other than the few times we spoke to arrange the deal we made. When I found out she double-crossed me and nearly destroyed the last of my family, I wanted her dead. I swore it was the only punishment fit for her crime. But wanting it was one thing. Carrying out the act myself, so brutally and so unexpected, is another.

The weight of my guilt settles over me as the medicine soaks into my veins and makes my eyes too heavy to focus. So I close them, and inevitably, sleep drags me away for a few blissful hours when nothing else exists.

When the light of day starts to creep into my window, the reality of my situation sinks in all over again. I wake up in a bed that's not my own, and one glance at my surroundings confirms I'm still living in a hell of my own making.

I squeeze my eyes shut and try to forget, but it's an impossible task. One complicated by the sound of my door opening. Miriam stands with a smug expression and a tray full of breakfast in her hands when I glance up.

Something about this woman rubs me the wrong way. I had a bad feeling about her from the time I stayed here before, but after last night, I know she can't be trusted.

"Time to get up," she announces with gleeful mockery in her eyes. She's enjoying this far too much.

"Just leave it." I nod at the tray. "I'll eat later."

"Afraid not." She hums as she moves to the seating area near the window and sets the tray on the table. "You've been ordered to get up. Take a shower, and then you can eat."

I glance at the clock next to the bed in dismay. "It's only six o'clock."

"Yes, and Mr. Montgomery wants you up. I suggest you follow his directives. Or don't. I suppose you're the one who will face the consequences, so it makes no difference to me."

I narrow my eyes at her. One thing's for certain. She could use a few lessons in manners from Antonia. At least our housekeeper knows when to bite her tongue.

"I'm going back to bed." I pull the covers tighter around me and roll onto my side. "Tell Judge if you'd like. It makes no difference to me either."

I could almost swear I hear her snort as she leaves the room, and for a second, I question what I'm doing. Am I really prepared to face his wrath before I've even had my coffee?

On the one hand, I'm certain I'm not. On the other, he's an asshole, and I want him to know I'm not going to make this easy for him just because he tells me to. If he had the first clue about my schedule, he would know that I stay up late just like Santiago. It's rare that I rise before noon, and I have no intentions of changing that just because some egomaniac beats his fists against his chest in a display of power.

I close my eyes, and my room is so quiet that I can almost believe I was right. Judge isn't going to waste his time coming in here this morning. Not when he has more important things to attend to, like lording over all the unfortunate souls who have to face him in court.

Five minutes pass, and then ten. With every additional second, my body begins to relax again, and my eyes grow heavy. I'm on the verge of sleep stealing me away when my door opens, and a chill moves over my spine. Without even looking, I know it's him. I can feel the darkness of his energy pulsing through the room, obliterating the sunlight pouring in through the windows.

I don't look at him. I lie there, frozen, my breath caught in my chest while I wait to see what he'll do.

"Get. Up." His order is issued in that authoritative voice that makes me shudder. But at the same time, it fuels my own ire.

"No."

"Mercedes," he warns. "Do not test me. I can promise you won't like the outcome."

"Just leave me alone!" I yell over my shoulder, the words dying off as I catch a glimpse of him.

He's standing there in a pair of riding breeches, boots, and a shirt that's hanging open to reveal his bare chest, glistening with the sheen of an early morning workout. I try to swallow the knot in my throat as my eyes unintentionally move over his muscular frame. I always knew Judge was strong. It's not a detail you can miss in his well-tailored suits. But knowing it is an entirely different beast than bearing witness to the broad expanse of his shoulders and the cut abs with that dark patch of hair that disappears beneath his waistband.

Oh, God. I can't look at him like this. Judge has always been my older brother's arrogant best friend. The type you tolerate because you have to. This feels wrong. All wrong. And I don't know why I'm still staring at him, or why I feel a rush of heat spreading down my neck and chest.

If I had to guess, it would be because I've never seen a man in this state of undress. Pathetic, I know. But rules are rules. Even when I was dating Jackson, I never once saw so much as a glimpse of his chest. I wasn't prepared for this, and I have no idea where I'm supposed to look, or what I'm supposed to do.

"Mercedes," Judge clips my name out with all the sharp delicacy he can muster.

My eyes move to his, and it's a mistake. Because I can see the fire in them. He's noticed me staring. He's noticed the flush moving over my skin. This can't be real. Not with Judge. He's never looked at me the way he's looking at me right now. Like he's about to crawl out of his skin and... *devour me.*

"Get up." His voice is rougher now. "I'm not going to ask again."

I stare at him, unable to speak. Unable to even formulate a thought. There's a tension between us I don't want to acknowledge. I think it's always been there, simmering quietly beneath the surface. I always thought it was a mutual hatred, but right now, it feels like something else. Something that's about to reach a boiling point.

"You have a way of getting what you want in life, little monster." He steps forward with determination, and I spot something in his hand.

It takes a moment to register that it's a riding crop. My heart slows to a heavy thud in my chest, and I try to shake my head, but it doesn't move. I'm frozen, terrified by what he might do, and it's a feeling I had long thought I'd put behind me. I'm Mercedes fucking De La Rosa. I don't back down from anything. I don't bow to anyone. But right now... it feels like that's exactly what I'm doing when he takes another step, and I bow my head to avoid his gaze.

"I knew you had it in you." He drags the rough edge of his thumb along my jaw, tipping my chin up so I have to look at him. "You can submit. You just need someone to guide you."

"No." I force the words between gritted teeth.

"Resist all you want," he says, his voice oddly calm. "I enjoy taming wild beasts."

His thumb skates dangerously close to my lips, and I suck in a sharp breath. At the same time, he freezes as if he didn't realize what he was doing. I don't know what to make of this strange interaction when things have only ever been strained or indifferent. This isn't the Judge I know and remember. This isn't the same man who looked at me as if I scarcely registered in his world. I had always felt he thought he was far too superior to really see me. But right now, it feels like he sees everything.

"Mercedes." He pulls his hand away abruptly, his face adopting a neutral expression that makes me wonder if I'm seriously losing my mind. Did I just imagine that?

"Judge." I return his name in a tone dripping with as much arrogance as I can squeeze into it.

His lip tips slightly at the corner, and if I didn't know any better, I might think he finds this whole situation amusing. But of course, he would. He's the one who has the real power here, and we both know it. Everything I do is for show, but I don't care. I want him to know what he signed up for. I want to make his life as hard as I possibly can.

"Kneel." He points at the floor with the end of his crop. "Now."

"Are you kidding me?" I glare up at him.

"Do I look like I'm kidding?"

No, he really, really doesn't.

"I'm not playing these twisted games with you." I

clutch the covers tighter around me. "Just leave me alone."

His eyes move to the clock and then back to me. "You're delaying the inevitable. Do as I say, or there will be further consequences when I get home tonight."

"I don't care." I hurl myself across the other side of the bed and drag the duvet with me, keeping cover as I bolt for the bathroom. "Find someone else to torture, you sadist. Go beat one of your willing courtesans at the—"

The words come to an abrupt halt when I feel the blanket being yanked out of my grasp. It all happens so fast, I don't even have time to steel myself before Judge seizes me and whips me around, baring my naked body to him as his eyes blaze with fire.

"What did you say?"

"You heard me." I keep my gaze locked on his even though it feels like my heart's about to explode. "You're so twisted, you can't even see it. Coming in to rescue me all high and mighty talking about discipline, when all you really want is to—"

Again, my words are cut off as he snatches me up and plants me face-first into the rug. There isn't time to try for a counterattack. Judge is showing me his true strength, his formidability, and his ability to dominate me so easily, no matter what I might throw at him.

Real fear streaks through me for the first time when he hoists my ass up and pins my hips into position with his muscular thighs, squeezing me like a vise.

"Is this what you're so afraid of?" He taunts me by dragging the leather crop down my bare back, skating over the scars I wish he hadn't seen.

"No!" I scream and buck against him, but he just squeezes me tighter with his legs, using his palm to shove my face back onto the floor.

"I think it's exactly what you're afraid of." He hurls the words as if he derives pleasure from the fact, like he gets off on seeing me so vulnerable. "What's the matter, little monster? Where are your accusations now?"

"Fuck you!"

"Fuck me," he echoes, his voice mocking. "You wish you could."

Before I can even attempt to formulate a response to that, the crop lashes against my left ass cheek unexpectedly, making me jolt. It stings and has the immediate effect of stealing my breath, but there isn't time to recover before he does it again.

"How many do you think you deserve for this morning's display?" he asks.

I clench my jaw and refuse to utter a word or make so much as a sound. I know that's what he wants. He wants my compliance. He wants to feel like he's winning, but I'll never admit defeat even when I'm down on my knees being humiliated by him.

When I don't respond, he slaps the leather against my skin harder, and it fucking burns. But again, I don't make a sound. Judge should know I've been through much worse. The scars are evidence of that. He thinks he can break me, but I've already been broken. I just refuse to let the world know it.

Slap. The leather hisses against my ass, and he grunts, picking up the rhythm, working both sides as he twists left to right, swinging the crop behind him. From my periphery, I can see his muscles straining as he loses himself to the moment, and if I were watching him in any other circumstance, I would think it's almost inhumanly beautiful the way he moves. As the thought occurs to me, I realize how deranged it is. But I've taken many beatings in my life. None of them were measured or well controlled. None of them were beautiful in any way. They were ugly and terrifying. Inexplicably, this time is different, and I don't know why. I just know I trust that Judge won't ever take it too far. He'll push me. He'll make me uncomfortable. But I don't believe he'd ever lay a hand on me just to cause me pain. There's a lesson in everything he does, and right now, the lesson in compliance will be had whether I like it or not.

"Say it," he grunts. "Tell me why you're here."

"Screw you!" I smirk over my shoulder. "That's why."

Whack. His crop hits me dead center between my thighs, and it shocks me so violently that I release an ear-piercing scream. The crop clatters to the floor in the aftermath, and Judge stumbles back, staring down at me as if he's just been doused in ice-cold water.

I release a silent sob as two realizations occur to me at the same time. The first is that he can see all of me right now, and I'm too weak to drag myself up and find even an ounce of dignity. The second is that perhaps I was wrong about him. Perhaps Judge isn't someone I can trust not to hurt me. Because even though I was more shocked than pained, I'm humiliated, and that's just as bad, isn't it?

I bury my face in the floor, trying to hide the moisture clinging to my eyes. I don't know what's wrong with me, but it seems as if a dam has opened, and now I can't stop it.

A long, heavy silence follows before I feel a gentle hand on my waist. I flinch at the contact, but then he scoops me up into his arms. The heat of his bare chest penetrates my skin, and it has the strangest effect on me. I want to hate myself for being so emotionally bankrupt that I could possibly derive any comfort from this man, but that's exactly what it feels like. His warmth surrounds me, and I can't help noticing the masculine scent of his sweat combined with the leather from his boots and perhaps even a hint of his cologne. It's spicy and warm, and I find it odd that I don't hate it. I should hate it.

I have to believe this is just a side effect of my fragile state of mind. Anyone else in my situation would do the same. Comfort is scarce in my world, and for once, I find that I need it. Even if it comes from the brute who made me show my vulnerability in the first place.

He carries me to the bed, laying me on my stomach before he pauses to stroke the hair gathered on my face. It feels almost like a silent apology, and I tell myself I should recoil from his touch, but again, I don't.

"Don't move," he orders, voice rough. "I'll get something to help with the pain."

"I don't need anything for the pain," I whisper. "It doesn't bother me."

He ignores my protest and disappears into the bathroom, and for a second, I consider trying to bolt for the door. Maybe I could make it if I wasn't so exhausted. I tell myself I could, but the truth is, I know he'll catch me. He'll always catch me. Judge is a hunter, and somehow, I've become his prey.

When he returns with a tube of cream, I try to turn over, but his palm comes to rest on the center of my back.

"No more fighting." His voice betrays a hint of

softness I don't think I've ever heard from him before. "Not right now."

"I can do it myself," I croak.

"But you won't," he answers. "It's my job to take care of you."

I bury my face in the pillow as he warms the cream between his palms and then starts to smooth it over the curves of my ass. It feels so intimate. Too intimate to be sharing with Judge. I can't make sense of him. This man is a Sovereign Son. He's practically royalty in The Society. He could have any woman he wants, yet he's never married. At thirty-one, I'm sure countless women have tried and failed to secure him as a husband. But Santiago has mentioned many times that Judge will never marry, and I have to wonder why. Why is it okay for him to refuse the expectations of The Society when I must abide by them? And what possible benefit could he derive by wasting his time on me when a plethora of beautiful women at the Cat House are willing to submit to his every command?

These thoughts occupy my mind while he rubs the cream into my skin, but as hard as I try, I can't distract myself enough from the feeling of his hands on me. He's meticulous. Careful. Treating me like I'm delicate when five minutes ago, he was treating me as if I were the bane of his existence. I don't understand him, and I can't stop myself from blurting the question that's been on my mind since last night.

"Why are you doing this? What's in it for you?"

His hand falters for a moment before he resumes his work, taking extra care to massage the sensitive skin I'm sure is red and swollen.

"There has to be something in it for you," I persist when he doesn't answer.

"There is," he says quietly.

Immediately, my thoughts go to the worst-case scenario. I already know from Santiago that if anything were to happen to my brother as head of the household, not only would Judge take over my care, but he would be paid well to do so. I can't imagine he needs the money, but do rich men ever turn down financial gains? Is that why he agreed to this? It's the only thing that makes any sense. And suddenly, this whole situation is even more mortifying than I imagined it could be.

"He's paying you, isn't he?" I demand. "Santiago is paying you for your trouble. That's why I'm here."

Judge doesn't respond, and I have my answer. I swallow my pride, ready to pull myself up and redraw the battle lines. But then his palm skates up my back, lightly grazing over the scars that have lived there for so many years.

"Who did this to you?" His question catches me off guard, and even more so when I seem to detect an undercurrent of rage in his tone.

"That's my business," I reply with less bite than I had hoped.

"Your business is my business." He resumes his stroking, massaging the skin of my back until his fingers skate over the curve of my hip and then around the globe of my butt down to the back of my thighs, where a few more scars reside.

I don't know how, but at some point, his endeavors to salve my inflamed skin turned into something else. Something more exploratory. Something darker and... more dangerous. When his thumb glides perilously close to my inner thigh, I draw in a sharp breath as a cascade of goose bumps breaks out all over my body, and my stomach clenches in anticipation.

I know he can't. He won't. I'm off-limits. That's no-man's-land until I'm married. It's the rule for Society women, especially women in the upper echelon. No man has ever dared touch me there before, and I can't imagine Judge testing the limits with Santiago's wrath. If he ruins me, no man would ever marry me, and he would have to face the consequences that surely aren't worth the trouble. It would be reckless and stupid, but a part of me also wonders if he wants to. That same deranged part of me is considering what it would feel like. Would he be rough, or would he be gentle as he is now? What would it feel like to have his hands all over my body? His mouth on my mouth. His cock deep inside me.

I shake away those horrifying thoughts, ashamed for even considering them.

"That's good enough," I choke out. "If I need more, I'll apply it later."

My words seem to bring him back to his senses too, and he drags his hand away, leaving me cold in the wake of the loss.

"You have an hour to rest," he says quietly. "Then I want you to shower. Your clothes are in the closet. Dress as you'd like, but you aren't to leave this room."

"My clothes are here?" I glance at the closet, wondering when they got delivered. It must have been while I was sleeping.

He nods, moving to the door, and I call after him. "What about my phone?"

"No phone," he replies, his face devoid of any emotion. "And no makeup."

"I need my phone, Judge. You can't just—"

"You'll get it back when you tell me why you're here. For now, you can use this time to think about that." He reaches for the handle and pauses after he opens it. "The rules are very simple, Mercedes. Good behavior earns you privileges. Bad behavior earns you consequences."

5

MERCEDES

Judge leaves the room, and emptiness engulfs me. It's a brittle feeling. I thought there would be some relief in his absence, but now I'm alone with my thoughts. Alone with the memories of last night and the knowledge that I deserve whatever punishment Judge can dole out. It still won't be enough.

I can't bring myself to eat so much as a bite of the breakfast Miriam delivered. I'm sure that will probably result in further consequences later, but right now, I can't find it in me to care. She comes again at noon with lunch, noting with raised eyebrows that I don't eat that either.

I try to find ways to pass the time. Things to occupy my mind. I shower and brush my hair and my teeth, trying to avoid the mirror as much as possible. I feel naked without the armor of my makeup, and I don't like it.

When I venture into my closet, sure enough, my clothes are there as Judge stated. Santiago had them sent over without delay, erasing all evidence of me from the manor. I swallow the painful lump that reality leaves me with and thumb through the racks of designer dresses I usually wear. But what's the point? I'm not going anywhere. There are no pretenses to keep. He's stripped me down and left me bare in more ways than one.

I grab a pair of yoga pants, a strappy tank top, and a cashmere sweater, opting for comfort over fashion. My room is cool enough that I can take solace in the soft fabric against my skin, at least for now.

Amongst all my other belongings, I find my purse. I rifle through it, half hopeful, but my phone is absent, and all that's left are the usual essentials I carry. A compact mirror, gum, lip conditioner, and my EpiPen.

I officially have no communication with the outside world unless I can somehow manage to get to a phone. But even if I could, I don't know what good it would do. Who even memorizes the numbers in their contacts anymore?

Solana and Georgie are sure to be blowing up my phone. I missed our customary Sunday brunch with them yesterday and didn't even have a chance to text them or explain. They've known something has been off with me lately, but I couldn't tell them the truth. They don't live in the same world I do, and there's no way they could ever understand the reality of The Society. All the rules, the expectations for my life. Poison and treachery are only things they hear about on TV. If they had any inclination of what my life was really like, they'd probably try to steal me away to a tropical island.

I miss them, and right now, I wish I could tell them everything. I wish I could hear Solana humming a happy little tune in her cozy apartment while she pours us mimosas and feeds us pastries. Georgie would hug me and tell me it's all going to be okay even though it isn't because Georgie never lets me believe anything else. He'd ask me who he needs to murder and then tell me how amazing I look.

I don't deserve them, truthfully. But they are a part of my life outside The Society that nobody knows about. I spend my free time at aerial yoga and dance classes with my friends, and in those stolen minutes, I am truly free. Then I leave them, donning my armor and going back to my world, spending time with my Society-approved frenemies. We eat fifty-dollar salads together and purge outrageous amounts of money trying to one-up each other's wardrobe, all while pretending we have any actual love and respect for one another.

I doubt very much that Giordana, Dulce, and

Vivien will even think twice about my welfare when I don't show up for tomorrow's weekly charity luncheon. They will gossip and speculate unkindly about my absence, but they won't seek me out.

Solana and Georgie, on the other hand, won't take it lightly when I completely ghost them. And if I'm being honest, I'm worried they will make a big deal about it when they can't find me. It's something The Society wouldn't like, and I have to tread carefully to make sure they are protected, but I'm just not sure how I'm going to do that yet.

What will Judge think if he looks at my phone and sees all their messages? Especially the ones between Georgie and me. We send each other selfies throughout the day and praise each other about how hot and fierce and amazing the other one looks with encouraging messages to slay the day. I jokingly dubbed him as 'boy-friend' in my phone, and I could see how that might be misconstrued. Especially taken out of context with the constant notes of affection and declarations of love for each other.

If anyone in The Society were to see those messages, they could easily conclude that I'm dating outside of our circle and, worse, that I'm no longer pure. It has the potential to destroy my reputation and further tarnish my family name. But how can I explain my friendships with Georgie and Solana in a way that any of them could even understand?

The upper echelon doesn't seek outside friends.

We don't mingle with the world that doesn't follow our ways. And I'm afraid if Judge sees those messages before I can get my phone back, the results could be disastrous.

I know it's a fruitless endeavor, but I walk to the door and check to see that it is in fact locked. The balcony too. I'm trapped in here with nowhere to go and nothing but these terrible thoughts rattling around in my brain.

I try to do some yoga to relax, but somewhere between downward dog and child's pose, another torrent of emotion floods over me. I end up curled up on the floor, rocking myself in an attempt to soothe the ache in my chest. When I close my eyes, I see that woman's face all over again. And when I open them, I see reminders everywhere.

The lamp shattering as it collides with her skull. The blood slipping down my fingers. I don't have to be in that room to feel those things. To hear them. They are on an almost constant feedback loop now, and I feel like I'm going to throw up.

I barely make it to the toilet before I heave and spew the only thing I managed to get down today, which was water. My stomach cramps, and I retch again, but nothing comes up. As it turns out, you can't vomit up your guilt after all.

I'm clinging to the toilet bowl, clammy and weak, when I feel a presence behind me. I lift my head to find Judge standing there, concern etched into his features. But as his eyes move over me, drifting down to my arm that's clutching my stomach, I see the question in them. He's concerned not only that I might be sick, but I'm certain he's also speculating about the reason.

"I..." My voice dies off as I pull myself up, and the room starts spinning.

"Fuck."

Judge's muffled curse is the last thing I hear before I stagger sideways and start to collapse, right into the strength of his arms.

6

JUDGE

She's not for you.

I lay Mercedes down on her bed. She's dressed in yoga pants and a sweater, her hair still loose, her feet still bare.

Not. For. You.

I swallow that fact down and sit on the edge of the bed, scrubbing my face. I wonder what my colleagues and those slated to appear in my courtroom thought of the half-moon-shaped marks on my cheeks from Mercedes's fingernails. No one dared ask. They know better.

She hasn't eaten all day. Miriam briefed me upon my arrival. It's probably why she passed out. That or the guilt I'm sure she's been reliving locked in here with nothing to distract her. That's the point, though. No distractions. The way out is through. Too many people expect shortcuts in life. But that's not how things work. Darkness touches all of our lives. The strong ones stand tall and walk willingly into the abyss to face down the shadows. The weak ones distract themselves so as not to have to face it. I won't let Mercedes be weak. She's not that.

"Mercedes."

Nothing.

I push the hair from her face. Her forehead is damp. I wonder if that's from the yoga—her mat is laid out on the floor—or from being sick. My guess is the latter when I see the puffy, pink skin around her eyes.

I've never studied her before. Never had the opportunity, really. And I realize there's something not quite right about doing it while she's passed out, but I shove those thoughts aside and find myself undressing her with the pretense that she's too hot under the clothes. But I do want to get a look at her—at those scars—and I doubt she'd allow it if she were awake.

And so, without much more thought, I strip off her sweater and pants, the tank top beneath, and set them at the foot of the bed. When I sit her up to remove her bra, she makes a sound, but her head lolls against my chest. Once the bra is unhooked, I cup the back of her head and lay her down. She quiets as I pull the straps from her arms and set the bra on top of her clothes.

I take in her breasts. Full. Perfectly round. Her large nipples darkening as they pucker. I clear my throat, then look over her chest, her stomach. Nothing here. Just perfect, unblemished skin. The sleeping beast inside stirs. I shift my gaze from her flat stomach to the lace panties just barely covering her. I slip my fingers into the waistband.

What would she think if she woke now? What would I tell her? The truth. Those scars are concerning. Santiago wouldn't have done that to her, would he? Does he even know about them?

I slide her panties down her long legs and am about to set them aside, but push them into my pocket instead. I stand. Take her in, my gaze again catching on the slit of her sex. She makes a sound, moves, but quiets again. Her legs part just a little. Just enough to give me a glimpse of the open lips of her pussy.

A rumbling inside my chest signals the beast's interest is piqued. I take a deep breath in, then slowly exhale. Adjust myself.

I tell myself that I am inspecting for scars. That's all this is.

And I find the first one. Just around the curve of her hip on her pelvic bone. As if the belt —and I know it was a belt—wrapped around and the buckle dug hard into flesh. It was wielded in anger. Uncontrolled. I know this, too. My jaw tightens as I reach down to touch it, scar tissue bumpy beneath my thumb.

The fronts of her legs are mostly unblemished, apart from two smaller marks like that at her hip from where the belt wrapped around when it struck.

Who did this to her?

I run my hand over the smooth skin of her thigh, knee, her shin. I move around the bed and take one foot in my hands, and when I see the underside of it, every muscle in my body tenses. And that rumbling from earlier, it's different now. Loud and possessive and enraged.

Both feet are heavily scarred. The bottoms whipped ruthlessly.

I hold them both, wanting to warm them. Heal them. They're small for her height, the nails polished to perfection in her signature red. Flawless on one side. Damaged on the other. Like her.

"What are you doing?" Mercedes asks. I look up to find her staring at me, eyes wide with horror. She comes up onto her elbows. "What the hell are you doing?" she demands, tugging her feet from my grasp.

I allow her to pull away and study her face. Her eyes. There she is, inside them. A broken girl.

"Who did this to you?"

She swallows hard, eyes misting, and sits up. She draws the duvet onto her lap, over her breasts. "Like I said last night, it's none of your business."

"Santiago?" I ask, not wanting to. It can't be, but what if I'm wrong? I'll kill him. I'll have to.

"No. God! Santi would never—" Her voice breaks, and it takes her a moment to compose herself and meet my eyes again. And when she does, hers are hard. Layers and layers of impenetrable obsidian. "What the hell do you think you're doing by stripping me when I'm passed out?"

Inspecting you and checking for scars sounds weak.

I wanted to see your pussy one more time is closer to the truth.

The image of her earlier this morning when I took the crop to her floats back into memory. Her hips trapped by my thighs. Her ass positioned to take my punishment. The reddening marks. Her most secret parts on display for me. For me.

Not. For. You.

"You haven't eaten anything."

"Answer my fucking question because I'm damn sure my brother would not have okayed this!"

"Does he know about the scars?" I ask, stopping that line of questioning because, honestly, she's right.

She falters. Hugs her arms a little closer.

"Does he?"

"No. And you're not going to tell him."

"Who did it?"

She sits back against the headboard and stares up at me, lips sealed tight.

"Tell me who, and I may not mention it to Santiago."

"You're going to blackmail me?"

"Mercedes—"

"Don't."

"Tell me."

I watch her. I can't look away.

"Don't tell him." She falters, shaking her head. "Please."

I study her for a quiet moment. I won't get an answer from her tonight, but I have time. "Why haven't you eaten?" I ask, changing the subject.

"Hmm. I don't know. Let's see. You locked me in a room. You whipped my ass. My brother just kicked me out of my own house and out of his life. I have a maid—a fucking maid—who clearly takes pleasure in my suffering, and my jailor is a sadist. I don't know why I have no fucking appetite!"

I watch the fury on her face. It's flimsy camouflage for her uncertainty. Her vulnerability. "Why are you here, Mercedes?"

She reaches for her sweater at the foot of the bed and pulls it on, then stands. It's oversized and comes to the tops of her thighs. "I'm here because my brother is paying you to deal with me while he plays house with that woman."

Does she know how much she's giving away?

There's a knock on the door. "Enter," I call out, not taking my eyes from Mercedes, who tries to keep hers on mine, although I see how she glances at Miriam walking in with yet another tray of food.

Miriam sets the large tray down on the table and leaves. Mercedes glances at it. Her forehead furrows, and she shifts her gaze to me.

I go to the table, see the cold scrambled eggs, the strips of unappealing bacon, a cold tomato soup, a sandwich on bread that's gone soggy from the roasted once-warm vegetables and goat cheese.

"Breakfast and lunch. You'll eat those meals before you're served anything different. If that's tonight, great. If it's tomorrow, fine. Next week? Again, fine. There's one thing I know, Mercedes. You will eat."

I pull out the chair and gesture for her to sit.

She exhales loudly, clearly deciding this is not a battle she will fight. Pain doesn't bother her. She said it herself. Not the pain of a whipping. Not the pain of hunger. But everyone has a threshold. I just have to find hers. And I will.

Mercedes glances at her clothes. She picks up the pants I stripped off her and searches for a moment. The panties burn a hole in my pocket as she pulls on the pants without anything underneath and walks toward me, but she doesn't sit. She eyes all the dishes, picks up the soup bowl, and looks up at me. Her eyes narrow, and she grins, then brings the bowl close, turns it over, and pushes it against my chest. She giggles as she pours cold tomato soup down my front and over my pants. It's a strange, almost unhinged sound. Soup drips onto my shoes and the once-pristine carpet.

She lets the bowl drop, wipes her hands with a napkin, and lets that fall too, then looks up at me. "There. One down. What would you like next? Eggs?"

"I liked this suit," I tell her casually, and there's that grin again.

"I'm sure the money my brother is paying you will be more than enough to order another."

But what she next sees on my face has her falter. It's as if the beast looks out at her from inside me. My muscles tighten, the darkness within casting its shadow, ensnaring us.

She takes one step backward, but before she can take another, I grip a handful of that luxurious, thick hair and tug hard. It feels good to do it. She cries out, and I catch myself. It's an involuntary sound. I'm sure she wouldn't give me the satisfaction if she could help it. She grips my arm with both hands as I haul her on tiptoe and pull her so close that our noses are touching.

"That was a mistake." I push her to her knees.

"Get off!"

"Pick up the bowl and the napkin."

"Let me go!"

"Pick. Them. Up."

"Fine! Just..." She stretches one arm to get both bowl and napkin, keeping the other on my forearm while still trying to tug free.

"Miriam," I call out.

The door opens instantly as if the woman had her fucking ear to it. "Sir," she says, her voice betraying no emotion.

"Mercedes has made a mess. She needs a bucket and a sponge to clean it up."

"Right away, sir." I keep Mercedes on her knees until Miriam returns and sets the bucket down, letting water splash out of the sides, then turns to leave.

"Stay," I tell her.

"Yes, sir."

I release Mercedes's hair, and she drops to her hands, then sits back to rub her head.

"Clean my shoes."

She grits her teeth but doesn't move.

"Get my crop, Miriam."

Miriam spins on her heel, but before she can take a step, Mercedes has the sponge and is wiping off my shoes. Smart girl. I'm sure she doesn't want her ass whipped in front of the help.

When she's done, she sits back and glares up at me. She has the good sense to keep her mouth shut.

I step away, then gesture to the mess on the floor. "Miriam will supervise as you scrub the carpet. I'll be back tomorrow morning bright and early to take you to the stables, where you'll clean the stalls. For starters. What's the expression? Idle hands are the devil's playground."

"You can't do this to me," she grits out.

I crouch down, take her chin in my hand, and tug her forward so she has to set her hands down to steady herself. "Do you remember what I said last night?" She tries to jerk free, but I only tighten my grip. "Good behavior earns you privileges. Bad behavior earns you consequences. If you think I'm playing a game here, let me be very clear that I am not. I take the Rite very seriously. And you, little monster, need to be tamed." She swallows, eyes searching mine. "I won't fail Santiago or you in my task. I promise you that. Now thank me for my lenience tonight."

Her eyes narrow to slits, but she says the words. Or more spits them. It's fine. I'll take it.

Releasing her, I get up and walk to the door, but I stop before I leave. I turn back to the two women—one on her knees and the other standing over her, relishing her task, this humbling of the great Mercedes De La Rosa. I'll have to remind Miriam of her place too. But not tonight.

"Miriam will leave once she's satisfied with your

work and only after you've thanked her for the opportunity."

"You fucking asshole," she says so low I almost don't hear it.

"What's that?" I ask, stepping back inside.

She leans away and doesn't open her mouth.

"I thought so," I say. "Good night, Mercedes."

7

JUDGE

I walk out of that room on wooden legs. She's under my skin. Even though I know she's testing. Pushing. She's acting out because she's out of options. A lioness backed into a corner staring down the all-powerful lion twice her size. She only has one option. Fight. It's in her nature. She's not one to lay herself down to be slaughtered. Devoured. Not by me. Not by anyone.

My room is beside Mercedes's. I enter, shut the door and strip off the ruined clothes. Lois, the housekeeper in charge of running the household, will let me know if we can salvage it. I doubt it, but I'll leave it for her. From my pocket, I retrieve Mercedes's panties. I don't know why I took them. The lace is soft in my hand. The scent subtle. Her scent.

There's that image of her again. On her knees. Squirming between my thighs.

Fuck.

I shove the panties into the nightstand drawer and take a cold shower, then put on dark jeans and a dark cashmere sweater. After checking the time, I walk out of my room, only pausing momentarily when I pass by Mercedes's room. I'm surprised it's quiet.

The house is lit by warm, golden light. I descend the stairs, and as I pass the windows in the foyer overlooking the main drive, I'm reminded of the beauty of this place. The oaks standing grand, the wide drive seeming to go on for miles.

I walk into the kitchen, and from one corner, my four beasts raise their heads from their lazy slumber and, excited, come to greet me. I smile. The sight of them is one of the few things that makes me smile these days.

"Boys. I hope you haven't been giving Lois too hard a time," I say, looking up at the housekeeper from my crouched position. Lois has been with my family for as long as I can remember, and she's too old to chase after four very energetic Dobermans.

"They've been fine," Lois says, coming over from the sink to pet Pestilence. "This one, though. Stealing food from the counter again."

"I thought Famine would do that," I say, petting

Pestilence's face, then taking it in my hands. "Don't make me put you outside."

He whines as if he understands and gives Lois puppy eyes.

She smiles, shaking her head. "Thinks he can get away with anything with those eyes."

"He can with you," I say, straightening. "Thanks for taking care of them while Paolo is out." Paolo trains and exercises the dogs, but he's been out sick for a few days.

"No problem, Judge. You know I don't mind. Dinner is almost ready."

I nod. "When my mother arrives, get her a drink. I need to make a call before I join her."

"What about the dogs? You know how she feels about them."

I glance at the four of them. Pestilence, War, Famine, and Death. Dramatic, I know. My brother named them. They're five years old now. Pestilence is licking the last of the food remaining in all four bowls while the other three play with a toy.

"Leave them."

Lois raises her eyebrows. "Are you sure?"

"She has to get used to them, and quite frankly, she invited herself, so I'm not inclined to make accommodations for her."

"And Ms. De La Rosa... I set a place for the three of you in the dining room."

"Ms. De La Rosa will be dining in her room.

His Rule

Miriam has already taken a tray up. You don't need to worry about her."

Lois studies me. "Miriam?"

"Is there a problem with Miriam?"

"It's just they didn't quite get along last time Ms. De La Rosa was our guest."

"Hm. I guess they too will have to get used to each other." I can just about picture how that's going.

Lois doesn't like Miriam, but not many of the staff seem to. I get it. And part of me wonders if I should have left her upstairs with Mercedes. If I should have done what I did because Mercedes's pride will be wounded. But then I remember the ruined suit. A little humility may be good for her. I have no doubt she'll survive.

Besides, other things are more important. Like where those scars came from.

I leave the kitchen and go to my study. This room has become my dark sanctuary with mahogany wood paneling, a black marble fireplace, and heavy, antique furnishings that date back over a hundred years. The smell of cigar smoke still clings to the walls from the time my grandfather, Carlisle Montgomery, used to occupy this space. I stop to take in the portrait of him. He's alone in this one. In the living room is another with my grandfather, grandmother and my father painted when he was fifteen years old. He looks like me, my grandfather. Or I look like him. Exactly like him.

Shifting my gaze, I put the thought out of my head. I am not my grandfather.

I walk around the large desk, glancing out of the windows into the garden. Warm lights showcase the large swimming pool, the curving patio with its three separate seating areas, and pots and pots of flowering plants. Beyond it, a path curves toward the stables that house my horses. Past those stables, and not visible from the house, are the cottages once used by staff. Some still are, and some are empty. My mother lives in one. She moved out of the main house after my father's death.

I sit down in the worn leather chair and lean back. It's been six months since my grandfather's death, but it's still sometimes hard to grasp that he's gone. That the house, its contents, the stables, the horses, and the grounds are all mine.

Theron's dark eyes meet mine from the framed photo on the edge of the desk. Theron is my younger brother. He's been gone for years. Left the night of his twenty-fifth birthday. He'll be back soon enough, though, now that grandfather is gone. He has to return. I cut off his allowance, so he'll show his face. And then we can have our reckoning.

But now isn't the time to think of them.

My mind returns to the woman upstairs. To how she'd looked this morning when I'd walked into her room after my ride. How she cast her eyes down submissively only after staring open-mouthed as if she'd never seen a man bare-chested before. Although perhaps she hasn't. The Society's rules are strict for women, especially those of her standing.

Another image comes into focus then. The one that had me jerking off in the shower this morning. That of Mercedes facedown ass up. The one of her from behind with everything exposed to me.

A low rumble comes from my chest. I draw in a deep breath and adjust myself.

Self-control. She'll test me. Just as I will test her.

I make myself think about the scars. Imagine what she endured when I remember her comment about pain not bothering her. No, I guess you learn to take it when you're beaten so badly that you're left that damaged. That broken. She has hidden them for years. I want to know what happened to her and when. They're old, so I believe her that it wasn't Santiago. And, truth be told, I am relieved. Santiago is a ruthless man, but he would never harm his sister. He loves her.

Was it Lorenzo De La Rosa, her father? Or Leandro, her brother. Two men who would have had access to her to beat her so brutally. Because this isn't something she would have walked away from. Hell, she wouldn't have been able to walk at all for days, if not weeks.

Lorenzo's hard face floats into memory. He was a

cruel man. I've heard some of the stories, the ones Santiago has shared. And even if I hadn't, I've seen his form of discipline. Santiago and I grew up together. But he wouldn't have laid a hand on his daughter, would he? Surely, he wouldn't have beaten her badly enough to scar her?

I pick up one of the two phones on my desk and scroll through my contacts to dial Santiago. He picks up on the second ring.

"Judge. How are things?" I hear the concern in his voice. No matter what Mercedes thinks, he is worried about her.

"As well as can be expected."

"Is she all right?"

"She's adjusting."

"Hmm."

"I have a question," I start, but something stops me from asking the one I want to ask. No, not something. Someone. Mercedes. Her face when I threatened to tell Santiago. She's desperate he doesn't find out.

"Go on," Santiago says when I pause for too long.

I clear my throat, then pick up the second phone on my desk. "The password to Mercedes's phone. Do you have it?"

"Yes. I'll text it to you. You'll take care of anything between her and this woman?"

"I give you my word. Nothing will get back to The Tribunal that can hurt her."

His Rule

"I can do it myself. You don't need to be involved."

"I think you have enough on your plate, don't you?"

"Thank you, Judge. You're a good friend."

Am I, though? My phone chimes with a text. It's the password. "Have a good night, Santiago."

"Good night."

Lois knocks on the door and peers inside. "She's here," she whispers and slips back out.

I draw in a deep, slow breath. My mother has come to dine with me. I wonder if she's heard about my guest and wants the latest gossip. Or if she just needs more money. Her allowance never seems to be enough. Although it could also be that she wants to come back to the main house now that grandfather is dead and gone.

Whatever it is, I can hardly stomach the woman who gave birth to me. Who hates me.

But I understand why, don't I? I know why she took Theron's side when he did what he did. And she is right about one thing. I chose my side too. Grandfather's. Knowing what he was capable of. Witnessing his rage. I, too, chose.

His portrait glares down at me.

What a family we are. Perfect on the outside. Vicious on the inside.

8

MERCEDES

Warmth moves over me. Something comforting. Something I want more of. Trapped in the clutches of my sleep, I lean into the feeling, soaking it in, wishing for more of it. How long has it been since I've found solace?

I can't remember. But it's here now, and it smells divine. Leather and spice and something so intoxicatingly unique, I can't stop myself from inhaling it. When I do, it gives me an instant rush, and I imagine this is what addiction must feel like. I've only taken one hit, but I want more. So much more.

A soft moan escapes my parted lips as the warmth spreads over my jaw and down my neck. Within the confines of my dream, it's safe to have these feelings. Nobody will ever know, and in the morning, I can pretend they never happened.

Only, after my visceral sound of appreciation, the warmth seems to freeze in place. Suddenly, it feels more tangible, and I find myself questioning my reality. I know I'm asleep, but I must be half-awake too. Is it a lucid dream? Or am I losing my mind?

The answer comes in the next breath when the familiarity of a rough voice invades my senses.

"Come on, little monster. It's time to wake up."

Horror washes over me as I come to my senses and realize I wasn't dreaming at all. The warmth I felt was Judge's hand gliding over my face. That hand was what I leaned into. That touch was what I moaned for.

Oh, dear God... I moaned for him.

A blast of heat floods my cheeks, and I'm grateful when he pulls away, but I also feel the loss immensely. Now he can surely see my face, see the embarrassment on the surface of my skin. It's too awful to consider.

In vain, I try to hold my breath. I try to sink back into stillness. Maybe if I can convince him I'm asleep, we can both forget this terrible event ever happened.

"I know you're awake." Amusement colors his voice. "You can quit faking now, Mercedes. Either open your eyes and get out of bed yourself, or I will drag you out and haul you to the stables naked. I can assure you it makes no difference to me."

My breath hitches at his threat, and I know this is

not something I want to test him on. So far, clothing does not seem to be a luxury he wants to allow. He's in the habit of undressing me for reasons I can't entirely fathom. We both know he can't ever touch me. But does he want to?

I try to shove the thought from my mind as quickly as it enters. He gives me another shake, and reluctantly, I open my eyes and glance at the clock to see that it's only 4:30 a.m.

"What sort of fuckery is this?" I glance up at him in dismay. "I only went to bed two hours ago."

"That's not my problem," he answers coldly. "While you are under my roof, you will learn to keep a schedule. Your days of sleeping in are a luxury that will not be afforded to you in my care."

"Of course not," I hiss. "Because you get off on this. What kind of a sick person do you have to be to enjoy torturing others?"

"That's rich." He snorts. "Coming from you. Why don't you tell me this, little monster? What kind of sick person do you have to be to enjoy it?"

"Enjoy it?" I narrow my gaze on his infuriatingly handsome face and that smug expression I want to smack right off it. "There is not one thing I enjoy about your company. And from what I can tell, I'm not the only one. That's why you have to pay women to do your bidding. And if I were to venture a guess, it must be the same reason nobody ever sees you in the company of your own family. Even they can't stand you."

Almost immediately, I can tell I've gone too far with my observations. Storm clouds roll into his normally calm eyes, and the control he wears like armor seems to fracture almost instantly as his hand whips out and squeezes my jaw in his palm.

"Don't ever mention my family or presume to know anything about me. Do you understand?"

His voice shakes the room, and if I'm honest, staring him down like this is terrifying. I've never seen Judge come uncorked. But a small, twisted part of me also gets a secret thrill knowing I've pricked a nerve with him.

That same part of me relishing in the small victory also wants to know his limits. How far can I push him? At what point will he truly snap?

The broken part of me understands these are important details. I need to know how far he'll go, as painful as it might be. I need to have a full grasp on how badly he can hurt me so I know how to prepare for it in the future.

So despite the fact that I'm shaking, I steel myself in his grasp and stare down the beast inside him.

"What's the matter, Judge? You can't swallow the taste of your own medicine? Is it too bitter?"

When he doesn't answer, I go on, trudging into a territory I know we might never come back from.

"Is it mommy issues? Is that it? Is that why you like to exert your power over me? Or was it someone else? They say the apple doesn't fall far from the tree. Are you taking a page out of daddy's book, or perhaps even your grandfather?"

His nostrils flare, his grip on me tightening to the point of pain. I know I'm throwing salt in the wound. It hasn't been that long since his grandfather passed, something that's common knowledge in The Society. But for a moment, I think it doesn't matter. He knows what I'm doing, and Judge has always displayed an eerie ability to remain calm in almost every situation I've seen him in.

Some of the tension in my body ebbs away when he releases my face from his grip, and I prepare myself for a biting remark. But that isn't what I get. Without warning, he lunges toward me, and my instinct is to flee. I scramble backward, getting tangled in the bedding, and he captures me far too easily. For the first time, real fear streaks through me as he pins me to the bed and climbs astride my torso, locking me in place between his muscular thighs.

"Judge—" I try for a feeble protest as he yanks my tank top up over my head roughly, dragging my arms with it. He uses the material to secure my wrists in place, stretching the fabric until it starts to tear before he ties me in a knot so tight, I know I can't escape.

I gulp in air, and he reaches behind him, shoving my shorts down to my ankles. When I buck up against him in resistance, he turns his fiery gaze back to me and pinches my nipple so hard I shriek from the shock of it.

"Enough," he roars, slapping my breast with his palm. "Is this what you wanted? Is that it, Mercedes?"

When I don't answer him, he slaps my other breast, and I jolt, my chest arching up off the bed as if I'm offering myself to him. I hate that display of weakness, but nobody has ever touched me like this. Nobody has ever shocked me this way.

"Answer me!" He slaps each breast again, his eyes flaring as my breaths come harder and faster.

"Fuck you." My voice trembles, and I hate that too.

I feel like I'm coming apart at the seams. I don't know what's happening to me, but I can't tear my eyes away from him as he puts me into my place in a way that nobody else has ever managed to.

"There you go, saying it again," he growls. "You should be careful what you wish for, little monster."

My breath catches as he flips me over beneath him, and my face falls into the pillow. He adjusts his position, moving his body lower to pin my legs again. I try to arch up, but he shoves me back down with a firm palm in the center of my back. And then that same palm thunders against my ass cheek with a ferocity I know will leave me thinking of him every time I sit for the next two days.

I try and fail to swallow my yelp, but it doesn't matter. He doesn't give me a second to recover before he smacks the same area, igniting a fire under my skin as heat blooms beneath the surface. This is worse than the crop somehow because it's unpredictable. He aims with purpose, but I don't know where he'll strike. At first, I think it's just the one side, and then he starts in on the other. He keeps going until I'm quite certain my ass is a giant red cherry, swollen from the artistry of his punishment. The thing that occurs to me as I'm lying there, panting like a dog, is just how true it is. Judge doesn't do anything sloppy. Even when he loses control, he does everything with purpose.

"Had enough, or shall I keep going?" He sounds breathless, his voice rough, and it doesn't escape my notice that when he leans forward, I can feel the warmth of his erection against my ass.

When I don't reply, he forces my legs wider and slaps my pussy again. Only this time, he freezes when he pulls his hand back and feels the undeniable evidence of what can only be my arousal. I don't know. It doesn't make sense. Logically, I'm aware of that. But I can feel it too. I'm soaked for him. Maybe it's biology. Maybe it's derangement. But the evidence of my body's betrayal is there, and I wish the earth would just open up and swallow me whole.

There's a long moment when the room falls into complete stillness. The only sound is our collective ragged breaths. His body is warm, trapping me against the bed, and I'm too exhausted to keep fighting. He's done what he set out to do by leeching every last ounce of my resistance this morning, but at what cost?

"No more," he grunts finally. "I'm taking you to the stables now, and you're going to do what I tell you. Understand?"

I'm so relieved he's not forcing me to acknowledge what he just felt between my thighs that all I can do is nod. But his mercy is not easily won, and he proves it when he removes the knotted fabric around my wrists, followed by the shorts around my ankles. He has me naked. Again.

"Judge—" I squeak when he drags me upright, wrapping one of the sheets around my body. "What are you—?"

He hoists me up over his shoulder, my legs dangling over his front while my head bobs over his back... with a perfect view of his ass. *Oh, dear baby Jesus.*

"You can't—"

"Don't fucking test me," he snaps. "I'm on a schedule, and already, you have delayed me for the second time this week."

I heed his warning, not because I'm afraid, but because I know it's fruitless. I'm only delaying the inevitable. And right now, all I can think about is if he's taking me outside, perhaps there's a chance at escape.

He hauls me out of my room and down the hall, winding his way through the house until we reach the front door. As my luck would have it, Miriam is about, smirking as she watches him carry me off like he's about to sell me at the market.

He doesn't set me down, even once we're outside. He hauls me like it's nothing to him, and I suppose it shouldn't surprise me, given his obvious strength. If he really wanted to hurt me, he could, very easily. Not that my ass isn't smarting, but I know it could be worse. So, so much worse.

He enters the stables and sets me down with a grunt, grabbing me by the wrist and yanking me forward. It's at about this point I realize how truly disgusting it is in here. It smells like horse shit, and the floor beneath my bare feet is undoubtedly filthy too. I thought the soup incident was bad, but I realize now it was nothing compared to this.

Judge stops at a supply closet off to the left, opens it, and retrieves what appears to be a large leather dog collar and two locks. When he turns to me, my instinct is to pull away, but he tightens his grip and halts me with little effort.

"Fight me, and I will make this so much worse for you," he growls. "I'm done playing, Mercedes."

I swallow as he yanks the sheet off my body, and it falls to the floor. Then he spins me in his arms and secures the collar around my neck, followed by a padlock that he loops through the ring and one of the spare holes, making it impossible to remove. When he's finished with that, he leads me to the center of the stables, where a large metal arm hangs from the ceiling with a chain dangling from the end all the way to the floor. On the bottom of the chain, there are four more individual attachments, one of which he secures to my collar with the addition of another lock.

When he's satisfied that he has me shackled like a dog, he returns to the entrance and retrieves a wheelbarrow, a shovel, and a thick broom.

"Start on that side." He points at one row of stalls. "I'll take the horses out of the other, and you can clean those while I ride. I want them all done by the time I return in an hour. Is that clear?"

"You must be delusional." I snort.

"Test me," he threatens. "Either you'll do this or I'll lock you up naked in the cellar where I kept Ivy, and I won't come back for you for a week."

This time, his warning sends a real frisson of terror through me. That place was so fucking creepy. There's no way in hell I'm going in there with all the skeletal remains of god knows what creatures. I actually felt pity for the woman when she was in there, and that's saying a lot.

"Do we have an understanding?" he demands.

"Yes." I glare at him. "I understand perfectly well." He turns on his heel, and I mutter under my breath. "Fucking asshole."

JUDGE DIDN'T LEAVE me with a lot of instructions, but he did add a few more while he was preparing the horses. I'll admit, it felt strange watching him in his natural environment. He was at ease, the tension leaving his body as he climbed astride one of the horse's backs and led the others along beside him out of the stables.

Once I was left alone with my thoughts and nothing else, of course, I tried and failed to release myself from the restraints he'd placed on me. The locks weren't overly large, but they were strong. I attempted to break them off by force, which was stupid in retrospect because it left me with little to show for it other than a bruise on my neck. When that didn't work, I considered trying to cut through the leather collar but noted with frustration that Judge had taken care to remove any sharp instruments from my immediate surroundings and locked the closet before he left.

I tested the limits of my chain to see how far I

could go, which, in the end, wasn't that far. It allowed me enough length to reach both ends of the stables but no farther. I was well and truly trapped, and given that I'd already wasted a considerable amount of time trying to find a way out, I had no choice but to accept my fate. It was either clean up horse shit, or have my ass thrown in the cellar with no creature comforts at all.

It was a painful task dragging myself back into the stalls. The smell of urine was overwhelming, and it burned my nostrils as I worked. But worse was the fact that I had zero protection on my body. The straw chafed against my skin as I stepped over it, and replacing it with fresh bedding was no easy feat. My entire body was scratched and raw. On top of that, I had stepped in a pile of manure when I wasn't paying attention, and I had slipped and fallen into the soiled bedding. So I was quite certain I smelled and looked disgusting.

It was truly awful, and I was really feeling sorry for myself until I remembered why I was here in the first place. That woman I had killed. As much as I didn't want to admit it, this was probably the best alternative I could have hoped for. If I didn't have the protection of The Society behind me, and my brother's swift cleaning of that mess before anyone could find out, I could easily be sitting in The Tribunal's prison for the rest of my life.

There are moments when I still wonder if it's

what I deserve. Those thoughts war with my justifications. The reminder that she tried to kill my brother. I want to believe she got what she deserved because it makes me feel better about what I've done, but it doesn't bring me any peace. Nothing brings me peace.

I'm exhausted and emotional by the time Judge finally returns. And worse yet, I'm not finished. I'm on the last stall, sniffling quietly, when I hear the clip-clop of the horses' hooves over the floor. I don't turn to look. Like a well-trained circus animal, I shovel faster, dreading that he might follow through on his word to toss me in the cellar.

I hear the stall doors closing as he puts the horses away, and my heartbeat quickens when the sound of his boots approaches me from behind. He doesn't say a word as I race to finish, but I can feel his eyes boring into my back. The undeniable evidence of my scars is on display in the light of morning.

"That's good enough for today," he clips the words out with a finality that makes me question if he will still punish me. I don't want to believe it, but I can't stop thinking about the possibility.

I turn toward him slowly, my head almost too heavy to lift. At the moment, it's painfully obvious that I don't have an ounce of pride left. As his eyes rake over me, I'm certain I'll see some satisfaction as he realizes that, but instead, there's mounting concern when he notices the rashes and scrapes all over my body.

"Why didn't you tell me you were allergic?" He frowns.

I glance down at the red welts on my body, my voice barely a whisper. "I'm not. My skin is sensitive, and I had no protection from the straw."

"Come." He joins me in the stall and grabs me by the arm, but this time, his touch is gentle.

I follow him into the center of the stables, where he unchains me from the large metal arm holding me hostage. After that, he carefully removes my collar and tosses it into the corner, along with the locks. For a second, I consider the possibility of running now, but realistically, I know he'd catch me before I even made it twenty feet. I'm too exhausted. My muscles are aching, and my head is throbbing. And all I want to do is fall into bed and cry.

Judge retrieves the sheet he hung on a hook outside the stables and wraps me up again before scooping me up over his shoulder once more.

"I can walk," I groan.

He doesn't answer, and I don't fight.

We make it to the safety of my room, and I'm hopeful that he'll just leave me to wallow in my misery, but of course that doesn't happen. Instead, he leads me into the bathroom and turns on the shower, testing the temperature of the water before he gestures for me.

"Get in."

It's one order I can't protest because I'm filthy, and I think it's very likely I'll probably need three showers before the day is through so I can feel like I actually washed it away. I step into the stone shower and under the spray, blinking through the steam as I wait for Judge to leave. Only, he doesn't.

Instead, he tugs off his shirt and kicks off his boots. When he reaches for the zipper on his riding breeches, I swallow so loudly, I'm convinced he heard it. But he doesn't seem to notice or care. And then before my eyes, he yanks off his breeches, leaving him standing there in nothing but a pair of black briefs.

I swallow again when he approaches, shaking my head infinitesimally. "I don't need any help."

He sighs. "For once in your life, just do as you're told, will you?"

He doesn't give me an opportunity to decide for myself, but rather he turns me in his arms and reaches for the soap. I'm frozen, my nerves unsettling me as I anticipate his touch. I don't know what it will be like. Nobody has washed me in a very long time. The last time was when Antonia tended to my wounds in those weeks following the beating that left me with my scars. But Judge isn't Antonia, and I feel the presence of his fingers on my skin in a way I'm certain I'll never feel anything else.

They are rough and large but gentle at the same

time. Like everything else he does, he washes me with a thoroughness that ensures he doesn't leave a single spot of skin untouched. I'm almost grateful that he started at my back so he can't see the expression on my face. But I'm certain he can still feel the soft shudder of my skin as his hands glide over it. My ass is still sore as hell, undoubtedly marked with his handprints, which he lingers to examine for a few moments before cleaning them tenderly.

I close my eyes and try to take myself to another place, but my mind drags me back to the present. To the hands touching my body. To the strange feelings stirring in my belly when he pulls me against the hard plane of his body and his fingertips edge around my ribs. I suck in a sharp breath when he washes my belly and then stop breathing entirely when his hands glide over my breasts, pausing there for a moment longer than what I'm sure is necessary. If I didn't know any better, I would think I heard him biting back the sound of a groan, but I can't see his face. I can, however, feel his cock against me, even through the material of his briefs. It's warm and... *huge*.

For a second, I find myself wondering what it looks like. What it would feel like in my palm. Or more importantly, buried deep inside me. Would it hurt? Of course, it probably would. But it would also feel good, I think. A good hurt.

My face flames with heat, and I shake my head

again, silently cursing myself. Judge doesn't acknowledge my strange behavior. He continues to wash me, not shying away from any of the areas on my body. When his palm glides down between my thighs, I almost buckle in his arms, and I don't know why. But the gentle caress of his fingers in such an intimate place is doing strange things to me. Things that shouldn't be happening. If Santiago ever found out he even did this much, my brother would murder him.

Still, it gives me a secret thrill I can't deny. We might hate each other, but there's no arguing a part of him wants me too. And I find myself wondering if a part of me wants him? Or am I just reaching for comfort in a terrible situation, even if it is from my captor?

That question is laid to rest when he releases me momentarily to let me rinse. When I'm done, he moves on to shampooing my hair, which is a whole other sensory experience. My hair is long and thick, but he takes his time working through each strand, even pausing to massage my scalp when he notices the way it gives me goose bumps.

He rinses me again, and, to be extra thorough, washes my body one more time. I'm grateful for that small gesture because I would have done the same. But I'm also slightly relieved that it's not over yet.

God, there is seriously something wrong with

me. By the time he releases me, my legs feel like jelly, and I can barely stand.

"Go dry yourself off," he says. "I'll be out to join you in a minute."

I do as he bids, stepping out to towel off, lingering in the bathroom for far too long. I'm curious if he'll undress completely, and I can admit that maybe a part of me wants to get a glimpse. Just to see what he's packing down there. To see the weapon between his thighs.

Judge turns away and doesn't acknowledge that he knows I'm still there. He yanks off his briefs and tosses them onto the wet floor, then turns the spray to cold. I freeze, unable to move as my eyes survey the perfect globes of his muscular ass.

Holy shit. It really is... beautiful. That's such a stupid thing to say about the man I hate more than anything right now, but I can't pretend it's not true. He has a gloriously sculpted body, like a piece of art. You can't help but stare at it. While my eyes are roaming over him, I catch a glimpse of some dark ink wrapped around his side and onto his back. At first glance, I think it must be the brand of the IVI tattoo we all have inked into our skin. Then he turns and catches me gawking, raising a brow as my eyes instinctively head south. And there it is in all its glory. The long, hard cock jutting out from that dark patch of hair. He doesn't even try to hide it, and I wonder if this is a test. If he wants to see how I'll react.

I want to believe I have a good poker face, but when I glance at him again, I can tell he knows. He hasn't missed the way my nipples have tightened or my belly has clenched. He can see that I'm curious. More than curious.

I'm... I don't know what the hell I am, actually.

9

JUDGE

I switch off the water and reach for a towel, Mercedes's eyes following my every move. Her neck and cheeks are flushed, and her eyes keep dropping south. I'm aroused. Still. Even after the freezing spray of water. Washing her, having her that close, touching her, well, fuck. I am a man.

A man who should know better.

I rode hard this morning. The truth was, I needed to after spanking her. I don't even know if it was the spanking or the fact that she was wet that did it. I can still smell the delicate scent of her arousal on my fingers.

When women are sent to me to be disciplined, I draw a very clear line. One I've never come close to crossing even when the opportunity arose. Mercedes, though, I don't know what the fuck it is with her, but all I can think about when I'm around her is how tight her pussy would feel around my cock. How she'd cling to me as I claimed her. How my name would sound on her lips when she came on my dick.

Fuck.

I need to stop this, or I'll need another cold shower. After scrubbing my hair with the towel, I wrap it low around my hips.

Mercedes clears her throat, and I look up to find her eyes on me. Her cheeks are flushed, and she's quick to shift her gaze away.

"Come here," I tell her.

She steps toward me. I notice how her pupils are dilated, her lips are parted, and her nipples are hard as pebbles beneath the towel she's holding loosely over her shoulders. She lowers her gaze again as I take the towel from her and dry her shoulders and arms, watching the top of her head as I do.

She reaches out, fingertips hesitantly tracing the skin of my chest, my abdomen. My muscles bunch beneath her touch, but I remain still as she tests.

"What are you doing?" I finally ask, though I don't stop her.

She looks up through thick lashes and watches me as she lets her fingertips slip toward the towel.

My dick responds, and I grab her wrist harder than I mean to. "What are you doing, Mercedes?"

"Nothing," she snaps.

I study her, keep her tiny wrist in my hand then turn her arm over to look at the delicate skin there.

"You don't want to touch me like that."

Her cheeks burn. She blinks several times, clearly embarrassed, her hand tightening around the knot of the towel as she tries to tug herself free of me but fails.

"That side of me you do not want to know, understand? It's not for you." *Just as you're not for me.*

It takes her a moment, but she steels herself and turns her narrowed eyes up to mine. "You can touch me, though? Any way you want."

"To discipline you. To clean you."

She tugs. "Let me go."

"Do you understand?"

She snorts. "Don't flatter yourself, Judge. I can have any man I want."

My jaw tenses, and I realize I'm squeezing her wrist too hard when she winces. I let her go, and she takes two steps away.

"Any man. Any time," she says, then cocks her head and grins that arrogant, self-satisfied Mercedes De La Rosa grin.

I close the space between us, relishing in the fact that she takes two away before her back hits the wall and she's out of room. I touch her chin and tilt her face up. "I have no doubt they drop to their knees on your command, little monster. But I'm not one of those boys you can wrap around your pretty little finger."

She jerks her chin out of my grasp. "As if I'd want to."

I grin. Good. This is good. We were moving into dangerous territory there. I turn to exit the bathroom, but before I'm even out the door, I hear her gasp, and I stop dead. Because fuck. I haven't showered with a woman in a long time. Too much intimacy. What just happened proved that, didn't it?

Without looking back, I continue into her bedroom.

She follows. "What is that tattoo?"

"It's nothing." In her bedroom, I see the tray of food Miriam must have returned. Still uneaten for the most part. Some of the bread has been picked at. It'll grow mold soon. "Your breakfast is here, Mercedes," I tell her as I reach the door to exit her room.

She's right behind me. "Judge?" Her fingers wrap around my bicep just as I pull the door open. "What the...?" She touches the spot. "There's a scar under there. What is this?"

I turn to face her. "The past. Get dressed, eat your breakfast, and think about why you're here or you'll be spending another day locked in this room."

She searches my face, hers unreadable. "Who did that to you?"

Is she taunting me? Using my own words to play with me? "Go eat your breakfast. Now."

"I'm not eating that. Tell me who did it? And why you'd hide it under a tattoo. Or can you ask me, but I can't ask you? Like you can touch me, but I can't touch you."

"You will learn to do exactly as I say."

"Fuck I will. You forget who you're dealing with. I'm not some courtesan working the Cat House. I'm Mercedes De La Rosa. You don't simply get to dismiss me."

"Is that so?"

I turn to her and close the door. There's a finality that comes with that sound. A shifting in the air, a weight to it.

I peel her hand off my arm and walk her backward to the wall, setting my hand against it and taking in the difference in size between us. I lean in close and scan her eyes, her flushed cheeks, and her mouth, noting the subtle signs of arousal. Both of her hands come up to grip the towel tight.

"You don't want me to dismiss you?"

Her pulse thrums at her neck.

"Alright. You want my attention? You have it. Now drop the towel."

She swallows audibly but doesn't obey.

"Drop it. Now."

Slowly, she does it, letting it fall to the floor and baring herself to me. I look down at her breasts and flat stomach. Then the slit of her sex. I return my gaze to hers.

"You're very beautiful. But you already know that, don't you?"

She bites her lip.

"And perhaps we're both forgetting the reason you're here."

"Judge—"

"Turn around and put your hands against the wall."

Goose bumps rise along her arms as she stares up at me, trying to understand what's happening. I'm not sure myself, to be honest. But I can't have her asking questions about my past. About the wound that almost killed me. So I will distract us both. And I'll put her firmly on the opposite side of the boxing ring while I'm at it because that's safer for her. For both of us.

"Do it."

She turns, hands shaking a little as she sets them against the wall.

"Now walk backward but keep your hands where they are."

"Judge, I—"

"Don't stop until I tell you." I give her space and watch as she does what I say, her fingertips trailing down the wall as she moves her feet farther from it, bending at the hips. "Stop," I tell her when her torso is parallel to the floor. "Spread your legs wider."

She glances back at me, eyes nervous but curious. She spreads her legs to shoulder width.

"Wider."

She hesitates but then does it, and from between her ass cheeks, I see the inviting mound of her sex. The glistening pink folds of her lips open. The tiny shadow of her other hole.

I swallow hard, pressing my palm against the length of my erection before moving closer to her and sliding my fingernails over the curve of her hip. With my other hand, I take a handful of hair and twist it around my fist. I press myself against her ass.

She gasps, but I don't move. Let her feel me. Let her know exactly the beast she's toying with.

"This is what the women at the Cat House do for me," I say in a low voice. "For starters. And anything else I ask."

Nothing. Not a word.

I tug the fistful of hair, straightening her, and wrap my other hand around her stomach to hold her to me.

"Is this what you wanted? You are curious about the Cat House."

"Let go."

I hold her tighter. "Tell me." She shudders as my breath caresses her ear. "Tell me, Mercedes."

"So I'm no different than a whore to you?" she asks instead of answering me, but I do hear the tremble of her voice.

I bring my jaw to her cheek. I haven't shaved yet, and I rub the scruff of it against her soft skin. "No, little monster. You are nothing like them. But you are impulsive and spoiled and arrogant. Those things I will break you of."

"Let me go."

"You sure you want that?"

"Let go, you fucker."

I snort and tug her head backward, forcing a cry from her. "Do I scare you?"

"What the hell do you want from me?" she yells.

"Are you ready to listen?"

She grunts, twisting against me.

"For starters, I'd like you to get dressed."

With a grin, I let her go and step backward. She spins to face me.

"Yet you're the one who keeps stripping me naked. What the fuck is that about? We're not in your courtroom, Judge." She emphasizes my name, my position.

"Get dressed, Mercedes. And eat your food. I'll be back tonight before dinner, and when I'm back, I'm going to ask you again why you're here. If you can't answer, you'll be spending another day locked in your room tomorrow. After cleaning the stables, that is, so I suggest you think hard. Can you do that for me?"

"I'll do nothing for you."

"For yourself then."

Her face falls, that vulnerability exposed again, at least momentarily. She hangs her head. I just reminded her exactly why she's here and what she did. All that talk about walking through the dark? I'm sending her there alone. She may be strong, but I get the feeling she's also been alone for a very long time, and I don't want that for her.

I sigh. And I decide to give her something. "Would you like to see the boys?" She knows instantly I mean the dogs. She loves them. I noticed that the last time she was here, which was shocking, considering, well, the dogs themselves are a frightening brood to behold. But Mercedes took to them instantly and they to her.

She glances up at me with both suspicion and hope in her eyes. She nods once.

"Get dressed. Lois will bring them up."

She doesn't say anything, but I'm pretty sure she thinks I'm lying. I walk to the door, open it, and step out into the hall. When I glance back, I find her still standing there, still staring at me, her forehead furrowed.

"Get dressed and eat. Understand?"

She nods.

10

JUDGE

Fuck. What am I doing with her?

I dress in my room, my usual three-piece tweed suit for the rare days I don't have to be in the courtroom. I could work from home, but I go to my office in town. I need to get away from here, away from her. Even with a wall dividing us, I feel her presence. And it's fucking with me.

It's my own damn fault. I should know better. Santiago trusted me to take care of his sister. He has put his faith in me. I'm sure showering with her wasn't something he imagined I'd be doing as part of her discipline. And the thing after? Against the wall? What the fuck was that?

I look up from the work on my desk and scrub my hand through my hair. It's the little things she does. When I woke her, how she curled into me, leaning into my hand, and moaning. The way my body reacted when she ran the tips of her fingers over my chest and abdomen. What having her near me does to me. It's nothing I've ever experienced with any other woman. And it's not just the fact of my dick getting hard at the mere thought of her. It's more. There's so much more to Mercedes than anyone knows. Than even her brother, the person closest to her, knows. There's a vulnerability inside her. She tries to hide it and usually succeeds, but I know she wants to give it over. Give it up and be held in arms strong enough to carry her and give her space to breathe.

I want to be that person. A part of me has always wanted to be that person for her.

But it's out of the question. I meant what I said. I'm dangerous for her. I have no intention of marrying. I know what I'm capable of, and I won't do that to her. But I can't ruin her for another, even if the thought of any other man touching her makes me want to punch my fist through a wall.

I'm reading the same document for the umpteenth time when my phone rings. It's my secretary. I push a button. "Yes?"

"Judge Montgomery, I'm sorry to bother you, but your mother has called three times. She insists she needs to talk to you."

My mother. Wasn't last night enough? "You're paid to handle things like this, Meredith."

"I'm so sorry. She's just…"

I sigh. Meredith is sweet, and I'm sure my mother bulldozed right over her. "It's all right. I know." I lean back in my chair. "Put her through."

"Right away, sir."

"Well, finally you can find time in your busy day to take my call," she starts.

"Mother. Good afternoon to you."

"Afternoon. It's evening. I've been calling all day. That dim-witted secretary you have—"

"What can I do for you?" I ask as I check the time. It's a little past seven. I didn't even realize how late it was. And Meredith was probably too nervous to say anything. I'll make sure she receives overtime for the extra hours.

"We didn't finish our conversation last night," she says.

"No, we didn't. And there's a reason for that. My brother is a grown man. I think it's about time he speaks for himself, don't you?"

"You cut him off, Judge. You can't do that."

"Why not? He was blackmailing grandfather."

I can almost hear her displeasure in the pause before she speaks. "He was protecting himself after your grandfather threatened to take everything away."

"And why did he do that, mother?"

Silence.

"Selective memory?"

"What he did was wrong."

"He almost killed me."

"And he'll apologize."

I snort. "An apology when my life almost ended... I'm not sure that goes far enough."

"What do you want from him?"

"I want him to face the consequences of his actions."

"What? You want for him to stand before The Tribunal? Imagine the shame it will bring to our family."

"That was grandfather's area. I don't care about appearances."

"Besides, they'll lock him up, and you know it."

"Maybe he deserves to be locked up." My grandfather kept tabs on him over the five years he's been MIA. I know what Theron's been up to, and it's no good.

"Your grandfather wanted to punish him for my mistake."

"For your extramarital affair, you mean?"

"Watch your mouth."

"What did I say? The truth?"

"He already punished me. You stood witness. Or have you forgotten? Selective memory, Judge?"

Fuck.

I don't have anything to say about that. I wish I'd

never seen it. I wish I'd never learned what my grandfather, a man I loved and looked up to, was capable of. But then again, I loved Theron too. We were close, but he turned on me and stabbed me in the back. Literally.

"Theron didn't choose his parents," my mother continues. I missed whatever else she said before. "It's not quite fair to punish him for that, is it? And besides, after what I've been through, don't I have a right to say where some of the money goes?"

"It doesn't work that way. Not for us. We've discussed this. Even if father was alive, the inheritance would have gone to me."

"You and your brother."

"I'm firstborn."

"Well, la-di-da for you."

"Mother, I don't have time for this."

"No, I guess you don't with your new plaything in the house. In a hurry to get back to her?"

I grit my teeth. She found out about Mercedes although it's not like I could keep that a secret. But the circumstances of her presence at my house? The plaything comment? What can she know?

"If Theron wants to return, he knows how to get in touch with me. In the meantime, if I find him on the grounds, he will be arrested. Understood?"

"My cottage is on the grounds."

"Exactly. Goodbye, Mother."

She mutters something, then hangs up. I put the

phone down. It doesn't bother me anymore, my mother's hate. Did she always hate me? She favored Theron, and for a long time, I assumed it was because he was the youngest. I know the truth now, though.

The thought of my brother brings me back to my conversation with Mercedes this morning. She isn't going to drop her questions. And she has a point. I want to know about her scars. She wants to know about mine. Except she can't know about this one. Ever. Not she. Not Santiago. Not anyone.

What do I want with my brother? What would I do if he came home?

I take a deep breath in and push the thought of Theron aside. He's too much of a coward to face me. Because only a coward would stab a man in the back.

I get up, pack my things, and put my jacket on. I want to go home. And there's only one reason for it. My little monster.

I'M NOT in my study at home twenty minutes before I hear a knock on my door, and Miriam enters, looking irritated.

"Miriam, how can I help you?" What did the little monster do now? The thought is amusing, actually. Mercedes will find every button to push with this woman. And part of me can't blame her. Miriam used to work for my mother, but she moved to the house a few months ago. I wonder if that's where my mother learned about Mercedes. If that's where the plaything comment came in.

"Sir, if I'm supposed to be in charge of Ms. De La Rosa, you need to tell Lois that she is to do as I say."

"Do as you say?" I raise both eyebrows.

She clears her throat, realizing her mistake, but collects herself quickly. "It's just those dogs are still in her room!" She doesn't like the dogs. And they don't like her.

"Well, I did give my permission. That's on me, Miriam."

"I'm certain she fed them her food."

"Mmm. I'm certain you're right." Pestilence would scarf down old bacon in a heartbeat. I guess they all would. "I'm sure she's hungry. I'd better go see to her."

"Well, that's the thing. Lois sent up food! A banquet! All her favorites."

It takes all I have to keep my mouth in a displeased flat line, although I find this so amusing. So typical for Mercedes, my spoiled little monster. My charming little monster. When she wants to be, that is. And she has charmed Lois.

"I'll discuss it with her. Let's remember this isn't a prison. She won't be fed bread and water." I walk her to the door. "And I assure you you're in charge of my houseguest. Why don't you take the night off? Go on."

"Sir, I don't need the night off."

"Take it anyway. I'll see you tomorrow morning. Bright and early. Good night, Miriam."

I leave her in the hallway and head upstairs, smiling as I go.

I change into riding clothes, then unlock Mercedes's door and enter.

"You could knock," she says from where she's sitting on her bed like a fucking queen surrounded by all four hounds. They're lying with their heads on her lap as she holds a magazine in one hand and eats a macaron from a plate of colorful macarons at her side.

"Well, look at you," I say as the dogs come to greet me. I pet them, taking time for each of them. I love these dogs. Have even before Theron abandoned them. I protected them from my grandfather when he would have drowned them. Theron had only brought the dogs into the house to get under his skin. But I wouldn't give them up.

"What?" Mercedes says from her place as she selects another macaron. "You didn't say I wasn't allowed food. Just that I had to finish my tray."

"And I'm sure it was you who finished it."

She grins like the cat who swallowed the canary and shoves an entire macaron into her mouth.

"These are delicious. Lois has outdone herself," she says around her mouthful.

"You're going to spoil your appetite for dinner."

"I'll be fine. I've been starved, remember?"

"Starved is quite the stretch." I walk over to her, the dogs on my heels, and pick up a macaron.

"Not that one. Pistachio is my favorite. Take the vanilla. Those are boring."

I raise my eyebrows and swallow the pistachio macaron, not missing the look she gives me. "You're something else, you know that?"

"Thank you."

"Most people would not take that as a compliment."

"I'm not most people." She grins up at me, and it's as if the woman I left here this morning is a distant memory. She's distracting herself. The dogs. The food. The magazine. I won't have that.

"Why are you here, Mercedes?"

Her expression falters momentarily but then her eyes narrow. "What? Can't stand to see me happy?"

"Are you happy?"

She shrugs a shoulder.

"Why are you here?"

She wraps an arm around her middle and looks away. In her profile, I see the vulnerable girl she hides beneath her armor. The damaged one. The frightened one.

"Mercedes." I touch her cheek and brush her hair away. "I'm not asking to hurt you."

She looks down at her lap, and Pestilence jumps up onto the bed as if sensing this shift. He whines and lays his head in her hands. I wouldn't normally allow them on the bed, but I think she needs this. She pets him, leans down to kiss the top of his head, then straightens back up.

"I'm dangerous," she says, swiping the back of her hand across her face.

I remain silent, watching her. Waiting.

"What I did to that woman." More tears. She still won't look at me. "I didn't mean to. But maybe, in a way, I did. I'm no good."

"Silly little monster." I tilt her face up. "You wanted to protect your family. You thought you were."

She shakes her head. "And then there's Ivy. I hate her. I hate her for taking Santi away from me."

"Well, that you're going to need to get over. She is your brother's wife."

The tears in her eyes freeze into ice. "Only for a limited time. Nine months. *If* he can stomach the idea of impregnating a Moreno. And that's a big if."

"Mercedes—"

"Can I get out of here now?"

"What if it happens? What if there's a baby? Will you hate your brother's child?"

She scrubs her face and pushes off the bed on

the other side. "I need to get out of this room." She turns to me. "Please, just for a little bit. Then you can lock me up again."

She's wearing yoga pants again. And another sweater. "Change into jeans and a warm, close-fitting jacket. We're going to go for a ride."

11

MERCEDES

Judge leads two horses from the stalls and dresses them while I entertain myself by playing with the four beasts at my side. War nudges my hand with his wet nose, jealous of the attention Death has been receiving. Their names are a little dramatic, even for my tastes, but I can admit they are beautiful creatures. I always wanted a dog growing up, but my father never allowed us to have pets. I'm sure most people would assume I'd be the type to tote around a Chihuahua in a fancy bag, but I like Judge's Dobermans. They're relatable in a way. When people who don't understand their temperament look at them, their instinct is to fear them. They look terrifying, and I'm quite certain they would be if the need arose for them to defend their owners. But they are so much more than loyal protectors. They are gentle-natured too. Playful.

Affectionate. Loving. It's what's beneath the surface that counts. And I believe in some ways, they are misunderstood the way I often feel I am.

Most people don't look past my tough exterior to get to know the other qualities I possess. Either my armor is impenetrable, or they don't believe I'm worth the effort. What I said to Judge was true. I could get any man I want, but their affection only runs skin deep. As soon as they realize they have to actually work at getting to know me, it isn't worth their time.

It's a lonely existence, and until I met Solana and Georgie, I didn't even know what it felt like to have true friends. But when I look up to find Judge watching me with the dogs, I know he's not like anyone else I've ever known. He sees... too much. With every day I spend here, he's slowly chiseling away at my armor. He wants to know my secrets. He wants to know everything. And I can't understand why. If this is just a job to him, why does he care?

"You can take Temperance." He leads the black mare with a glossy coat toward me. "She's a retired racehorse, but she still has some get up and go."

"Hello, Temperance." I greet her softly, then move toward her in a gentle manner so I don't spook her. "What a beauty you are."

I let her sniff my hand, and Judge gives me a curious glance as if he's surprised by my actions. Temperance returns the gesture with a snort and a nose boop to my palm. Once I have her approval, I stroke her face, and she closes her eyes, silently soaking it in.

"She likes you." Judge observes as if he didn't expect it, and I arch an eyebrow at him.

"What can I say? Not everyone has poor taste like you."

He doesn't smirk at my sarcastic remark, and if it weren't for the tension between his eyebrows, I wouldn't even be sure he heard me.

"Come." He holds out his hand. "I'll help you put on your helmet."

"I think I can manage." I reach out and take it from him, still smarting from his rejection earlier. He made it clear where he stands, and I don't want or need the confusion of trying to complicate this situation any further. The more distance we can keep between us, the better off I'll be.

Once I have my helmet secured, he offers me his hand to help me mount, but I ignore it. That unnerves him, and I can feel him watching me as I reach up and grab the reins with one hand and the saddle with the other. I ease my left foot up into the stirrup and hoist myself up, swinging my other leg astride the horse and mounting myself comfortably.

"You've ridden before?" Judge's question betrays his disbelief.

"You forget we grew up in the same circumstances." I stare at him incredulously. "I think our parents would have agreed that it's all part of being a well-rounded member of the upper echelon. A child simply cannot have one or two extracurriculars. They must excel at everything."

Judge frowns, his features tightening as he seems to recall a memory from his own past. I can't be sure, though because a moment later, it's as if it never happened. He mounts his own steed, one who seems far more spirited than mine. But why should that come as a surprise? I think Judge enjoys a challenge in all his endeavors.

"You ready?" He glances over at me, and I nod.

He clicks his tongue and gives the horse a light squeeze with his boots. I secure the reins in my grasp, and Temperance takes her cue from Judge, following along without requiring me to do anything.

We settle into an easy gait, heading for the field of open grass behind the house. The grounds of Judge's estate are huge, and I'm quite certain he explores more difficult terrain every morning when he goes for his rides. But I suspect he doesn't want to throw anything too tricky my way just yet, regardless of my assurance that I'm capable.

"How long has it been since you last rode?" he asks.

"I had lessons most summers from the age of ten," I tell him. "And then I'd still often visit my horse over the years. But I haven't been back since he passed away."

I can feel Judge watching me, and I don't know if I admitted too much. Perhaps it comes as a shock to learn that despite all appearances, I do have a heart. I have real feelings, and I am capable of caring about other people and animals too. Although, admittedly, animals are easier. They don't require much from you. All they want is your affection.

"I've forgotten how much I missed it," I add, the gentle breeze blowing against my cheeks. It feels refreshing after being locked in my room.

"What kind of horse?" Judge asks, seemingly interested in keeping the conversation going.

"A Percheron." I smirk at him. "They were a team actually. Prince and Duke. Prince was the one I rode often, although they were both magnificent. My instructor made the mistake of letting me ride him once for fun. After that, I never wanted to stop."

"Why am I not surprised you took on the mammoth?" Judge smirks.

"He was seventeen hands," I recall wistfully. "But a gentle giant, nonetheless."

He eyes me carefully, and I realize it's because I'm relaxed for the first time since I've been here. This feels natural to me. It feels good to be outside, breathing in fresh air while doing something physical. My body is in tune with the solid weight of Temperance beneath me. I trust her, and she trusts me, and there's something beautiful about that simplicity.

For a moment, I consider that I shouldn't be telling him how much I enjoy riding because that will just give him something else to leverage against me. Perhaps I should have played it smart and told him it was stupid so he'd make me do it every day. But what's done is done, and I can only hope that the warmth in his eyes means he approves of my willingness to ride with him. At least it will give me something to do. Something else to focus on.

"Shall we pick up the pace?" he asks.

I smile and give Temperance a gentle squeeze, and she breaks into a trot before I can even call out over my shoulder. "I thought you'd never ask."

When Judge comes for me in the morning, I'm already prepared. He smirks at his small victory when he sees me dressed and ready, and it grates at me, but I know resistance is futile at this point. If I don't go freely, he'll make me go naked again. And I can imagine few things worse than falling in a pile of horse shit with nothing to buffer it. So I go along with this charade, deciding that I have a new plan of action.

I realized last night when I was lying in bed, trying to forget the events of the past few days, that

His Rule

I've been going about this whole situation the wrong way. I've learned quickly that putting up a fight with Judge isn't going to get me anywhere, no matter how satisfying it might be to test his patience. What I need to do is earn my freedom and a small sliver of his trust. If I can access the grounds, I can find a way out of here and put this whole situation behind me.

Those are my best-laid plans. But patience isn't one of my virtues, and when Miriam comes to my room in the afternoon looking like she sucked on a lemon, it sours my mood.

"Sorry, princess. No buffet for you today." She sets the tray of what I can only describe as prison food onto the table. It looks like some sort of gelatinous loaf of cat food, and there's no way in hell I'm eating that.

When I glance up at her, she's wearing a cruel smirk, waiting for a reaction.

"Hey, Miriam." I smile at her sweetly. "Do you ever worry your face will get stuck like that?"

My victory is small but glorious, when she narrows her eyes at me and spits out her reply. "You think you're pretty special, don't you, Ms. De La Rosa? But I think you know there's nothing special about you. That's why you're still on the shelf at twenty-five. Nobody can stand to be around you. You can't even find some poor sap to marry you even with all your money and the trappings of your last name. Lord, what a poor soul the unfortunate bastard would be."

When I don't reply, her lips curve even higher, sensing that she's struck a nerve. But she doesn't stop there.

"I heard all about how Jackson Van der Smit kicked you to the curb and married his pretty wife instead. What's her name? Collette? I bet that didn't feel so good, being passed over like that. But I'm sure you're used to it. I guess that sort of thing must happen all the time when you have a pretty face and a rotten personality. I suppose that's the same reason your brother and his new wife wanted you out of the house. It didn't take long—"

"Get. Out!" I scream at her. "Get out of my room, now!"

When she doesn't move, my anger bubbles over, and I can feel it flooding my veins, taking over my senses. I know it's stupid, but I reach for the loaf of food and stare her down, my voice shaking from the force of my rage.

"I'm not going to ask you again," I threaten.

"You wouldn't dare—"

She can't even finish the sentence before I'm hurtling the goop across the room. It splatters across her face and chest, sliding down her cheeks and onto the floor with a satisfactory plop.

For a full second, Miriam is too stunned to move, and then she decides to show me her teeth. She stomps toward me, and I dart around her, narrowly missing her claws as she tries to grab me by the shirt. I'm faster than her, and she made the mistake of leaving my bedroom door open, so I bolt out of it and start running down the hall.

I'm thinking about how easy that was and wondering if I might actually make it to the front door. There won't be a thing she can say to stop me if I do. That's what I'm telling myself when I hear a war cry from behind me right before something heavy sails into the back of my head.

It happens so fast that I barely have the awareness of toppling forward. My knees bang against the floor first, followed by the side of my face bouncing off the hardwood. Pain streaks through me, and then everything goes black.

I don't know how long I'm out for. A few seconds. Maybe more. But even as I stir, consciousness doesn't seem to be fully within my grasp. My body feels heavy, impossibly so. And my arms ache as Miriam drags me along the floor by my wrists, my shoulders straining like they're going to dislocate. I can hear her muttering to herself as she pulls me along, pausing to grunt and catch her breath.

My instinct is to call out to Lois for help, but I can't seem to get my mouth to cooperate. My head is throbbing violently, and I feel like I might puke. God, what the hell did she hit me with?

It doesn't take long to answer that question. I see

the weapon lying on the floor of my room when she finally gets me inside. It's a solid wood paperweight from the desk. And for the first time since I arrived here, I wonder if maybe Judge isn't the real enemy. Because Miriam didn't hesitate to hurl that thing at the back of my head. I may have started it, but she could have easily finished it with that. As it stands, I'm fairly certain I have a concussion.

She slams the door shut and turns her venomous gaze on me, hurtling a wad of spit from her mouth onto my face.

"How does it feel to be the scum for once?" she hisses. "What have you got to say now, you little bitch?"

I moan as I try to wipe her saliva away in disgust, but it hurts too much. Everything hurts. And it only gets worse when Miriam continues her assault by kicking me in the ribs.

"You want to fuck with me? See what happens. I can make your life a living hell."

I can't move, and clearly, she can see that, but it doesn't stop her from kicking me again. My only defense is to try to curl into a ball, but it doesn't protect me when she grabs me by the hair and drags me farther into the room. For such a small woman, she's freakishly strong, almost demonic.

I don't want to cry, but her reign of terror won't end as she leans down and grabs a glob of the food off the floor and smears it all over my face before forcing it into my mouth.

"Stop," I protest weakly. But even speaking that much makes the throbbing in my head increase to the point of no return.

Miriam doesn't stop. She continues to scoop up the food with her hands, forcing it into my mouth until my body's involuntary reaction takes over, and I vomit it all back up.

"You're pathetic," she snarls. "And I'm going to enjoy watching you rot."

With that, she finally leaves me.

12

MERCEDES

I'm still lying on the floor in a heap when Judge comes to my room two hours later. When I see him, relief floods over me, bringing tears to my eyes. That is until I notice the expression on his face.

"What the fuck have you done?" he clips out.

I stare up at him in confusion, and his eyes rake over me with contempt that turns to something else when he sees the pile of puke beside me. That same suspicion I noticed before flares again, but I couldn't explain it even if I wanted to right now. I'm too weak. In too much pain to move. It feels like my head is going to fucking explode.

"Why did you do it?" he demands. "Why, Mercedes?"

I shake my head, not understanding. At least not until Miriam appears behind him with two black eyes and a cut adorning her cheek. He turns and gestures her inside, his anger palpable.

"Why did you attack her?"

"I... didn't," I heave the words out, but they're barely audible.

Whatever happened to her is a result of what she did when she left my room. That becomes painfully clear when she smirks behind Judge's back. Judge isn't paying attention to her, though. He's looking at me the same way everyone always does. Like I'm a disappointment. Like all I ever do is ruin everyone's lives.

"Miriam, you may go rest," he tells her. "I will handle this."

"Are you sure?" she asks. "I can help you get her to the cellar..."

Panic takes over me, and I try to shake my head, but another streak of pain forces me to stop and cry out. Some of the anger in Judge's eyes ebbs away as it turns to concern.

"Leave, Miriam."

She does, reluctantly, and I feel like I can finally breathe again when she's out of my sight.

Judge kneels beside me, his eyes moving over my face in confusion. "Why do you keep throwing up?"

My only response is to release a quiet sob, which doesn't help the situation. He's never going to believe me. Not after Miriam made sure of that. And why should he? That's the whole reason I'm here, isn't it? Because I lose control and bad things happen.

"Get up." He reaches for me and tries to sit me upright but stops abruptly when I cry out in agony.

"What is it?" he demands, his eyes searching mine.

"My head," I croak.

He frowns. "Miriam said you tried to escape, and you fell in the hall. Did you hit your head?"

"She's lying," I rasp, but it doesn't sound believable, even to myself.

"So you didn't try to escape?" he challenges.

"I did, but—"

I stop because I know there's no point. He's already made up his mind. I can see it in his eyes. The irritation swirling with his desire to punish me. I don't have the energy to argue right now. He could drag me to the cellar, and I wouldn't be able to put up so much as an argument.

"I'm going to sit you up," he says. "We'll go slow."

I give him a tiny nod, and as he promised, he goes very slow, but it doesn't stop the pain shooting through my skull. I'm wincing in agony, and Judge doesn't miss it. Nor does he miss the bruise on the side of my face when he tucks my hair back behind my ear.

"Is this where it hurts?" He presses his fingers against the area gingerly.

"No. The back."

He keeps my body supported with his hands as he moves around behind me to examine the area, and I hear his sharp inhale when he feels the egg on the back of my head.

"You're bleeding," he says gruffly.

"It hurts," I whisper. "Please—"

I don't even know what I'm asking for. But I need his help, as much as it pains me to admit it.

He moves around me and gathers me up in his arms, his eyes darker than I've ever seen them. "Don't worry, little monster. I'm going to take care of you."

AFTER HOURS of tests and observation at The Society hospital, the verdict is as I suspected. I have a concussion, and they had to give me a few stitches for the gash on the back of my head. They send us home with instructions to rest and a prescription for the pain. But that isn't the extent of my injuries, and I know Judge is still thinking about them as he drives me home.

When they asked me to change into a gown, there was no hiding them from him. He saw the bruises on my ribs and knees, and I know he's questioning why I would do that to myself. I want to tell him I didn't, but that fear is still there in the back of my mind. Just like when I tried to tell Santiago that I killed the courtesan in self-defense. He didn't believe me, so it's doubtful Judge will either. He probably thinks I got what I deserve for trying to escape in the first place.

I stare out the window, numb and exhausted. I want to cry, but it hurts too much to do that. I'm just hoping Judge will be merciful and leave me to the comfort of my own room tonight rather than tossing me in the cellar like Miriam mentioned.

The answer to that question comes when we arrive back at the house. He doesn't take me to the cellar, but he doesn't take me to my room either. Instead, he takes me to his. And again, I find myself under his care as he gently sets me into a bathtub and washes my body, cleaning the filth of the day's events away. I don't protest, and the gentle touch of his hands and the warmth of the water lulls me into a state of comfort I can't deny myself. By the time he carries me to his bed, I can barely keep my eyes open.

When he drapes me over the expensive sheets and covers me with the duvet, I sigh. It smells like him. So does the pillow. And I find that I'm strangely okay with that.

"You're going to sleep too?" I murmur.

I think I see a hint of a smile on his lips as he shakes his head. "No, Mercedes. I'm going to watch over you. Get some rest now."

With a nod, I close my eyes, and everything else fades away.

When the light of morning pours into the room, I realize that Judge let me sleep in. I know because he's been waking me up when it's still dark outside. But today, it's the warmth of the sunlight on my skin that wakes me, and it feels good. I feel comfortable in Judge's bed, and I can already tell my head is much better, though it still aches a little and probably will for a while.

As I try to sit up, I notice Judge is in the chair beside the bed, staring at his phone. And he looks pissed.

"Judge?" I force his name from my dry throat.

His eyes snap to mine, relief blotting out any other palpable emotions, but only for a moment.

"How are you feeling?" he asks.

"Better," I acknowledge, although I'm not sure that's true. Because right now, the way he's staring at me makes me feel like I should crawl under the covers and hide.

"Good," he grunts. "That's good."

"Is... everything okay?" I ask reluctantly.

"No." His eyes flash with irritation he's struggling to contain. "It's not okay, Mercedes. It seems you've made yet another mess for me to clean up."

"What are you talking about?"

"This." He tosses a creased piece of paper from the nightstand onto the bed.

When I unfold it, dread curdles my stomach. It's a missing person's report... for me. Complete with a terrible photo, a description of my physical appearance, and a statement that I never showed up for a planned brunch, nor have I been seen or heard from.

"Oh, shit," I whisper.

"Yeah," Judge growls. "Oh, shit."

"It's not what you—"

"I've been going through your phone." He tosses that onto the bed too, and when I glance at it, I can see he's been scrolling through my messages with Georgie.

I swallow, and my head spins as fear takes an ugly hold on me. He said he has to clean up the mess I've made. Clearly, it was Solana and Georgie who reported me missing. Nobody within The Society would think twice about it. My two worlds are colliding, and I know this won't be good. But what I don't know is what will happen with my friends if Judge manages to track them down. If he hasn't already.

Oh, God. That's a horrific thought.

I look up at him, trying to find the words to plead my case, but he doesn't give me the chance.

"I just have two questions for you, Mercedes." He lowers his voice to a deadly calm that terrifies me more than his rage. "Who the fuck is Georgie, and are you fucking pregnant?"

13

JUDGE

"Pregnant?" Mercedes asks, half sitting up, wincing as she does. She closes her eyes and takes a moment. I watch her, gripping the edges of my chair so tight my fingernails make crescent shapes in the leather. I'm so angry. So fucking angry.

"Yes, pregnant. It would explain the vomiting."

"Vomiting? I was... Christ, Judge. Miriam threw a fucking paperweight at my head and gave me a fucking concussion. That's the vomiting."

"Miriam threw a paperweight at your head? Why are you lying?"

"You know what? Never mind." She takes a deep breath and shakes her head, looking disappointed. Disheartened. "You're right. I gave myself a concussion. After giving her two black eyes. And I kicked myself in the ribs too. That's what you believe, right?" She sits up against the headboard, pulls the blankets closer and glances at her phone on the duvet. "You went through my phone? You have no right. How did you even get the password?"

"Santiago."

She opens her mouth, closes it, looking hurt and betrayed. I understand. "Did he look through it too?"

"Are you pregnant, Mercedes? You need to tell me now."

"Oh, my God, you're serious. No, Judge, I'm not fucking pregnant. How would I be pregnant?"

"Your texts with this man—"

"You don't know anything!" She shoves the blankets off, taking a moment to look down at the unfamiliar shirt she's wearing. It's mine. I put it on her last night. She swings her legs over the side of the bed. "I'm going to my room." She stands but wobbles.

I reach her in time, catching her just as her knees give out. "You're not going anywhere."

I put her back in the bed, and she doesn't argue. But I think that's because she's too weak. And I can see she's nauseous. I see it in the way she clutches her stomach. How she squeezes her eyes and mouth shut.

"Un-fucking-believable," I mutter and walk away, raking a hand through my hair as I wear a hole in the carpet. I glance at her to find her watching me and go into the bathroom to wash my face. I haven't slept more than a few hours. I've been keeping an eye on her, waking her every couple of hours on doctor's orders. And it shows in my reflection. Mercedes De La Rosa will age me.

Mercedes watches me with cold indifference when I return to the bedroom. Someone knocks on the door.

"Enter."

Miriam pushes in and smiles at me. "Good morning, sir. I brought breakfast."

"Un-fucking-believable," Mercedes mutters.

I give her a look to shut her up. "Thank you, Miriam. I'll take it from here."

Miriam glances at Mercedes, who's staring daggers at her, but then turns to go.

"Just a minute," I say.

She stops and turns back to me.

"Mercedes. I think you owe Miriam an apology."

Mercedes snorts. "When hell freezes over. I didn't do that to her."

"Mercedes," I say again. She's not looking at me, though. She's still glaring at Miriam. "Apologize."

She shifts her gaze to me. "No. I don't care what you do to me, but I won't apologize for something I didn't do."

"Do you apologize for things you do do?"

She folds her arms across her chest and looks away, the line of her jaw tight as she clenches her teeth.

"We'll try again tomorrow, Miriam. Perhaps Ms. De La Rosa will be feeling better by then. Thank you."

"Sir." She nods, turns to exit.

I bring my attention to the tray of food. If that's what you can call it. It's a lump of some unrecognizable slop. I pour coffee for Mercedes and carry the mug to her. She takes it and brings it to her lips, pauses to inhale as if she thinks it may be poison, then sips.

"I will punish you in front of her if you don't apologize."

She looks at me, quiet for a moment. "I didn't hurt her."

"Who gave her two black eyes then?"

"I don't know. I'm sure there is a line of people wanting to do that. She's a horrible woman."

"I will punish you in front of her, Mercedes. Understand that."

"And if you do that, I will never forgive you. *You* understand *that*."

"So be it." I carry the tray to the bed and set it on the nightstand, then push her blanket off. "Up."

"Why?"

"I will help you to the bathroom, then I need to go, and you need to get some sleep."

"I'm fine." She tries to cover herself again.

I take her wrist. "Up, Mercedes."

"Fine." She moves more slowly this time and

leans into me as we walk into the bathroom. Once we're inside, she turns to me and raises her eyebrows.

I raise mine, too, and lean against the doorframe, folding my arms across my chest.

"Oh, no. I'm not going to the bathroom while you stand there."

"Yes, you are."

"Judge—"

"It's either me or Miriam. You can't get out of bed on your own. You could fall, hit your head again."

"I didn't hit my head! She threw..." But she stops, makes a sound like it's pointless, then pulls down her panties and sits on the toilet to pee.

I look away, giving her that little bit of privacy. When she's done, she flushes, washes her hands, and shoves me off when I try to hold onto her to take her back to bed. She climbs in herself and lies down, giving me her back.

"I need to take care of this missing persons report. You will remain in my room. In my bed. Do you understand?"

Nothing.

I lean down so my face is inches from hers. The things I'm feeling right now, the betrayal, it's strange. And more painful than I imagined it could be.

"Do you understand?" I ask again.

"Yes. Just do me one favor and lock the door so

that woman doesn't come in here and smother me in my sleep."

I straighten and draw a deep breath in. "I'm trying to help you, but you're so fucking tiring sometimes, you know that?"

She turns her head so she's looking up at me, dark eyes misty. "You mean I'm not worth the trouble, right?"

"That's not—"

"Don't bother. It's fine. I understand. Just go."

"Mercedes—"

"What the hell do you want from me?" she snaps, sitting up, squeezing her eyes shut with the swift movement. It takes all I have not to go to her. A part of me hates watching her like this.

"What I want is for you to be the woman you try so fucking hard to hide. I see her. You think I don't, but I do."

She shakes her head. "You're mistaken. There's no other, better woman. And you're right. I'm not worth the effort. So just please get the fuck out of my sight and let me rest." She drops back down, and I know this is done. For now. Her phone is still on the bed, and I pocket it, then walk out the door and lock it, leaving instructions she's not to be disturbed under any circumstances. Because I don't want Miriam going in there.

14

JUDGE

I should tell Santiago what I found on her phone. Tell him about this Georgie. What the fuck kind of name is Georgie anyway? I scroll through their texts again, their photos. Lips puckered to send kisses. Showing off cleavage or abs or biceps. Telling each other how fucking awesome they are. How they own the world.

Something burns inside me as I shove her phone into my pocket and make a call with mine while heading out the door and into the waiting Rolls Royce. I hand Raul an address and sit.

"Is it handled?" I ask the man on the other end.

"Yes, sir. The missing person's report has been canceled, but I have to tell you I'm fielding calls from a woman, Solana Lavigne, and a man named George Beaumont. They're the two who filed the report in the first place."

"Forward those to my office. I'll take care of them later. And thank you for your discretion in this matter."

"Anytime, Judge. You know that."

I disconnect. I had to call in a favor to get the report taken down, but it would be an embarrassment to Santiago and to IVI if it got out. We do things differently within The Society, and our members have enough pull to make that happen, but every now and then, something leaks through the cracks. I'm just surprised to find it's Mercedes.

I scroll through the photos on her phone again. Fucking Georgie. He's younger than me. Her age. Good looking if you like that pretty-boy type. Looks to me like he spends too much time in front of a mirror.

I glance at my reflection in the rearview and rake my hand through my hair to tame it. See how tired I look. Fucking Georgie.

At least she's not pregnant although I should make sure. She may not know herself. I make another call to Dr. Barnes. He's a Society doctor. He's with a patient, though, so I leave a message for him to call me back.

"We're here, sir," Raul says as we pull up in front of a modest development of condos in the heart of the city. A dozen homes are set in a semi-circle with a parking lot in the middle. Each condo is two floors and has a private garden. It's, in a word, quaint with the white picket fences and the beds of flowers. Not at all what I'd expect from Mercedes.

"Thank you. I'll be out shortly."

"Yes, sir."

I walk up to number 39, opening the small gate, taking in the flowers and shrubs that look like they're well-tended. Mercedes? No. I can see her standing over the gardener and giving orders but not getting her hands dirty. She'd mess up her nails.

Fuck.

I'm angry. I'm angry as hell. Those texts. This condo. A whole other life outside of The Society. What else is she hiding? And why the fuck do I care? For Santiago? Because I'll have to tell him. But no, it's not that. I'm angry for me.

Last night, that horseback ride, it was good. Fun. I felt like we were starting to get somewhere. But then I come home to find her on the floor puking after she tries to escape. Escape! Where would she go? What the hell was she thinking? But I have a clearer idea now. At least on the where. Into her life outside of The Society. Right here to 39 Wooded Way.

I find the key easily enough. She'd told Georgie where she hides it. I unlock the door and enter, then close it behind me. Sunlight pours in through the large windows, making the space bright.

The downstairs is a grand room with living and dining rooms separated from the kitchen by a curving counter where three barstools are lined up. My shoes echo on the hardwood floors as I make my way into the kitchen, recognizing the scent of her perfume lingering in the space. There's a coffee mug in the drying rack, and in the refrigerator are basics, not anything that would spoil. There's a half-bottle of expensive vodka in the freezer, and in the decorative cabinet against the wall, I see mismatched crystal wineglasses, shot, and cocktail glasses. I open the door. It's lightweight and artsy with faded paint that I think was scraped off for effect. Not anything I'd expect Mercedes to like, but I can see it's good quality and the glasses are expensive crystal. I have some of the same brand myself.

Closing that cabinet door, I look through the others to find dishes, pots, pans, all perfectly normal. I then walk into the living room with its comfortable couches. Again, high-end and nice enough but not what I'd call luxurious. A TV hangs over the fireplace, and on the coffee table are yoga and fashion magazines and well-read books. I pick up one of the magazines. On the cover is a woman wrapped in silks doing some sort of circus move. Aerial Yoga. Hm. Not what I'd expect Mercedes to read. But isn't that what I'm discovering more and more? I don't know her. No one does.

Two sliding glass doors on either side of the fireplace lead out to a deck. I open one and step outside to hear the gentle flow of a creek hidden in the thicket of trees. The deck is only big enough for a small, round table that would seat three, and there are two plush chairs set beside a small mosaic-topped table looking out into the woods. Flowers bloom in pots, and I put my hand inside one to feel the soil. They've recently been watered.

Back inside, I go upstairs. There are two bedrooms. One is clearly an unused guest room where clothes in Mercedes's size hang. More color here rather than her usual black and red favorites. But maybe they don't belong to her. Maybe they belong to this Solana. But I sniff the sleeve of one and pick up the scent of her perfume.

Closing the door, I go to the master, where I'm surprised to find the bed unmade and clothes on top of it like someone got dressed in a hurry. Several pairs of jeans and tops, a couple of dresses.

A man's suit.

And beside the bed is a laundry basket full of folded clothes. Not hers. Men's clothes. Boxers, T-shirts, jeans. All designer. One loud pink shirt I recognize. I take out her phone to confirm that it's Georgie's. Fucking Georgie.

My chest tightens, and it's hard to swallow down my anger.

I turn to the double doors that lead into a large bathroom. They stand open, and I can see the huge tub with bottles of bubble bath and various shampoos and conditioners for both men and women.

Does he fucking live here with her? What the hell is going on?

Just then, my phone rings, and I pull it out of my pocket. I answer more sharply than I intend.

"Judge Montgomery. This is Dr. Barnes. You'd called my office, but if it's a bad time, I can call you back."

"No. Sorry." I shake my head. "It's fine."

"What can I do for you?"

"I need your help with a personal matter."

"Alright."

"I need you to conduct a virginity test."

"I see."

"Tonight."

"Tonight?"

"Yes."

He clears his throat. "Well, you can bring the young lady—"

"No. You'll come to my house. Alone please."

"But as you know, such a test requires at least one witness to be present. My assistant—"

"This is a delicate matter, Dr. Barnes. One that will require your discretion."

He clears his throat. "Of course. But the witness?"

"I'll be the witness."

He is quiet for a moment. "What time suits you?"

"Seven."

"I'll see you then, Judge."

"See you then, Doctor."

I disconnect the call and walk out of that house, not quite sure what this commotion in my gut is about. Why am I so fucking bothered by all of this? If Mercedes isn't a virgin, she'll be punished. By Santiago. Not me. She isn't my fucking problem. So why the fuck am I so unsettled by this discovery of her secret life? Why do I care? Because there is no doubt that I do fucking care.

15

JUDGE

I spend the afternoon in my study. I don't go upstairs to see her. I don't ask about her. Instead, I sit here and drink my scotch as I scroll through the photos on her phone yet again and grow angrier and angrier.

At seven o'clock on the dot, Lois knocks on my door to let me know Dr. Barnes is here. I'm in no mood for conversation and want to get this done and over with. Because I'm questioning my motives for doing it in the first place.

Would I, if I were to take a wife, subject her to a virginity test? Would I care about her purity?

I'm a modern man. And as much as The Society is ingrained in my very being, some practices I find archaic. And the virginity test is one.

So why am I doing it? Is it to punish her? And for

what? For wanting a man? For being with a man? For that man not being me?

Doesn't that make me what I accused her of being? Arrogant? Worse?

No. I push those thoughts from my mind. If Santiago knew what I'd found, he'd order the test himself. That's what I tell myself as I get to my feet to greet Dr. Barnes and lead him upstairs to my bedroom where Mercedes has pulled a chair up to the open window and is sitting there with a blanket wrapped around her, her feet up on the windowsill as she stares out at the night sky.

She turns her head when I enter, and for a moment, the look in her eyes makes me want to stop this. But then whatever it was I glimpsed there moments ago morphs into a cool indifference, and she's about to turn back to the window when Dr. Barnes enters.

"Mercedes," I say.

She looks at the man. He's in his forties and not as hardened in expression or personality as some of the other Society doctors. It's why I chose him.

"This is Dr. Barnes. Dr. Barnes, Mercedes De La Rosa."

"Ms. De La Rosa," Dr. Barnes says, bowing his head in greeting.

Mercedes looks suspiciously from him to me and sets her feet on the floor. She tugs the blanket closer.

"Dr. Barnes," she says, turning her gaze to him.

"It's nice to meet you, but if you came to check on me, I can assure you I'm fine. My headache is gone, and I feel like myself."

Dr. Barnes glances at me, confused.

I clear my throat. "That's not why he's here."

I think her plan was to ignore me outright, but this makes it impossible. "Then why is he here?" she asks, getting to her feet, the thick duvet making her appear small.

"He'll be conducting a virginity test."

It takes her a minute. "Pardon?"

"A virginity test. It's standard practice with The Society, as you know."

"Are you serious?" she asks me.

I turn to the doctor. "Would you give us a minute?"

"Of course." Dr. Barnes steps into the hallway, and I close the door behind him, then turn to Mercedes.

"What the fuck, Judge?"

I step closer, my breathing somehow normal even through this rage growing inside me all day.

"So, 39 Wooded Way, Mercedes?"

She opens her mouth, stunned, color leaching from her face.

"Georgie. Is he your fucking boyfriend? Are you living together?"

"Wh... what?"

"I saw his clothes. In your house that I'm certain

Santiago knows nothing about. Your behavior, the vomiting—"

"I'm not pregnant! I told you that."

"Even if you're not, if you're not a virgin—"

"I know the rules, Judge. I wouldn't do that to Santiago. Shame him like that."

"You know the rules, yet you're living a second life outside of The Society."

"A second life is a bit much—"

"A life I'm not sure I understand."

"How could you? You're a man. The rules, you have none. Me? I can hardly breathe without permission. There are expectations of me that are so outdated, you can't even begin to understand. You? You have the fucking Cat House to fuck around as much as you want, and we have to submit to a fucking virginity test? Does that seem remotely fair or normal to you?"

Her eyes are bright with rage and something else, something like hurt. And for as much fight as Mercedes has in her, there is something submissive about her. Or maybe she's learned sometimes it's easier to submit.

I go to her, close my hands over her shoulders.

"Don't touch me!" She shoves me off.

"The texts between you and this man."

"He's my friend. My friend!"

"You call him your boyfriend."

She looks at me like I just sprouted a second

head, then chuckles, and it's that same unhinged sound as when she dumped the bowl of soup on me. The one that warns she's coming undone. It's what I want, right? To break her down so I can build her back up.

I shake my head, wrap my hands around the back of my neck.

"Fuck, Mercedes."

"Have you looked closely at those photos, Judge?" she asks, shoving the duvet from her shoulders and standing tall, hands on her hips. She's still wearing my T-shirt and has a pair of my socks on her feet. She must have gotten cold.

"I have."

"Did you notice anything?" She raises her eyebrows and looks oddly amused.

"Like what?"

"Georgie?"

"What the fuck kind of name is that anyway?"

She stops. Exhales a quick, short chuckle and studies me, one corner of her mouth quirking upward. "Are you jealous?"

I swallow, look down at her. "I am concerned."

"Well," she says, cocking her head and walking around to my side of the bed where she opens the nightstand drawer and fuck me. Because I'd forgotten it. Forgotten I'd dropped the panties I'd pocketed, *her* panties, in there.

She slips them out now. "Are you sure about

that?" she asks, walking toward me and dangling them between us.

I clench my jaw but remain silent.

She smiles, shakes her head, and shoves them into the breast pocket of my vest. "You enjoy those," she says and bends to slip the thong she's wearing off. "Have these too," she says, slapping them against my chest so hard she rocks on her heels when I don't budge. I take them, her hand slipping through mine as she walks away and climbs up on my bed. "Bring the good doctor in," she says, settling back against the headboard and setting her feet on her mattress, spreading them wide. "You can both have a good look at what you will never ever fuck."

16

MERCEDES

My heart thumps erratically as I wait for the doctor to finish the exam. I've never been so exposed, and it's humiliating, but it will be worth every second when I get to watch Judge choke on his own words.

He was so convinced of his ridiculous notion that I'm looking forward to disabusing him of it. If he wants to hurl accusations at me and tarnish my reputation, he needs to learn to come better prepared. All of this is because I have a life outside The Society. The audacity to have my own free space, a place to call mine.

If Georgie could only hear how worked up the very mention of his name had gotten this man, he would laugh. We would both laugh, and then Georgie would probably shamelessly flirt with me in front of Judge just to provoke him. God, I miss him and Solana. That's what I think about to get me through the exam, which really doesn't take long, but it feels like forever.

The doctor pokes and prods, and then turns to Judge, who's standing like a sentry next to the bed, his tension palpable. I'm quite certain he's already concocting ways to punish me for the imaginary results in his head. Although he would deny it, we both know what this test is really for. He can't stand the thought of anyone else ever having me. But he'll never admit it. He's too goddamn proud.

"She's intact," the doctor tells him.

Judge glances at me, swallows, and nods. "Thank you, Dr. Barnes."

The doctor hands me a towel to clean up, and I take it to the privacy of the bathroom. I don't know why I'm still in Judge's bedroom, but if I'm being honest, I'm grateful for the sanctuary. I don't think I'd find a moment of sleep in my room, thinking Miriam might decide to come back and finish me off at any moment.

When I glance at my reflection in the mirror, the bruising on my face is a painful reminder that just like now, Judge didn't believe what I'd told him about Miriam. No matter what I tell him, I doubt he'll be swayed, and I can't endure him looking at me like I'm a liar all over again. I know he's taking it easy on me right now, but it won't last. Once he knows I'm recovered, there will be a reckoning, and I don't know I'm prepared to face it.

I consider all the things that might happen between now and then. There are other things to worry about too, like Georgie and Solana. What will he do about them? How can I protect them when I can't even warn them?

I swallow the bitterness in my mouth and make my way back to the bed reluctantly. The doctor is gone now, and it's just Judge and me. He's standing at the window, staring out at the grounds, deep in thought. I know he heard me return, but I'm hoping he'll pretend he didn't because I'm so annoyed by him I could scream.

But annoyed isn't the right word, really. I'm fucking hurt. I'm hurt that he expects the worse from me. It cuts me deep, and I don't know why. Why should I care what he thinks? He means nothing to me in the grand scheme of things. I have to remember that. No matter what happens here. No matter how much he twists me up inside.

He turns to face me, and more emotions I don't want well up within me. I'm sure as hell not expecting an apology, and he doesn't offer me one.

"Who is Georgie to you, Mercedes?"

"I owe you nothing." My voice trembles slightly as I force the words out, and I hate myself for it. "You don't get to know about my life. You got what you wanted. I proved that I'm untouched, and still, all you can do is interrogate me."

He's quiet, but a storm is brewing behind his eyes, and I don't know if it's because of me or his own choices today.

"Why don't we talk about your life, Judge?" I hurl the words at him. "Why don't we talk about the women you fuck. The virtues you endorse so diligently while you're partaking in the oldest temptation in the book. I've always wondered how that double standard tastes. How does it feel to be so weak you can't even uphold yourself to the same standard you expect of me?"

"Mercedes." His voice is a warning, but I don't care.

"I hope you enjoy it," I bite out. "Because those shallow, empty encounters are all you'll ever have. As for me, I'm going to marry a goddamn Sovereign Son, and you know what, Judge? I'm going to fuck his brains out every night for the rest of my—"

My words die in my throat as he snarls a curse and stalks toward me, dark and deadly. When his hand snakes out to grab my face, I flinch, and it makes him pause, but only for a second.

"You haven't learned when to keep your mouth shut," he growls.

"I'm just telling it like it is." I smile up at him, even though I'm shaking in his grasp. "In fact, you can let me go now. I'm sure there's another of Santiago's friends who'd happily take over my care until I'm married. Perhaps one of the Augustine brothers. I mean, I know they live in Seattle, but I could use a change of pace—"

"You. Belong. To. Me!" he roars.

I stare up at him, stunned by his claim, but he ruins it almost as soon as he realizes his mistake.

"For now," he utters, releasing me with a ragged breath. "You are in my care, Mercedes. That's not going to change. And if or when you ever do decide to marry, I will be the one to give my approval."

"You're a goddamn liar." I blink rapidly in an attempt to dispel the tears I feel building behind my eyes.

"I will hand you over myself." He says it so callously that there can be no doubt about his words. "And I will do it with pleasure."

His assurance stings, but I can't forget what he just said. Or the expression on his face when he said it. I pushed him to that point, and he slipped. He wants me. He just can't admit it to himself.

"Get some rest." He turns and heads for the door. "You're going to need it when the time comes to receive your punishment."

Judge lets me rest in his room for a full week. He doesn't come to drag me from bed to clean the stables. He doesn't come to argue with me and tell me to eat. He doesn't come for anything, as far as I can tell. And I know it's because he's steeling himself. When I do see him again, there's no question he'll punish me.

Lois is the one to deliver my meals, and I can be grateful for that at least. They are not only edible but also delicious. However, I don't have faith that it's going to last. Any day now, Miriam will return, and things will go back to shit. Unless I can find a way to leave first.

When I'm tired of sleeping, I spend my time trying to find a way out. But just like my room, this one is locked up tight. The only chance I'd have of escaping right now is to push past Lois, and I can't bring myself to do that to her. She's kind to me, and it's such a rarity these days I need to maintain our connection for my sanity.

On occasion, she sneaks the dogs up and lets me pet them. She brings me desserts. She even made my favorite, tiramisu. She's been spoiling me, and I'm honestly surprised Judge hasn't put a stop to it, but I have a feeling he doesn't want to know.

It's a cozy Saturday morning in bed when he finally does make an appearance. When I see the dog collar and leash in his hands and the expression on his face, I know this is it.

I'm already shaking my head when he approaches. "No, I won't do it."

"You don't have a choice." His voice is hard, probably harder than I've ever heard it. It proves that I was right. He has been using this time and distance to regain his control, and his well of empathy, if he ever had any, has dried right up.

I try to scoot across the bed, and he wraps a steely hand around my wrist, halting me.

"Don't make this more difficult than it needs to be," he clips out. "You owe Miriam an apology, and you're going to give her one."

"I would rather die," I hiss. "I won't fucking do it. I won't. No matter what you say or do! I don't care!"

Judge sighs, tossing the collar and leash onto the bed before he removes his phone from his pocket. "I'm sure I don't have to tell you how many friends I have."

"Good for you." I glare at him. "You want a fucking gold star?"

"Police, politicians, government officials. The district attorney is one of my biggest admirers," he goes on. "We have an understanding between us that keeps things simple."

"What's your point?" I ask.

He shows me a photo on his phone, and I swallow, my resistance dying in my throat. It's a snapshot of Georgie outside of his work. But that isn't all. Judge swipes, and another one pops up. Georgie at his apartment. And then at the studio with Solana. At the police station, presumably trying to figure out where I am. There's an entire reel of their lives right here. Which means Judge knows where they live and work. He probably knows everything about them.

I drag my eyes up to his face, noting the tension in his jaw. The vein in his neck is pulsing too, and I want to believe that means he doesn't want to do this. But the truth is, I don't know.

"I can make their lives very difficult," he tells me. "You know I can make them absolute hell."

Tears prick my eyes because I do. I really fucking do. Judge is in the unique position of working in the court system, where corruption runs deep. I'd venture a guess that probably half if not more of his connections are Society. They have a power outsiders couldn't possibly understand. I've heard the stories. They can complicate anyone's life. They can have them arrested for bogus charges. They can have them sentenced to lengthy prison terms because they looked at someone the wrong way. They could even make them disappear with a simple phone call if they really wanted to.

I don't think Judge would ever go that far, but does it really matter? Any consequences he decides to throw at Solana and Georgie aren't acceptable. I can't allow them to be punished because of my mess.

"You can't hurt them," I answer in a brittle voice. "Please."

He shoves his phone back into his pocket and reaches for the collar. "Then do as you're told."

17

MERCEDES

Judge finishes securing the collar around my neck and then attaches the leash. He can barely look at me. I know because I've been staring at him for the last two minutes. There must be some level of contrition in his heart for doing this, but if there is, he's not caving to it.

"Ready?" he asks gruffly.

I stare up at him, silently pleading with my eyes. Searching for one scrap of humanity, one ounce of the comfort I know he's capable of providing. But I come up empty.

"I meant what I said," I whisper. "If you make me do this, I'll never forgive you."

His eyes move over me, and I can see the war in them. I want him to change his mind. I want him to tell me that he trusts me, that he believes me. But he doesn't.

"I don't negotiate with emotional terrorists," he answers. "Now come."

I follow him from the bed because I have no choice. He has a hold on the other end of the chain-link leash attached to my collar, and fighting him at this point will only result in more pain for me.

I try to remember why I'm doing this. It's impossible to forget his threat against Solana and Georgie. But it doesn't make it any easier to accept when he stops and points at the floor.

"Kneel."

I meet his gaze, steeling mine as I slowly drop to the floor and do his bidding.

"Good," he murmurs, his hand coming to rest on my head. "That's good, little monster."

For a moment, I can't help closing my eyes and allowing myself to feel the warmth of his touch. It's the comfort I need, even if it's from the same man who's making me suffer. But all too soon, it's gone again.

"Now crawl." He gives the leash a gentle tug, and I lurch forward with no choice but to follow his command.

I'm not sure what to expect or what he's going to make me do, but when he opens the bedroom door, and I see Miriam standing there, I really just want to die. He nods at her, and her eyes sparkle with satisfaction when she sees that I've been quite literally brought to my knees before her.

I want to spit at her. I want to fucking scream. But I keep repeating the mantra in my head. Georgie and Solana. I'm doing this for them.

"You're going to spend some time in Miriam's shoes today," Judge informs me as he leads me down the hall with the bitch at my heels. "Perhaps it will make you learn to respect what she does for you."

My anger feels like a hot poker in my chest, stabbing me over and over again as I crawl along the floor like a dog without an ounce of dignity left. I don't have to look at Miriam to know how much she's enjoying this. I can feel her gaze boring into the back of my skull.

Judge leads me into my bedroom, and then to the adjoining bathroom. He nods to Miriam again, and she steps around me, staring down at me like I'm the dirt on the bottom of her shoe. She produces a raggedy-looking toothbrush and a pair of gloves, which she reluctantly hands over. Judge's doing, I'm guessing. I'm sure if it were up to her, she'd probably make me lick the floor clean.

"You can start with the toilet," she says, her tone haughty. "Don't skimp on the scrubbing."

Judge drops the leash from his hand, and it clinks against the floor as I stare at them both incredulously.

"You want me to clean the toilet with a toothbrush?"

"Details matter," Miriam chirps. "Everything needs to be spotless."

My gaze moves to the toothbrush, and for a moment, I wonder how it would feel to make her choke on it. But then I remember why I'm here. I despise Miriam with every part of my being. There's no debating that. But my hatred of her doesn't outweigh the love I have for my friends. I have to keep telling myself that as I crawl toward the toilet and peek over the bowl.

There's already some blue cleaning solution in there, so at least there's that. Despite what they may think, this isn't the first time I've ever cleaned a toilet. I did my fair share of cleaning in boarding school when I got mouthy. But I've never had to clean anything with a toothbrush.

Regardless, I get to work because I just want to get it over with. I scrub the bowl for a solid ten minutes, and when I think I'm done, Miriam is quick to point out areas she wants me to redo. Meanwhile, Judge watches on in silence, and my resentment of him only grows.

When I'm finished with the toilet, she makes me wipe down the exterior with a cloth and then hands me another toothbrush and a bucket of soapy water for the floor. That takes me at least a full hour to clean because Miriam won't shut her goddamn piehole about invisible specks of dirt she claims exist.

I'm shaking with bottled-up rage by the time I finish the bathroom, but it doesn't end there. Next, they drag me to the kitchen, where I'm put on dishes and floor duty again. When that's done, she makes me polish all of Judge's shoes, and then to my horror, hers. Just when I think it might finally end, I'm told I have to clean her bathroom, which is truly fucking disgusting. It's obvious she's waited the entire week for this, and there's piss all over the tile floor that makes me wonder if she even bothered using the toilet.

I'm on the verge of tears by the time I finally finish, but I don't let them fall. I won't let them see that they've won. I feel disgusting, humiliated, and beat down. All I want to do is crawl into the shower and then bed. But nothing with Judge is ever that simple.

"Now, tell her how sorry you are," he says. "Tell her how much you appreciate everything she does for you here."

I stare up at him with flamethrowers for eyes, wishing I could fucking strangle him right now. But I have to bite my tongue. If I can just do this one last thing, I'll be done, and then I can get back to figuring out how the hell to get out of this place.

"I'm sorry you wound up with two black eyes." I grit the words out as I glare up at Miriam. "I appreciate all that you do. The food, really, is top-notch. Michelin Star, I'd go as far as saying—"

"Mercedes." Judge gives me a warning, but it's cut off by his phone ringing.

He glances at the screen and then at me. "I have to take this. Don't move."

I watch him walk into the adjoining bedroom, where he's still in view but out of earshot. Miriam's lips curl into a wicked smile, and she cocks her head to the side, staring down at me as if she's examining a bug.

"How did those words taste coming out of your mouth?"

I try to ignore her, but she's not about to waste this opportunity.

"You know where you stand now. I've worked for this family for years, princess. He's always going to take my word over yours."

I clench my jaw, trying to contain myself. I know she's goading me. She wants a reaction. But it doesn't make it any easier to accept.

"If you think you mean anything to him, you'd be sadly mistaken." She flicks her gaze to the other room, and I follow it, noting the way Judge is smiling at whoever is on the line.

"I'd venture a guess that's probably his favorite courtesan. He's been meeting with her every night since you've been here. I've never seen him take a liking to anyone the way he has to her. Who knows, maybe he'll even marry her."

"You're a liar," I hiss.

"Am I?" She shrugs. "Believe what you want. It makes no difference to me. I'm not the idiot who thinks he actually wants you here."

Her words hurt me, and I know she knows it. When I don't say anything, she takes it upon herself to keep poking that wound.

"I wonder how much your brother paid him," she ponders aloud. "In my opinion, there's not enough money in the world to make it worthwhile. How does it feel to know that men have to be paid just to tolerate your company? I suppose that makes you no different than a whore."

"Screw you," I snarl. "You don't know anything about my life."

"Oh, I know plenty." She offers me another evil smile. "These walls are... surprisingly thin. You'd be amazed at what one overhears. And you'd do well to remember that. It would be a shame if any of that information got out. Like your little secret about the courtesan you killed? I wonder what that would do to your reputation. I don't imagine it would be a good look for you or your brother."

My face blanches as I realize she's actually threatening me. As much as I want to pretend it doesn't matter, we both know it does. She shouldn't know that. She should never have had the opportunity to hear any of it. And the only reason she did is because of Judge. Because of his carelessness in trusting her and his blindness to what she really is.

I have never been one to take threats lightly. But I can't fight fire with fire right now. She has the upper hand, there's no denying that. I'm locked up like a prisoner with zero resources. It seems as if overnight, my entire life has been taken away. I have no access to my friends. My brother can't even stand to look at me. And Judge isn't an ally, no matter how much I wanted to believe that maybe he could be. Miriam is right about one thing. I'm only here because there's something in it for him financially. And the rest, well, I don't know. Maybe he is meeting with a courtesan every night. I'd have no way of knowing. But I'd have to be delusional to think he wouldn't. He's told me himself he won't touch me. That I won't know him that way. Whatever jealousy I thought I saw in him... whatever is going on with him stealing my panties... none of that matters. Because he doesn't care about me, and he never will. He's proven that today.

"Alright." His voice drifts closer as his shoes clip across the bathroom floor when he returns. "I'll see you tonight then."

Miriam smirks at me as if to say she told me so, and I dip my head so she can't see the emotions on my face.

"Everything good in here?" Judge asks.

"Oh, we're just fine," Miriam tells him. "Ms. De La Rosa offered me a very sincere apology. She promised she won't be making any more trouble for me, sir."

He seems confused by her declaration but doesn't question it as he grabs my leash and turns me around. "Very well. We'll leave you to it, Miriam."

My knees ache as I crawl back down the hall to my bedroom. I guess Judge is done letting me stay in his room, and I'm glad for it. I don't want to smell him. I don't want to see him. I just want to curl up and die, if I'm being honest. I have nothing and no one. It fucking hurts, and for the first time in my life, I'm questioning why I'm even here. What purpose does my existence even serve?

"Let's get you cleaned up." Judge reaches for my arm and tries to pull me up, and I yank away, shoving at his hand.

"Don't touch me," I snarl.

He stares at me, bewildered by the violence in my tone, and makes the mistake of reaching for me again. This time, I scream.

"Don't ever fucking touch me again! I hate you. I fucking hate you. Leave me alone!"

"Mercedes." He stands there, shocked, and I know what it looks like. It looks like I'm losing my mind. But I don't care. Maybe I finally am.

"I don't want to see your face," I choke out as I pry the collar off my neck and toss it onto the ground. "I don't want to hear your voice. And if you touch me again, I will murder you too. So do us both a favor and just stay the hell away from me."

I stagger into the bathroom and slam the door behind me, locking it in place. And then, I cry.

18

JUDGE

The next two weeks pass quietly. To anyone who was to only look into my house, that is. It may appear peaceful even. If not for the near-catatonic woman who is my houseguest.

Since her outburst after her punishment, Mercedes has barely spoken two words to me. She hasn't looked at me. She's refused to eat a morsel of food that Miriam brings her, and I admit, it's forced my hand, so I've let her eat with Lois in the kitchen. I didn't like to see how gaunt she was becoming. How quickly she was losing weight.

She's stubborn to the point that she will hurt herself, and I need to figure out how to get through to her.

But this isn't just being stubborn. Something broke in her the day I punished her. And I hate myself for it. For not having understood what a humbling as great as that would do to her psyche.

She's depressed.

And I'm worried.

I haven't talked to Santiago about it yet, but I will need to very soon.

Each morning at five o'clock, I knock on her door to find her dressed and sitting on her bed ready to go to the stables and do her work. She doesn't look at me. Doesn't answer me when I say something. Just obediently gets to her feet and walks ahead of me to the stables as if she were the prisoner and I were her guard.

Seeing her sitting on the bed is unnerving. I still haven't given her her makeup so her face is still free of it, but where before she was taking care of herself, showering, brushing her hair, changing her clothes, everything is different now.

If I don't tell her she needs to shower and stand there to watch her do it, she doesn't. She simply strips off her clothes—the same jeans and long-sleeved T-shirt she's worn every fucking morning to clean the stables—and gets back into bed to sleep until evening when Lois can get her downstairs to eat the little bit she'll eat. The only time she changes into clean clothes is when Lois or Miriam take the dirty ones to wash.

Her hair is losing its gloss. I'm not sure when she last brushed it. I have tried to, but she screams bloody murder when I go near her, so I stopped. Her skin too, for as much sleep as she's getting, has grown sallow, dark circles appearing under her sad, distant eyes.

A part of me, the one that sounds exactly like my grandfather, tells me it's fine. That she's trying to manipulate me with this little show of rebellion. This is the voice that worries me. That has made me swear to never marry. And watching Mercedes come undone so completely, it's just evidence that I'm right. Proof of what I can do. What I'm capable of.

I call her my little monster. There's a certain affection that comes with that. I don't know if she realizes that.

But what I am? Inside me lives the real monster, the true beast. And I need to keep very tight hold of the reins because it cannot be allowed to breathe. It's why I'm so disciplined in every aspect of my life.

It's Sunday evening, exactly two weeks after the night of her punishment. I carry two large boxes into the house. A rush order. My peace offering. She'll probably think it comes from the money Santiago is paying me to look after her, but the truth is, there is no money, no payment. I refused it. I'm wondering now if I should have told her the truth about it. Or at least not let her believe an untruth. But it was another way to keep her at arm's length, and I need all the help I can get with that when it comes to Mercedes.

I enter the house and climb the stairs. I hear Lois and Paolo talking in the hallway. They're both on their knees, looking closely at something when I approach.

"Evening, Judge," Paolo says casually. He's been back to work for the last week.

"Evening. What are you doing here on a Sunday night?" I ask him. He usually only works during the week, and even though he lives in a cottage on the property, I try to respect his time.

"I'd come to check on the hounds, and Lois mentioned a repair, so I thought I'd get a head start."

"Repair?" I ask Lois.

"I noticed it this morning. It's small enough, but..." She trails off and touches a spot on the hardwood floor close enough to the runner that I'm not even sure how she found it.

I set the boxes down and crouch to examine it. There's a divot in the hardwood, a small depression.

"How did you see it?" I ask.

"I was vacuuming, and it caught my eye. I've told the girls to let me know about things like this, but well, you know how that goes. They mean well, but their heads are in their phones half the time."

I touch it. My first thought would be a woman's heel. I've seen it before, especially when the rubber at the end of the heel has worn down and it acts like a nail on the wood, digging divots into it with each step. But this isn't that. For one thing, it's a perfect half-circle. No breaking of wood, more of a pushing in. For another, it's too big to be a heel.

"I'm sure I can repair it, sir. Don't you worry," Paolo says.

I straighten. Think. I remember the comment Mercedes made about Miriam throwing a paperweight at her. It sounded so ridiculous, so outlandish. So unbelievable.

"Sir?" Lois says, holding on to the banister to stand.

"Sorry, what?"

"Dinner's almost ready. Will you eat with Ms. De La Rosa tonight?"

Was she telling the truth? No. Why would Miriam throw a paperweight at her? It makes no sense.

"I've made Italian. Her favorite. And tiramisu for dessert." She's worried. I see it on her face, in her eyes. "Maybe she'll eat a little more tonight. If you're there, perhaps—"

"No." I swallow down a lump. "Let her eat with you. I think she'd prefer that. I'll eat later. Just take care of her."

She sighs and nods.

"Has she eaten anything today?"

"Just a few bites of an apple and tea."

"Thank you."

I pick up the boxes, thoughts swimming in my head. Lois's and Paolo's voices fade into the distance as I knock on Mercedes's door. As usual, there's no answer, so I open it and enter. It's unlocked now. Has been for two weeks. But I'm not sure she's left it apart from when I take her to the stables in the morning or when Lois comes to get her for dinner in the evening. Miriam still delivers breakfast and lunch, which Lois prepares, but those trays go back untouched.

"Good evening," I say as I enter. I set the boxes down on the table by the door.

Mercedes has a chair pulled up to the open window and is sitting with a heavy sweater wrapped around her, her knees tucked up under her. She doesn't bother to turn around or acknowledge me.

It's raining and colder than usual tonight. It's been raining for the past few nights, and the prediction is for more wet, gloomy, and cold weather in the next few days.

"It's too cold to have your window open," I say when she shudders at a gust of wind. I move to close it. "If you want fresh air, let's get a jacket on you, and we can go for a walk."

I look down at her, waiting for her to reply. And it takes all I have to tamp down whatever the fuck it is that seems to be creeping up from my gut to my chest, casting a shadow over everything.

"Mercedes? Would you like to go for a walk?"

She blinks, slowly, so slowly. She drags her gaze from the window to me as if she's just realized I'm here. Just noticed I closed the window. She takes a breath in, looks away, and shakes her head. She gets up, makes a point of walking in the narrow space between the chair and the wall to avoid having to pass close to me, and gets into bed.

"It's early for bed," I tell her.

"I'm tired."

"You need to eat dinner."

"Tomorrow." She turns her back to me and pulls the blankets up high.

I pick up the boxes and walk around to the other side of the bed so I can see her face. "I have a gift for you," I say, trying to inject a smile into my words.

Nothing.

I set the large, embossed gold boxes down on the bed. They're from a specialty shop in town. I'm sure she recognizes them, but her eyes are still blank.

"I didn't see any riding clothes in your closet, and since you used to enjoy it, I thought I'd order you some. I hope I got the size right. And if you don't like something, we can, of course, exchange it. They're especially made for you."

Nothing.

"Would you like to open them?" I ask, irritation creeping into my voice.

"Tomorrow."

"I went to a lot of trouble, Mercedes."

She closes her eyes.

I stand, hands clenching, unclenching as I pace.

"What do I have to do to get you back?" I ask, my voice low. Calm.

Nothing. No acknowledgment at all.

"What do I have to do, Mercedes?" I move to stand right over her bed and look down at her.

"I'm tired. I want to go to sleep."

"At least open your gift."

Mercedes is a clothes horse. She loves fashion. Loves high-end clothes. Has a million designer, specially made dresses, shoes, bags, jewelry, you name it. More than any woman can ever need. In another life, I think she'd be over the moon to receive the gift I have for her but this version of Mercedes? Nothing.

"Goddammit!" I rip the bow off the box and hurl the top across the room, tearing the tissue paper as I lift out her jacket, the pants. "At least look at it!" I yell, throwing her covers off and grabbing her arm, startling her. Finally. Finally fucking startling her enough to get a reaction. Any fucking reaction.

Her eyes fly open as I drag her up to sit, and she opens her mouth to scream when I realize what I'm doing and let her go. I turn from her, stalking away, hands pulling at my hair.

"What the fuck do I have to do to get you back?" I ask, no longer calm or quiet.

She's watching me, and it takes all I have to remain where I am. To not go to her and shake her out of this catatonic state.

"This has to stop. You have to get out of bed every morning. You have to wash yourself. You have to brush your hair. Dress in clean clothes. You have to fucking eat."

She blinks, then looks down at the clothes, the jacket half in the box. She touches it. "It's nice. Thank you."

I nod.

She gathers the blankets up and lies back down. "I'm tired now. I'll try them on tomorrow."

"Tomorrow. Tomorrow. Tomorrow. Fuck tomorrow!"

She doesn't seem to care, though. She just closes her eyes again. Closes her goddamn eyes.

"Tomorrow, I'm calling Dr. Barnes. Hell, I should have called him a week ago."

At that, I get a reaction. "No."

"If we need to put you on medication to get you out of this, so be it."

She shakes her head and pulls herself up to a seat. I see the effort it takes her, and I hear my grandfather's voice in my head. My hands fist.

She's manipulating you. Take control of her.

I know what he'd do. I know exactly how he'd take control.

I dig my fingernails into my palms. Let myself feel the pain of it as I recall her scars. Someone has already taken control of her in the past. I won't repeat history.

"If you don't want the doctor to come, then I need something from you. I need you to give me some sign that you don't need him."

She looks up at me. Meets my gaze and holds it, although the fire that used to burn in her black eyes isn't there. Not even close.

"I need my Mercedes back. The Mercedes who fights. The one who doesn't back down. The Mercedes who has given me a run for my money since she got here."

She blinks. Rubs her face and just looks like she wants to sleep. Like all she wants in the whole world is sleep.

There's a knock on the door, and Lois opens it to peer around. I'm sure she heard me lose my temper.

I drop my gaze to the carpet, take a deep breath in, and slowly exhale.

"Dinner's ready, dear. And the boys are anxious to see you," Lois says to Mercedes after a sad little glance at me.

Mercedes nods, looks at the boxes, the second one which contains her boots is still closed. For a moment, it's like she's not sure how to get out of the bed and moves to the other side to climb out. I notice she's barefoot. And I've seen those yoga pants about a dozen times already.

Angry, I cut her off on her way to Lois.

She stops and looks up at me. One hand wraps

around the footboard of the bed, and I'm not sure if it's to steady herself or to not back away.

"You're going to eat every bite of your dinner tonight. And you're not going to throw it up. Do you hear me?" Because she's done that the few times I've forced her to eat. "Lois made you your favorites. You're not going to waste it."

She looks over my shoulder at Lois, her eyes dull. She's not even crying anymore. Not that I've seen at least. Like the effort of tears is too much.

"Come on, dear," Lois says, stepping closer.

Mercedes takes a step around me, and I lose it. I just lose my shit. I grab her hard and give her that shake. "Do you fucking hear me?"

Her head flops on her neck, and she cries out.

Something. Finally, some fucking reaction. I do it again.

"Judge!" Lois's voice is alarmed. She puts a hand on my arm.

I lean my face close to Mercedes's. "Do. You. Fucking. Hear. Me?"

Tears spring from her eyes. Again. Victory. I'll take it.

She nods.

"Sir. You need to let me take her now." Lois's hand on my arm tightens. "You don't want to hurt her."

Fuck.

No, I don't.

I loosen my grip a little. I can't let go just yet, though.

"You'll stay with her after. Until she's asleep. Make sure she doesn't make herself vomit."

"I will. She won't do that. I know it," Lois says. Although she doesn't know it at all, and I can hear that in her words.

"Or I'll have Miriam watch her."

"I'll be here with her. It's no trouble." Her tone is gentler when she next speaks to Mercedes. "Let's go see the boys, dear. They're hungry. Come on, come with me. Just you and me."

Lois takes her hand, and I'm forced to step away. And I watch from my place as she walks across the room with Lois, her steps slower than the older woman's. She doesn't speak, doesn't answer Lois even as Lois prattles on, and when they're gone, I sit on the edge of her bed, my head heavy in my hands.

I have fucked this up so royally. I have more than lost control. Never before has this happened. But Mercedes? She's under my skin, and I am fast losing control of the situation.

A few minutes later, I get up. I set the riding clothes on the bench at the foot of her bed. Maybe if she sees them laid out, it'll inspire something. I don't know. I'm on my way out the door when something catches my eye. On the desk in the corner is a paperweight. A solid wood paperweight.

I tilt my head. It's probably been here for years,

and I wouldn't have noticed it except for what Mercedes said about Miriam. When I thought she was lying. I pick it up, weigh it. I take it with me when I leave and head to my study to read through the staff applications and their files and learn what I can about Miriam, whose last name I can't even recall.

19

JUDGE

The threat of the doctor does its job. Mercedes eats, and she manages to keep it down for the next few days. It's raining again, the ground sopping after a week of unrelenting rain. It's so bad I won't even ride. I don't want the horses to injure themselves on the soft ground.

I get home late in the evening and head toward the kitchen, where I hear Lois and Miriam talking. Neither of them notices me.

"You're spoiling her if you ask me," Miriam tells Lois.

I stand just outside and listen.

"She needs a firm hand, that one. All this sulking around," she says.

"She's depressed, Miriam. You just leave her alone."

"But it's my job to look after her."

Lois snorts.

"She's an attention seeker, that's all. She'll get over it. Just needs a firm hand to give her a shove."

I don't miss the ugly turn at the word *shove*. I clear my throat, and Miriam startles, almost spills the coffee she was bringing to her lips.

"Ladies," I say as I study Miriam. She pushes her chair back loudly to stand. I almost expect a salute from her.

"Sir," Miriam says. She bows her head rather than saluting.

"Well, you're late tonight, Judge," Lois says. "You must be starved. Come on, sit down. It'll just take me a minute to warm up your plate." She wipes her hands on her towel and moves to where a covered dish has been set aside.

"Thank you, Lois," I say, taking the scotch from the cabinet and pouring myself a glass.

"I'll be off to bed then," Miriam says and brings her coffee cup to the sink for Lois to set in the dishwasher.

"Stay a minute," I say.

She looks nervous but nods and sits opposite me.

Lois brings over my food and returns to cleaning the dishes.

"How has Mercedes been?" I ask her.

"Same," she says. "Refuses to touch any food I bring her. Gives me an evil look whenever I offer to help her with anything."

"Hm. Lois?"

Lois is watching us from the counter. "I think she's doing a little better. Eating a little more. The boys are good for her. That Pestilence can nudge a smile out of anyone."

"I'm glad. Where are the hounds?" I notice their place is empty.

"She took them out for a little walk," Lois says proudly. "Her idea."

"That's good to hear." It is an improvement although the time is concerning. I hope she's not doing something stupid like looking for an exit. I check my watch. "How long ago?"

"Fifteen, twenty minutes. She took an umbrella and a warm jacket. Said she'd check on the horses too. They've been cooped up in their stalls what with your busy week and this weather we've been having."

"You know what, I'll go see if I can't catch up with her." I get up, switch out my shoes for an old pair of riding boots I reserve for just this weather, and grab my Barbour from the rack by the door. It's perfect for this weather. "I'll eat when I'm back. Don't worry, I can heat it up again myself. You two go to bed."

"Are you sure? I can stay," Lois says almost at the same time that Miriam murmurs a good night and disappears.

"Go on, Lois. You've been putting in a lot of hours with Mercedes as it is, and I appreciate it."

"It's no trouble. I love that girl like she's my own."

"You should tell her that. I'm not sure she hears that often enough."

"I have. I'm not too shy to share my feelings."

"Good. I'll see you in the morning."

I step outside just as the rain seems to pick up and open my umbrella. I glance around and whistle for the dogs. But if they're at the stables, they may not hear me over the rain, so I head in that direction, hurrying my steps. I'm about halfway there when I hear barking. I pause to listen. Rain comes down heavy, but there it is again. Barking. It's getting closer, and I start to run toward the sound because something feels wrong. And I have a feeling of dread in my gut like I've never felt before.

Would she hurt herself? Is she so far gone that she'll hurt herself?

I'm almost to the stables when Famine and War come charging toward me, barking their warning. I stop dead, my heart pounding heavy against my chest.

"What is it? Where is she?" I ask them when they reach me, barking their warnings, their panic.

"Mercedes!" I call out over the rain as I hurry toward the stables where the lights are on and the door is open. "Mercedes!"

I rush inside, Famine and War at my heels, and my heart drops to my stomach when I see the open door of my horse, Kentucky Lightning's, stall. His saddle hangs where it should be, but the bridle is gone.

"Fuck!"

The dogs whine, and Temperance neighs as I open the door to her stall. I slip her bridle on. I don't bother with the saddle. There's no time. She shouldn't be riding at night and in this weather. In her state. And she should definitely not be riding my horse. She may be experienced, but he's too big. Too fast.

"Where is she?" The dogs leap out ahead of me barking and charging in what I hope is the direction she went. I call out to her as I ride hard, my torso laid over Temperance's back to hurry her into the woods. Why would she go into the woods? Rain soaks me, pouring through the collar of my jacket. I can only imagine the state she's in, and just when panic is setting in, I hear the other dogs. Hear the thundering of Kentucky Lightning's hooves as he rides fast, too fast.

And then I see them. They're in a clearing coming up to the creek. He's used to the jump, but the ground is too muddy, too slippery.

"Mercedes!" She turns her head so I know she hears me. But she's determined. I can see it from here. Body laid low over the back of the horse, hands tight around the reins.

When I'm close enough, I whistle my command to Kentucky Lightning to stop, but she urges him on.

"It's too wet! You can't make the jump!" I yell, but I'm too far for her to hear, or maybe she just doesn't want to listen.

The dogs are going wild, circling, howling, anticipating. And Mercedes keeps riding like the wind.

It's what I wanted, right? The old Mercedes back. The fierce woman I know.

I'm almost to them. If I can get close enough, Kentucky Lightning will obey my command. I can stop this. I whistle, and when the horse hesitates, she glances back at me, eyes bright in this darkness as she tugs on the reins urging him on.

But I'm close enough now. And I only have a moment before the jump. Either he's going to stop and throw her, or he's going to jump it and lose his footing in the mud. Either way, at least one of them is getting hurt, if not both.

I bring Temperance up alongside Kentucky Lightning, and he slows just enough at my presence, giving me the moment I need to leap onto his back. Mercedes screams as she almost topples over the other side of the giant beast, and Temperance neighs as we leave her behind. I wrap one arm around Mercedes's waist and take the reins from her, whistling my command for Kentucky Lightning to slow to a stop, rain pelting us as the dogs bark and whine around us, confused.

"Get off me!" Mercedes yells, pulling at my arm to free herself. "Get off!"

"Are you trying to kill yourself?" I yell over the rain as Kentucky Lightning slows to a trot, and I guide him around, whistling for Temperance to follow as I grip Mercedes hard and lead the horses back to the stables.

Paolo runs out as we approach, coat half-zipped, boots muddy, hair soaked.

"I heard the commotion," he says as I slide off Kentucky Lightning and carry Mercedes down, hauling her over my shoulder and slapping her ass hard when she won't stop fighting.

"Can you take care of this?" I ask.

He looks at us and nods. "I'll bring the dogs in. Go. Take care of her."

"Thank you." I hurry back to the house, Mercedes pounding at my back, legs kicking. It doesn't matter how much she fights. Her strength is nothing compared to mine, and I'm as determined as she is. I get her into the house and set her on the kitchen counter. I'm so angry, so fucking angry that I can't speak as I rip off her boots then mine and throw the muddy things on the floor, discarding our jackets on top of the boots before I scoop her back up and carry her up to my room. She still fights me every step of the way. Still screams bloody fucking murder.

But I don't care.

I don't give a single fuck.

Because what the fuck was she doing out there? Trying to get herself killed? Maim my horse?

"Are you fucking insane?" I finally spit as I walk into my bedroom through to the bathroom and stand her up in the shower. I switch on the spray, and she yelps at the initial splash of icy water. Again, I don't care.

I strip off her clothes, ripping them to shreds, then I strip naked and step into the shower with her. We need to warm up and get clean.

The shower stall is big enough for two with two showerheads, but I crowd her, looming over her. Even as tall as she is, she's nothing next to me.

"Answer me!"

"Get away from me!" She shoves at my chest, energy burning in her black eyes. Making molten lava out of them.

Rage.

Fucking rage.

I'll take it over catatonic any day.

"No!" I grip a handful of hair and force her beneath the flow. "When was the last time you washed your hair?"

"It's none of your business."

"Your business is my business, little monster."

"Fuck you, you asshole."

I tug her head backward and bring my face to hers. "Be careful what you ask for."

Her eyebrows come together, but then she glares.

The shower steams around us. "I should whip your ass."

"Don't you dare."

"You could have been killed."

"Like you care."

"And if you'd made it, you could have maimed Kentucky Lightning."

At that she stops. No smart-ass comment. I wonder if she'd thought about that. But it's only a moment of silence before she's slapping at my chest and shoving to get around me.

"You want to fight? Do you?"

"Yeah, dickhead. I'd love a fight."

"You got it. Maybe this is exactly what you need." I switch off the water and lift her off her feet, hauling her over my shoulder as soon as I step out of the shower.

She kicks. I slap her ass once, twice, three times, the sound of my hand on her wet cheek reverberating off the walls as she pounds against my back, nails digging in to scratch rivulets into my skin.

"I'll give you some fresh scars to go with the one you're trying to hide," she tells me when I throw her onto the bed.

She bounces twice, and before she's up on her elbows, I'm on top of her. I fist her hair. She buries her fingernails in my chest, digging mercilessly.

"What did you want out there? Tell me."

"You don't get to know what's in my head. You've

more than proven you don't give a fuck about me! Besides, what are you afraid of?" She asks as I tug on her hair. She winces, hands coming to my forearm to pry me off. "That you won't get your payday if I'm dead? Or that you'll have to answer to my brother? Because he will fucking kill you if you hurt me!"

"Is that it, then? You wanted to kill yourself?" I release her hair and sit back, keeping my weight on my thighs as I straddle her to keep her pinned.

"Like I said, you don't care!" She slaps my chest. I let her. A look of surprise crosses her features when I don't stop her, and she does it again, then again, then again. "Fight me, you bastard!" She slaps my face this time, but it's hesitant.

"Stop, Mercedes."

"Fight me!" She slaps harder, making my cheek sting.

I catch her wrists, grip them in one hand, and lay on top of her, my weight partially on the bed, partially on her.

"Fight!" she screams, and I look at her, seeing the sadness of it all, the truth of it. She would have hurt herself. Worse. That's how far this has come.

"No," I tell her. "Enough fighting."

She struggles beneath me, eyes wet with hurt and tears and hopelessness.

"Mercedes."

"Hit me!"

"Mercedes. Quiet."

She shakes her head violently, tears unleashed.

"I do care about you. Don't you know that?" I cup the back of her head and hold her to me. When I release her hands, she presses against me, slapping my chest, but it's half-hearted. She's spent.

"Quiet now."

A sob breaks from her throat. And I just hold her for a long, long time. And then... and then... I don't know what happens next. We're so close, both of us naked, wet from the shower, from exertion, and I don't fucking know, but I'm kissing her. I'm kissing her, and it's like something inside my chest quickens, my heart faltering. She's soft and inexperienced and yielding, and there's a sudden stopping of time.

But I don't stop. I can't.

I kiss her again and feel her breath, the warmth of her. Her taste salty with tears. Tears that belong to me.

Her hands curl around my shoulders, and I slide one of mine down over her stomach until it's between her legs. I draw back to look at her as I close my hand over the mound of her sex, and then my fingers are opening her, feeling her warm dampness. The stiff, swollen clit. She stares up at me, eyes wide, mouth open, and I watch her as I play with her, fingers sliding through her folds to dip inside her, to carry that moisture back to her clit. I listen to her sharp intake of breath and watch her pupils darken.

"Judge... I..."

I find I'm holding my breath, and I pull back, dip my head to her breast, and lick then take her nipple into my mouth.

She gasps and clings to me, hips arching into my hand as I close my teeth around the hard nub and draw it out, then release it to do the same to the other. Her hands move into my hair, clutching it, and I take her clit between my thumb and forefinger and draw back to watch her.

Mercedes bares her neck, biting her lip hard enough that a drop of crimson appears. She pushes herself into my hand and closes her eyes.

"Open them. I want to see you. I want to watch you come."

She does as she's told, and it's moments before she's panting, legs squeezing around my hand as she whispers my name, closing her eyes again and pulling me to her with the last of her orgasm.

I'm still hard as a fucking rock as I take my wet fingers from between her legs, and when her small hand wraps around my shaft, I capture it to halt her, groaning with my need. Battling with my duty.

"Mercedes..."

"I don't... know how," she says, her voice uncertain and quiet.

I open my eyes to look at her, and I'm not sure I've ever seen her so vulnerable. So beautiful. So fucking perfect. And as wrong as I know this is, as much as I know I am betraying my best friend to do it, I find myself pressing my cock between her folds before letting her wrap her hand around it again and closing mine over hers.

I make a promise then. An oath.

One time.

Just once.

This will happen exactly once. Because I think we both need this.

But I will leave her pure. Untouched.

One time. That is all I'll allow the beast inside me.

I repeat it like a fucking mantra as I guide her hand. Her eyes are locked on mine in wide fascination, and when I feel her slide her free hand between her legs, I am undone.

"Fuck. Mercedes. Fuck."

My breath is ragged when I come, hearing her surprised gasp as I cover her with ropes of come. I watch her slide her hand from between her legs to scoop it up and then return it to her clit, smearing my essence into herself.

I kiss her. My little monster is a dirty, dirty girl.

She does it again, and I groan, gripping her tight as I empty the last of it, and she shudders beneath me, coming again.

20

MERCEDES

Judge blinks at me as if he doesn't understand how the hell that just happened. It makes two of us. His warm body is still pressing down onto mine. I'm covered in his come, and I'm still soaked with the evidence of my body's betrayal. The want I shouldn't have felt for him.

It was intense. It was... all-consuming. And now, it just feels confusing. But when he rolls over and collapses beside me, I feel the loss of his warmth immediately. I hate that I miss it, but even worse, I hate that I allowed him to touch me in the first place. Because now that it's all catching up to me, I realize how stupid it was for me to give in. I can't pretend I've forgotten everything I know about him. I refuse to be another Society woman who turns a blind eye to what's happening right under her nose.

"So how does this work, exactly?" My voice is

dripping with the bitterness I can't hide. "You take the edge off with me and then call up your courtesan later tonight?"

Judge glances over at me, his brow furrowed as if I'm being ridiculous, and it only serves to irritate me even more.

"Don't expect to have us on a rotating schedule," I snap at him. "Because that's not going to happen."

He leans up on one elbow to examine me. "You know, your jealousy might be cute if I even knew where the hell it was coming from, little monster."

"I'm not jealous." I glare back at him. "It's called respect. I'm not going to be your side piece."

He chuckles softly then, shaking his head. "I'd have to have a main piece for you to be my side piece, Mercedes."

"Don't treat me as if I'm stupid." I grab the covers to pull them over myself as I sit up. "I know what you do at night. The staff talks. If you think discretion is a thing, you're seriously deluded."

Irritation flickers across his features. "What do you mean the staff talks?"

"Are you really going to make me spell it out for you?"

"That would be helpful, yes."

"Miriam," I bark. "She told me all about your nighttime proclivities. That's who you were on the phone with the other day, isn't it? Making plans for your nights while you spend your days torturing me?"

For a moment, he looks so stunned by the accusation that it makes me question my sanity. If I'm being honest, I hate that I'm even pursuing this. That I need an answer from him. But I do.

"Miriam told you I was talking to... who, exactly?" he asks.

I roll my eyes and look away. "Who do you think, Judge? Your favorite courtesan."

He snorts, and it pisses me off. I move to leave, but he grabs me, dragging me back onto the bed and forcing me to look at him. Our eyes lock, and the amusement slowly slips away from his.

"There is no courtesan keeping me company at night," he says softly. "You keep me more than occupied for that. But what just happened between us? I need you to understand that won't happen again. Those intimacies are for your future husband. I shouldn't have crossed that line with you."

His words leave a sour taste in my mouth, and when I swallow down the emotions I want to hide, I hope he can't see them. I know he's lying. He has to be lying because, on some level, he feels what I feel. That's the only explanation for this dysfunctional attraction between us. As much as he pretends to be okay with the idea that I'll marry someone else eventually, I can't accept that it's true. And part of me feels like he keeps throwing it in my face as a way to keep me at a distance.

He touches my face as if he's trying to soften the blow. "Don't retreat back into yourself. I need to know you're not going to do that again."

I blink away the stinging pain behind my eyes and shake my head. Again, I want to ask him why he cares, but I know it doesn't matter. Judge can't even be honest with himself in this situation, so he's certainly not going to be honest with me.

"I wasn't trying to hurt myself," I whisper. At least I don't think I was. Admittedly, what I did was reckless, but it wasn't like I was really trying to kill myself. "And I would never, ever want to hurt one of your horses. I've seen what a bad jump can do to a horse. I wouldn't do that. It wasn't even my intent. I just wanted to see how fast he would go. I needed... something. But the terrain was unfamiliar, and I could hardly see in the rain. When you came out of nowhere, I didn't want you to catch me. I didn't even realize what was happening until you jumped on to stop us."

I truly feel fucking terrible, and Judge must see it because he doesn't scold me again. Instead, he comforts me, his hand rubbing circles into my back. It feels so good that I don't want it to end. I don't understand it. How can this man who infuriates me so often bring me this kind of peace as well? When I look at him, I wonder if he's questioning it too.

"Just don't try it again," he says, his voice absent of derision. "You don't ride unless you're with me, or I give you permission."

I could bite back, but I don't. There's something about when he shows me even an ounce of softness that makes me wish for more. After the hell of the last few weeks, I shouldn't want or need these moments from him, but I do. I know I told him I'd never forgive him for what he'd done, and a part of me still hasn't, but right now, it's overshadowed by my basic human need for comfort.

"I want you to tell me what happened with Miriam."

I lift my gaze to his, already prepared for a fight, but he stops me with a shake of his head.

"I'll listen this time. Please, tell me."

"I did tell you." My lip trembles, betrayal prickling my nerves all over again. "I'm not in the habit of repeating the truth when it only serves to earn me a punishment."

I learned that the hard way long ago, with my father and even Santiago. The men in my life all have a tendency to believe what they want, regardless of what I say. When someone challenges your truth, it makes you start to question your own reality. It invalidates everything you experienced. And I'm not about to let Judge do that to me all over again.

"Mercedes." He tries to coax more from me, but I shake my head.

"No. I'm not repeating it. You betrayed my trust. You accused me of lying when I wasn't. I'm not going through that again."

I'm not sure if I should expect a fight from him, but he doesn't give me one. Instead, we fall into a tense silence until he finally breaks it with the touch of his hand. At first, I'm not sure what he's doing as his fingers move over the skin at the nape of my neck. Then it occurs to me, that's where my IVI tattoo is located. Like every other member, I have one. But that ink isn't what Judge is quietly contemplating. He's touching the empty space above it. The one reserved for my husband's family crest when I marry.

I turn toward him, and our eyes clash, and abruptly, his hand falls away. He knows I know what he was doing. That he was thinking about it. And I can't tell if he's already mourning the loss of me, or if he's thinking something else. Something that... could be.

My answer comes when his features harden again, his voice regaining the steel edge he's known for.

"Come on. Let's get you cleaned up."

21

MERCEDES

True to his word, Judge hasn't touched me again. More weeks have passed. I don't even know how long it's been. How long ago was it that I even had a life of my own? In some ways, it feels like an eternity. In others, it feels like no time at all has passed.

As part of Judge's program for keeping me at a distance, he seems to find ways to occupy my time. I still rise every morning to clean the stables, and he's been letting me spend more time with the horses and dogs too. It seems as if slowly, he's giving me more and more responsibility. Now, in addition to the stable duties, I'm also spending my days brushing the horses and helping with feedings, as well as walking the dogs.

I've been exploring the property, which is vast.

Of course, one of the first things I did when I had the opportunity was to look for a way out, but it appears the entire grounds are gated. Not only that, but Judge has staff who lives on-site, and I'm fairly certain there's a security system in place, like there is for most Sovereign Sons. I would be a fool to believe otherwise.

In one of the old stone outbuildings, I found what appears to be a door at the back, and it caught my curiosity. I was tempted to go inside to see what was there, but I haven't worked up the courage to do it yet. Every day, I keep telling myself that I will. But something has been holding me back, and I'm not entirely certain yet what it is.

My mood has improved since Judge has allowed me more freedom to roam, and I spend my days doing physical activity. I missed it. I miss my friends and my aerial classes, and I want to ask Judge when I can see them. But that would require him grunting more than one word to me. Or even really looking at me, for that matter.

When I'm not outside, I've taken to wandering the house. Miriam is still always lurking around what feels like every corner, but she's not as involved in my day-to-day life anymore, and that's one small thing I can be grateful for. I eat my meals with Lois and the hounds. And then, in the afternoons, I sit down at the piano and play.

When Judge first told me I was to resume my piano practice, I was ready to hurl the music sheets right at his head. I hadn't played since my father and brother died in the explosion that rocked our family to its core. That event was the result of the Moreno family's scheming, an event Santiago swore we would avenge when he married Ivy Moreno. But instead of the revenge I was promised, I was given a front row seat to my brother's infatuation with the woman he vowed he would destroy. He seems to have forgotten all about how our father and brother died, and the grief that stole our mother shortly after. Almost overnight, our lives changed drastically. For so long, I felt like I was drowning in that grief because it was the right thing to do. And for Leandro and my mother, that was true. But there was another part of me. The one that felt… slightly relieved when my father was gone.

It's a messy type of love when you still care about the person who hurt you the most. Biologically, we're programmed to love our parents. We depend on them to nurture us, but when that system fails, it doesn't alter the needs you have as a child. You still crave their protection. Their love. Even when they are the ones to harm you.

My father was the one who insisted I play the piano every day. For hours upon hours, he was merciless in his directives that I perfect this skill. It was the one talent I seemed to possess naturally, and he homed in on it, deciding this would be the thing that made me stand out from all the other Society daughters. I was only a child when he treated it as if it were a full-time job. He would force me to play until my fingers blistered and bled. And if I ever dared to resist, I was whipped, paddled, or caned. Beatings weren't uncommon in the De La Rosa manor, and sometimes, it felt as if there didn't need to be a reason to justify them. It was simply that children needed to be put in their place.

Leandro and Santiago tried to protect me as often as they could. But, like me, their schedules were busy. Sometimes, they were away at school, and I was left alone to fend for myself. It was during one of these times that I worked up the courage to tell my father I no longer wished to play the piano at all. What a foolish notion that was. My ten-year-old brain was too immature to understand the consequences of such bravado. Yet I went to him, prepared to plead my case and stand my ground, the way I had seen my brothers often do.

I walked into his study when he was drunk one night. That was my first mistake. I thought perhaps it would actually work in my favor. He might agree to my request in his inebriated state, and then there could be no going back on it.

I sat down across from the man who was supposed to love and protect me, and I recited the speech I'd prepared, complete with an array of alternative skills I could spend my time perfecting. Dance was my favorite, I told him. He laughed as if it was ridiculous and told me to go away, but I didn't. I went on to beg him the way I knew I shouldn't. I told him piano wasn't fun anymore. He had made it not fun anymore.

I'll never forget the look in his eyes when he rose from his seat that night. Like a demon straight from the depths of hell. He asked me if I thought anything worth doing was fun. Of course, I didn't know how to answer that. I told him about the other girls in my class who spent their time doing fun things. He snarled and said I wasn't like the other girls. I was a De La Rosa, and I needed to live up to the name. Somehow, even then, I knew that I never would. Nothing I did could ever please my father. Nothing would ever be good enough.

My second mistake was trying to pursue my argument, determined to show him that I was a De La Rosa because I wouldn't back down. I didn't doubt I'd be punished for it. I was always punished for speaking my mind. For being too willful. For just existing. But that night, when my father dragged me to the chapel and took out his instruments of torture, something was different. He hit me harder than I expected with the belt right from the start, and I did the one thing I was never, ever supposed to do.

I cried. It only fueled his rage. He hit me again,

harder yet, screaming at me not to be weak. But as much as I tried, I couldn't hold back the tears that time. I couldn't understand why it was okay for the boys to stand up for themselves but not the girls. I couldn't understand why I wasn't free to choose my own path in life, and my only reason for existing was to be the talented doll of a wife to a Sovereign Son someday.

I had dreams, and at that moment, they all shattered because I knew they'd never come true. Whatever innocence may have existed in me died that night. Beneath the weight of my father's wrath, I quickly came to understand my role in life. I came to understand that I was nothing more than a decorative chess piece for him to control. To move around the board as he pleased.

I mourned for the loss of the things I wanted, and he beat me savagely for it. For every tear I shed, he returned it with the crack of his belt so violently, it split my skin and flayed me wide open. But that didn't stop him. It only seemed to make him angrier, as if I should show such a weakness. As if a De La Rosa could ever bleed.

By the time he finished, I couldn't move. He left me sobbing on the floor of the chapel, too broken to ever be whole again. Antonia was the one who found me, and I was grateful for it. She cleaned my wounds, stitched me up, and tended to me for weeks while I recovered. During that time, my father took my mother to Barcelona so she wouldn't see what he had done. My brothers were away at school, and when they returned, they'd be none the wiser. The implication was clear. My father never explicitly told me not to say anything, but then he didn't have to. If I had, that would have proven how weak I was.

So I kept it in. I shut my emotions off. And I learned to toe the line of being who I was always meant to while hiding my truest self whenever I was in his shadow. I played the piano. I honed my craft. And I perfected every challenge he threw my way until the day he died.

But once he was gone, I swore I'd never play again. Until Judge asked me to. At first, I was angry. I was grief-stricken, and not just for my family or the memories that stirred when I associated them with my performances. I was also grieving for the loss of myself. The little girl who wanted to choose her own path.

I told Judge no that first day and many more days after that. Until one night, I couldn't sleep, and I was wandering the house when I came upon the piano by myself. When I glared down at the offending keys, I realized the only person I was punishing was me. Because truth be told, I had enjoyed it once. I had loved the way my fingers flew over the ivory, whipping into a frenzy as my body swayed with the music. There had been a time before the pain when it had brought me pleasure. That night, I told myself I would only do it once, for old times' sake.

I sat down, and I did play once. But it didn't give me the closure I was hoping for. It gave me something else. And oddly enough, I think that thing was peace. Because I wasn't doing it for anyone else. I was doing it for me. The music I wanted to play, how I wanted to play it.

I stayed up until the late hours that night, and it was only when I turned to leave that I caught Judge watching me. He seemed to be ensnared by the very sight of me. Moonlight poured in from the window, bathing my skin in an ethereal glow, and I imagine in many ways, it was like watching Frankenstein come alive. I felt alive for the first time in as long as I could remember, and Judge could see it too.

After that, new sheets of music started to appear. He didn't demand anything from me. He didn't even ask. But every night, when I would sneak down to play, I'd feel his presence behind me, watching me from the darkness. Inevitably, those sessions crept into my daylight hours too. And now, I find myself spending afternoons in front of the beautiful instrument. Judge will ask me to play something difficult, and I don't deny him. I'm not sure why, but this feels like something special between us. Like a secret language. A gift.

This afternoon, when I hear his footsteps approaching somewhere between Moonlight Sonata and Gaspard de la nuit, I'm expecting him to throw me another challenge. He likes to do that, and secretly, I like to rise to meet them. But instead, when I glance over my shoulder, my fingers come to a halt on the keys, and I suck in a sharp breath.

It isn't just Judge watching me today. Standing beside him is my brother, looking so melancholy it makes me want to cry. But there's something else in his eyes. Something I can't mistake for anything other than pride.

"Don't stop," he tells me. "Finish the song."

I give him the tiniest of nods and turn to finish, giving the performance my all. Perhaps it's my version of an apology. Perhaps I just need to know he still loves me. Regardless, when I finish, whatever it is I think I need from him is absent from his face.

"You came to see me?" I ask.

"Yes." The softness disappears from his features, returning to stone. "I came to ask you about the aspirin you left in my wife's room."

"Aspirin?" I echo, trying to discern the meaning behind the question.

"Yes," he grits out. "The aspirin you gave her. The aspirin she used to try to kill herself and my child."

"Child?" My voice fractures, betrayal crawling beneath my skin like insects. "You... you got her pregnant?"

The very idea of it makes me rage. And I can see now that he never wanted me gone because of what

I did. He wanted me gone because he's fallen in love with her. After promising she would pay for her father's sins, after all his assurances that our family didn't die in vain. He comes here to tell me she's pregnant as if he didn't ever plan on killing her to begin with.

"How could you?" I sneer at him in disgust. "She's the enemy, Santiago. What part of that don't you remember?"

It isn't Santiago that responds. It's Judge. He stalks toward me, reaching out to take my face into his palm, and it completely disorients me. Because I had tried to reject the notion that I had missed his touch. That I had ached for it. But feeling his grip on me now, his power and his possession, I can't deny it. When he leans down to whisper his threat in my ear, it sends a shiver of pleasure down my spine.

"Behave."

I close my eyes for a moment, trying to steady the erratic beat of my heart. I don't understand how he has this effect on me. It makes no rational sense. A part of me is tempted to disobey just so I can guarantee more of his touch, even if it comes in the form of punishment. But not with Santiago here. Not when there are important matters to be discussed.

I release a shuddering breath and nod, and Judge hesitates to release me. When I open my eyes to meet his, it's like nothing else exists at this moment. He overshadows everything. That is until he seems to snap out of whatever spell he's under, and his fingers fall away from my face, leaving me cold again.

I can't begin to unpack those feelings right now, so I return my focus to Santi, determined to face his allegation head-on.

"You think I gave them to her intentionally," I say. "To kill herself. That's why you came here."

"It isn't out of the realm of possibility," he answers bitterly. "I need to know what other schemes you may have left unfinished."

Emotion burns my eyes, and I dip my head to hide it before regaining control of myself. "I didn't have any other schemes, Santi. I gave her the aspirin for pain. That was my only intention. I never meant to hurt your precious wife or child."

"For your sake, I hope that isn't another lie." He turns to go, but something gnaws at me. Something else I've been hiding. And I want to show him I'm trying. I want to be honest, even if I know it will probably only make him more upset.

"Goddammit, wait a second," I blurt out. "I have something to tell you."

He halts and turns, the uneasiness on his face an obvious sign he's preparing for another painful blow of my betrayal. I suppose I should expect nothing more at this point.

"I'm not telling you for Ivy's sake," I announce, wanting to make that perfectly clear. "I'm telling you because I want to show you that you can trust me."

"What is it?" he asks.

For a moment, my nerves get the better of me, and then my gaze drifts to Judge as if to seek his approval. He seems to understand, nodding at me silently, giving me the assurance I need to go on.

"It's about Chambers, that doctor." The first words are difficult to get out, and Santiago looks pissed already. So I rush to explain everything while I have a chance.

I tell him how I started following Ivy's brother after Santi was poisoned. I go into details about the storage unit I tracked him to several times and how it seemed suspicious. I had no way of knowing it at the time, but I suspected Abel had something to do with the attack that almost cost my brother his life. The attack he blames me for, regardless of who really gave the order. I explain how I broke into the storage unit to see what he was hiding, and as I do, both Judge and Santiago glower at me in unison.

Ignoring their silent disapproval, I continue, hurrying to get the words out. I talk about the evidence of the doctor's demise. The bloody wallet I found. All the files from his office. Abel was hiding them for a reason, and I need my brother to know that regardless of his feelings for Ivy, her brother can't be trusted.

"He's dangerous, Santi," I croak. "And I overheard him say something on the phone. Something I can't stop thinking about."

"What was it?" His rough voice betrays his concern.

"He said he would sooner rot than let you impregnate Ivy," I confess. "And if you did, he would cut the baby out of her himself."

22

JUDGE

Once Santiago leaves, I rejoin Mercedes. She's standing beside the piano still watching the spot where her brother was. I saw the hope in her eyes when she first saw him. And then the disappointment that followed almost immediately.

"Are you all right?"

She shakes her head as if to clear it, then looks at me. "Fine," she says coldly. She turns away from me and closes the piano lid.

I go to her and place my hand over hers, pressing my front to her back. There's a moment when she softens against me, leaning into me. But it's brief, and I think she'd pull away if she wasn't trapped between me and the piano. "Mercedes."

"What?" she snaps, trying to take her hand from mine.

I tighten my hold and brush her hair off the nape of her neck, setting it over her shoulder. I'm so close I can smell her shampoo, and I hear her short breaths as my fingers play over the IVI tattoo. The space above it. She shudders, and I draw in a deep breath before taking a step backward.

One time. It was allowed one fucking time. Looking Santiago in the eye was already hard today. I can't complicate things more.

Mercedes sighs and walks away from me.

"Why didn't you tell me about Chambers earlier? And why in the world would you think it was safe for you to pursue this alone? To follow Abel when you know how dangerous he is?"

She folds her arms across her chest, her defenses up again. I'm sorry for it because this space, this room and the piano have become a haven for her. Watching her when she plays, listening to the music she makes, it's, in a word, sublime. She is at ease. Relaxed to the point she drops her defenses, her anger, her hurt, and is perhaps herself more than at any other time I see her.

"It's fine. Nothing happened. I'm fine. Excuse me." She walks toward the exit, but I capture her arm.

"I don't excuse you." And there it is again, the friction between us. A charged tension I've never before felt with any other woman. "And you don't walk away from me until I do."

She looks down at my hand, then up at me, and I see how her eyes darken as she licks her lips. It makes my dick twitch, and what I'd like to do most in the world right now is rip off her clothes, bend her over the piano, and fuck her until her knees give out and my name is the breath she breathes.

A low rumble from inside my chest breaks the silence. The beast is rattling its chains. It wants out. It wants her.

One. Fucking. Time. That was all.

"And what will you do if I don't obey your command, *your honor*? Is that what you make them call you in the courtroom?"

I grin. "I like that. You may start using the honorific, Mercedes."

"Fuck off."

"Careful."

"I won't be careful." She tries to jerk free. "What are you going to do about it? Bend me over the piano and spank me?"

"Close." I tug her to me and let my gaze drop to her mouth, to the expanse of skin exposed by her top and the soft swell of her breasts in the push-up bra.

She grins. "Do it then. I dare you."

I grit my teeth. "Be careful, Mercedes. I mean it."

She shrugs the shoulder of her free arm. "You won't. You don't dare touch me because you're afraid."

"Afraid?"

She leans up on tiptoe. I feel her breath on my face when she speaks. "Yes, you're afraid, Judge. Afraid you won't be able to stop yourself from taking what we both know you really want."

I shift my hand from her arm to her back, brushing fingers up along her spine until I get to the base of her skull where I grip a handful of hair. She drops to flat feet, and I tug her head backward.

"And what is it I want, little monster?"

"Me." She grins. "My pussy, to be exact."

My response, a growl, makes her smile. Confirmation. As if it's a secret. It was a ridiculous notion to ever try to pretend I didn't want her.

I tilt my head and walk her backward so she's standing against the piano. She swallows hard. I spin her around so fast, she yelps, not expecting it. Her hands come flat to the top of the piano so she's half bent over it.

"Stay," I tell her when she struggles. It's her default. Fight. Every time. And I'll still take it over flight. Her retreating into herself is not what I want to see ever again. And I'll do whatever I need to do to make sure I don't.

"You keep telling yourself that," my grandfather's voice says. *"You want her. Have her. She's yours for the taking."*

I flip her dress up over her ass. She's wearing a

dark red G-string. "Your ass does beg to be spanked, doesn't it?"

She clenches her cheeks, then softens them as if offering them to me. My cock grows hard at the sight of her, at the sound of her quickening breath. I slip my fingers into the waistband of her panties and tug them up.

She gasps, rising on tiptoe as the string digs into her folds. "What the fuck?"

I lean over her, slide one hand between her torso and the piano, and cup her breast, pinching her nipple.

She yelps.

"What I want, little monster, is for you to be safe."

She turns her head, wincing as I tug her panties higher. "Can I ask you a question, Judge?"

"Of course, Mercedes."

"How do you picture me when you're jerking off at night? Am I on my knees at your feet? Worshipping the great Judge Lawson Montgomery's big dick? Or am I bent over taking it from behind? What's your preferred scenario?"

I pull her up straight and turn her to face me but keep a tight grip on her panties. She braces her hands on my shoulders for balance. "Thank you for asking. I enjoy both. How about you? I hear you, you know? I hear you moan when you make yourself come at night."

She blushes wildly and shoves against me. "I don't!"

"No need to be embarrassed, little monster. It's perfectly natural." I release her abruptly, and she stumbles sideways, posture twisting as she tries to muster some dignity without actually reaching under her dress to pull the string out of her pussy. "And I like listening to you come. I like it very much."

"You're such a jerk!" She spins to walk away, but I grab her arm again. I need to address something.

"Paolo said he saw you near one of the outbuildings on the property. You're fine to wander, but I don't want you going into those buildings."

"Why? What are you hiding?"

"I'm not hiding anything. It's not safe. You keep out, Mercedes. Do you understand?"

"Fine. Let me go."

"One more thing."

"What?"

"You and I will be attending a party at IVI on Saturday night."

"What party?"

"A dinner."

"Why?"

"You need to show your face. People are talking."

She raises her eyebrows. "Aren't you afraid they'll talk about you when they see me on your arm?"

I don't answer that. "I'll send a dress up for you."

"Fine. Whatever." She walks toward the exit but stops and turns back. "Did you know?"

"Know what?"

"That she's pregnant?"

After a long moment, I nod.

She snorts, then curls her lip in disgust and stalks off. I hear her slam her bedroom door, and I don't see her for the rest of the day. Which is a good thing because I can't seem to be around her without touching her. And she's right about what I want. What I imagine at night. And it needs to stop because no matter what, I cannot have her. Not the way I want. Not ever.

23

JUDGE

Paolo has been working for my family for a long time. I know exactly the outbuilding he spoke of and why he mentioned it. And I know Mercedes well enough to know if she's told she can't do something, she will do just that. It's her nature, and I need to protect her from herself.

I walk through the woods to the building. I want to be sure myself that she can't get in there. How did she even find it? It's a hike from the house.

The property contains several stone structures. The cellar I'd put Ivy in is one. They were primarily used for storage in the past, but my grandfather had converted this particular one for his personal use. I'd been there a time or two while growing up. We all have, my mother included. It's not a place you ever wanted to be summoned to.

My father was a kind man. The only offspring of

Carlisle Montgomery after too many miscarriages to count. But he was a disappointment to my grandfather. Too weak. Too little like him.

My mother, Margot Hawkins, was an only child. The daughter of a low-ranking Society member. The men of her family were not Sovereign Sons. My grandfather arranging a marriage between Margot and my father was a boon to Margot's father. She would marry a Montgomery. A Sovereign Son for his lowly daughter. It was higher than he'd ever have thought to strive. They married quickly, and when they produced the first male heir—me—Grandfather knew he'd done the right thing.

Then Theron came along, and my grandfather had all he required of my father. Two sons. No daughters necessary. If anything happened to me, Theron would slip into my place. And so my parents were told they would not have any more children. I wonder if it bothered my mother. She has always been a vain, selfish, and ambitious woman. A woman for whom Society life as the wife of a high-ranking member with its lunches and parties and money was all she needed. She's still the same today.

My father obeyed the decree laid down by my grandfather, but I know he wanted a large family. I think he even loved my mother. I can't say the same for her. I loved him, but I also knew he was weak. No match for a man like Carlisle Lawson Montgomery.

I have to pass my mother's cottage on my way to

this particular outbuilding, but I don't stop to see her. I still wonder if Grandfather gave her this cottage on purpose. A constant memory. When I get to the building, I take my phone out of my pocket and switch on the flashlight. I don't hesitate to enter even though it's been a long time since I've been here.

The building is made of stone. It's an older, simpler structure than the cottages though it's just as sturdy and possibly more so. The entrance to the room itself is set farther back, and I shine my flashlight along the walls as I make my way toward it, wondering what Mercedes thought of it as she walked in. How deep did she go? The natural light fades quickly to pitch black, and without a flashlight, you'd be walking blind. I can't imagine she wasn't afraid.

My steps echo off the stone floor and walls as the passage grows narrow for several minutes, then, unexpectedly, it opens up again, the ceiling higher as I reach the closed door.

I test it and confirm it's locked just as Paolo said. Good. Even if she'd gotten this far, which I doubt, she wouldn't have gotten past the lock.

From inside my pocket, I retrieve the key. My heart thuds against my chest as I hold it, feel the weight of it. I inherited this, too, along with everything else. To continue the tradition with my own family, I guess. What does it say about me that I haven't burned it to the ground?

I slip the key into the lock and turn it, that sound, too, echoing. Although I think it's in my head. Memory. The very real panic some memories elicit.

I touch my forehead and wipe the sweat that's broken out. Then I chastise myself mentally for my weakness as I open the door.

For one terrifying moment, it's as though he was just here. As though I am a boy in this room again. I can still smell his cigars and the leather of his boots and his whips. It all clings to this place, making it hard to breathe. I enter and switch on the light. The room is wired for electricity even though the entrance isn't. The bulb flickers from lack of use, but a moment later, a cold, unforgiving light washes over the space.

I close the door behind me and slip my phone into my pocket, taking a moment. Needing that time to remember that it was the past. He's gone. Dead and buried. We all survived. Well, almost all of us.

With a deep sigh, I open my eyes. It's a simple room. Cold. I remember how cold it always was at first as we shivered before we were even told to strip but how quickly it would grow too warm. How had I forgotten that? I go straight to the cabinet where he kept the scotch. The bottle he never got to finish is half-full. I drink a healthy swallow, then another, right from the bottle before capping it. I wipe my mouth with the back of my hand and look around the room. It's all the same. Everything is in its place. My grandfather's leather wingback chair and the small table beside it are both covered in dust. As is all the other furniture. The tools of his punishments. I never got rid of anything. I just locked it up and should probably have thrown away the key.

My father was the only one to escape his wrath. The rest of us, even my mother, even well into adulthood and married herself, submitted to him. To his rage. And what he did to her when he learned the truth about Theron, it turns my stomach to remember it.

He made me watch, though. Made me bear witness. To teach me that no one can be trusted. That all women are whores, including my mother. That weak men deserve their fate.

And then he made me choose. I was sixteen at the time. Theron fifteen. Theron didn't know about the beating our mother endured. Didn't know that my grandfather knew something about him that he would later use as a weapon. I didn't understand that part, not then.

I think back then, my mother thought that through her submission she paid the price for herself and Theron. Misguided, really. She should have known better.

It's how I recognized the marks on Mercedes. My grandfather lost control punishing my mother.

Someone lost control punishing Mercedes. I see the panic in her eyes now and again if I move too swiftly or raise my hand in a way that she interprets wrongly.

My grandfather had never beaten Theron or me to the point he beat my mother that night. He punished us thoroughly but never like he did her. And I know he punished my grandmother ruthlessly too. I remember her weeping. I can hear it still. Maybe it's just that he hated women.

I still wonder whether my grandmother's death was truly an accident.

But the night I learned the truth about my brother, I made a choice. I pledged allegiance to my grandfather. My mother was punished, then banished to one of the cottages. My father was sent away on business he would never return from. My father didn't protect her from him. When he learned the truth about Theron, he betrayed her to my grandfather. I don't think he realized what my grandfather would do. What he was capable of. I think he was just so fucking terrified of him that he was no longer a man.

I pick up one of the canes. My grandfather's preferred one. It's worn from use. I still remember its bite. We were raised in a similar fashion as many within The Society are. But Carlisle Lawson Montgomery was meaner than most. And what scares me is how many traits I share with my grandfather. How like him I am. Everyone says it, too, even my mother. But I suppose her hate of me is warranted since I chose him over her.

My phone vibrates in my pocket. I draw it out, grateful for the interruption. It's a text from the private investigator I hired. He just emailed me a file.

I reply with a thanks and walk out of that room, switching out the light and thinking I should put a padlock on the door to be doubly sure Mercedes never gets in here. I head back into the forest, grateful for the fresh air, and return to the house, glancing up at Mercedes's window. The light is on, and she's standing there watching me. She wouldn't know where I was. But I do wonder if she'll do as she's told and stay away from that outbuilding. It will force my hand if she doesn't. The thought of stripping her bare and punishing her has its usual effect on my cock. And this is the very reason I can't touch her. Can't have her. It's not because I'm afraid. It's to keep her safe from the beast within.

24

JUDGE

I enter Mercedes's room on Saturday evening to find her applying the last of her makeup. Her signature crimson lipstick. The makeup is just for tonight. It will be removed from her room once we're gone.

Her back is to me, and I see how the dress drapes to just the right length to hide any scars. Only the unblemished skin of her back is exposed. Her hair is pulled up, and I can see the IVI tattoo, and the empty space above it where her eventual husband's mark will be placed.

I can't think about that, though.

Mercedes's eyes are on me in the reflection. She knew I was watching and waited, letting me. "Too much?" she asks, standing to her full height.

She's stunning. Black hair swept high, one tendril left to be tucked flirtatiously behind her ear.

Skin glowing. Eyes lined heavily. The scarlet dress hugs her the way it was made to. She has brushed gold dust on her shoulders and at the deep V between her breasts that allows for a glimpse of their fullness, but it's unnecessary. She's already too beautiful. Too alluring.

"My eyes are up here, Judge."

I look up to find her grinning like she's amused. The old Mercedes De La Rosa will make an appearance tonight. All her armor is in place. I had worried about her going back to a Society event, but I know now I don't need to be. She will dominate.

"Not too much, no," I start, taking her arm and tucking it into mine. "Stunning. But you already know that."

"I do, but I love hearing it." She smiles wide, and I walk her out of the room.

"Vanity is not an attractive trait."

"Neither is cowardice."

I help her into the back of the Rolls, and Raul drives toward the compound. "Are we back to that?"

She turns to me, eyes calculating, and I remember what she'd said in the beginning. How she could have any man she wanted. Any time.

I had no doubt then. I have no doubt now.

"It's just that if you can't be honest with yourself, well, it's cowardly, don't you think? All the *why are you here, Mercedes*," she says, mimicking me, "when you can't admit to yourself what you truly want."

"Your pussy."

"Exactly. My pussy."

I lean toward her to whisper the next part. "Thing is, I do want it, little monster. I'd love to feel that tight virgin cunt of yours squeezing my cock."

Her mouth falls open at my inelegant response.

I straighten, victorious. "But one of us has to be the adult here. Think of what's best for the little monster."

"Stop calling me that!"

"What's the matter? Have I ruffled your feathers?"

"Fuck off." She folds her arms and turns to look out the window.

I chuckle as we pull in through the compound entrance where cars are already lined up, dozens of elegantly dressed men and women mingling in the courtyard.

I climb out of the car and extend my hand. "Shall we?"

She places hers inside mine. "Let's." She smiles wide, putting on the mask she reserves for Society events. The socialite. The wealthy, gorgeous young woman who hasn't a care in the world. It must be exhausting.

I slip a hand to her lower back and don't miss the looks we're getting as I lean close to her ear. "Ivy will be here tonight. I expect you to behave. Or else."

She stops and looks up at me. "Is that why you

brought me? A repeat of my punishment with Miriam?"

My jaw tenses. Does she see it? "On the contrary. She has agreed to come to show her support of you. She doesn't want you going before The Tribunal any more than I do."

Her face loses some of its color then, and I rub a circle into her lower back.

"It won't come to that," I say.

"How can you know that?" she asks, looking up at me, that vulnerable girl beneath the armored woman before my eyes.

"I will make certain of it. I promise, little monster. I will protect you."

She looks momentarily confused, but before she can comment, we're interrupted. As soon as we enter the ballroom, Mercedes shines brighter than the chandeliers, the center of attention, laughing, telling stories, being the Mercedes they all know and love to hate.

It's a little while later when Santiago walks in with Ivy. I know Mercedes has been watching for them, and I hear the small pause in her speech when she sees them. No one else would notice it, though. She's quick to recover.

"If you'll excuse us," I say to the group and take Mercedes's elbow to lead her toward Ivy and Santiago, giving Ivy a moment as she realizes who I am. In the time I kept her in that cellar, she never saw my face. But she did hear my voice. And I'm sure she's memorized my walk, my posture. I know the moment she recognizes me from her body language. She stiffens and all but turns to leave when Santiago stops her. Her expression is one of horror as he talks to her, whispering in her ear. I can imagine what he's saying. And when we get to them, I nod in greeting to her only to watch Santiago draw her closer when she stutters an attempt at a greeting.

"Well, well," Mercedes says, a wide grin on her face, drink in hand. Her gaze drops to Ivy's stomach before meeting her eyes, and I am sure both Ivy and Santiago see her disdain.

I squeeze her elbow.

"Santi," Mercedes says. "So nice to see you two out and about together, a little family in the making." She swallows what's left in her glass, sets it on a passing server's tray, grabs a full flute, and brings it to her lips.

"Easy," I tell her. I think she'd knock the drink back if she could.

Councillor Hildebrand's secretary approaches us then. I try to remember his name but fail. We greet him, and he asks for a moment with Santiago and me.

"Do you ladies think you can behave yourselves for five minutes?" I ask. This is as good a time as any to see if my little monster can do it.

I get the feeling the answer is no when Mercedes,

beaming, takes Ivy's hand. "Don't worry about us. We'll catch up." I give her a warning look she ignores and turns to walk Ivy to a private sitting area. Santiago and I both watch the women as the secretary discusses what he came to tell us. A trivial matter.

The women speak for a few moments, and Ivy tries to disengage herself, rising halfway but then sitting back down. I don't miss Mercedes's bloodred nails on the other woman's thigh. Someone Mercedes knows walks by. One of her circle whose name I don't know. Mercedes greets her, then returns her attention to Ivy while wearing a frosty smile as they speak.

"If I were a fly on the wall," Santiago says.

"I can probably take a guess at what is being said."

"Sadly, so can I."

They speak some more, and finally, Ivy, forgetting or not caring she's in public, shoves Mercedes's arm off and stands. She only gets about two steps in before whatever Mercedes says stops her, and Santiago and I move just a little closer. Close enough to catch enough of the words that will condemn Mercedes to her fate tonight.

"In nine months' time, I'll be back in my rightful place," Mercedes hisses.

"What did you say?"

"Or eight months, I guess?" She sips from her drink.

"What are you talking about?"

She stands and walks toward Ivy, her approach that of a predator.

Santiago sighs in disappointment as we hear the rest of their conversation.

"What did you think? That you could steal my family from me?" Mercedes asks Ivy.

"I'm not stealing anything. Your brother made a choice. He chose me."

Mercedes pauses, then cocks her head to the side to study Ivy. And she laughs. "Oh, my God! I don't believe it. You're in love with him. You are seriously in love with him."

"I—"

"Well, poor, stupid Ivy," she says, leaning closer, twirling a strand of Ivy's hair around her forefinger. "He doesn't love you. He could never love you. Not after what your father did to him. To us."

Ivy's face pales.

"So enjoy your little victory for now. But remember what you are to him and what he needs you for. Once you give him his heir, it's bye-bye, Ivy."

25

MERCEDES

"Mercedes." Judge's voice is thick with warning as I try to pull away from him before we can even reach the car.

I know whatever punishment he has waiting for me at home won't be pleasant, and right now, in my tipsy state of mind, I'm questioning if I can actually outrun him. The answer comes when I do break away from his grasp and nearly topple face-first into the sidewalk. Judge's steely arm catches me from behind, hauling me back against him with little effort before he drags me back toward the Rolls Royce.

I resist him, trying like hell to pry him off me, but people are starting to stare, and humiliation burns me alive as I notice three familiar faces watching the scene unfold from the courtyard. Giordana, Dulce, and Vivien are all sipping from their flutes of champagne, their eyes glued to my face as they revel in my anguish. Those women are supposed to be my friends, but I can see now they never were. They made it obvious tonight when they didn't even bother to ask where I'd been for all this time. Concern for my welfare was nonexistent in our brief conversation, and it was plain to me that they'd enjoyed my absence. That bitter truth stings, but if I can be grateful for one thing, it's the indignation on Vivien's face.

She has always carried a torch for Judge. I doubt he even knows she exists, but I can recall vividly how she'd try to get his attention at social events. How she'd pine over his dark, handsome features and his powerful, dominant personality. She had delusional dreams of converting him from a perpetual bachelor to her husband someday, and I can see now that I've inadvertently ruined that for her.

Maybe it's my cold, black heart, or maybe it's the alcohol circulating in my bloodstream. Whatever it is makes me bold, and before I can overthink it, I thrust my palms against Judge's chest without warning, slamming him back against the car. He grunts in surprise, and I swallow that sound when I press my body against his and capture his lips with mine.

If there's one thing I know, it's that The Society is all about appearances. Not only will this little display leave my frenemies with something to gossip about for weeks but it will also turn things around in my favor. If they think I want to be with him... that this is some kind of fiery, dysfunctional relationship, then I will be lauded by every Society daughter for claiming the one man who's never dared to court anyone publicly. I'll be a goddamn legend, and Judge will have to face the consequences of my very public exhibition.

His friends will raise eyebrows. Every eligible woman will whisper our names. They will question his morals. They will look at him with certain judgment, and he will know what it's like to be on the receiving end for once.

Those are my best-laid plans. But when I drag my fingers through his hair and press my pelvis against his, feeling the length of his undeniably hard cock, Judge doesn't break away as quickly as I anticipate. Instead, he seems to almost... freeze, as if he can't help himself. He wants this, and that becomes ragingly evident when he groans into my mouth, his fingers clutching my hips possessively.

What started as a stunt evolves into something else, and my motives become background noise to the fire he stokes inside me when he deepens the kiss. I make a bold move, my tongue sweeping over his lips until he grants me entry and then sucks me inside with an agonized sound. I want to play that noise on repeat. I want to hear him make it again and again as he breaks every rule with me. But before I can make that happen, Judge seems to snap back to his senses. He pulls away on a ragged breath, his eyes darting around us before narrowing on me.

"You're playing a dangerous game here, little monster."

I smile up at him sweetly, and he drags me into the car, slamming my ass onto the leather seat and forcefully buckling me in. By the time he's got the door closed and plants himself next to me, I've already got my seat belt undone again.

I crawl onto his lap and grab his face, trying to take back control, snatching what I can't admit I want. I can see him battling with himself, torn between giving in and holding on to the rules that govern us. He keeps telling himself he won't ruin me, but I know he wants to, and more importantly, I want him to.

"Just give in," I whisper against his lips as he tries and fails to secure both my wrists in his grasp.

I yank one of them away and shove it down between us, cupping the bulge in his trousers before I drag my fingernails over it, making him shudder.

"I won't tell anyone."

"You just told everyone." He growls. "Fucking Christ, Mercedes. What were you thinking?"

"I'm thinking I want to feel your cock inside me," I murmur as I kiss my way along his jaw.

"You're drunk," he answers flatly as if that will stop this nonsense.

"And I'm wet, too." I reach for the hem of my dress, trying to drag it up, but his hand catches mine in an iron grip, and he shakes his head.

"No."

"No?" I taunt him. "What are you going to do about it?"

His eyes flash with what I'm certain are a few ideas, but I don't give him space to breathe life into them.

"Give me what I want, or I'll find someone who will."

"Like hell you will." He releases my arm to grab my jaw, branding me with the heat of his fingers. "Think long and hard before you make those kinds of threats. Because I have no problem ending any man who tries to touch you."

I think that's supposed to scare me, but all it does is make him even hotter right now.

"Give me what I want." I grind my hips against him. "Or so help me God, I will go up to my room tonight and finger myself so hard there will be nothing left of my virginity. Then when I'm lying in my marital bed, and my husband is fucking me with his hard cock—"

"Enough!" he roars, the blistering heat of his anger searing my lips. "You watch your goddamn mouth, Mercedes. I'm not going to tell you again."

"Is that an order, your honor?" I purr against him. "What will your verdict be if I don't?"

"You don't want to find out." He releases my hands to pry me off and put me back into my seat, but I squeeze my thighs around him and resist.

"You said it yourself." I stroke his erection with my palm, and his anger falters, eyes shuttering. "You're going to give me away to another man. You're going to hand me over yourself. Maybe I should invite you to stay for the wedding night so you can watch him fuck me. That will give you something to remember me by."

His lips curl into a cruel smile. "What a good idea, little monster. You know two can play that game, right? Perhaps I should take you to the Cat House, and you can watch me fuck my favorite courtesans all night long. Watch the way they kneel before my cock, worship it, and then swallow my come—"

"Fuck you." I shove against his chest, and this time, he captures me and hoists me back onto my side of the car without an ounce of gentility.

"That's what I thought," he murmurs darkly.

I turn to face the window, my jealousy eating me alive. I hate that he knows it. I hate that I don't know if he really means it. Just because he gave me his assurances once doesn't mean anything. There's nothing to stop him from going to the Cat House every night and partaking in whatever or whoever delights him. I have to assume if he hasn't been touching me, he must be getting his pleasure somewhere else. And even though I was the one to start this game, Judge quickly proved that he's always going to be the one to finish it. Because he has all the power, and I am merely a pawn.

The drive is tense and silent, and he doesn't try to change that. Not until we pull through the gate at his property and the driver delivers us to the front entrance.

"No." Judge clips out as I try to exit myself and make a dash for the house.

He grabs me by the arm, hauls me out, and leads me toward the stables.

"What are you doing? Leave me alone."

"What you did tonight with Ivy isn't going to fly." His voice is colder than I've ever heard it, and I suspect the anger behind it has nothing to do with Ivy at all, but rather the things that were said in the car.

"I hate her," I snarl. "Just like I hate you."

"Ten minutes ago, you wanted to climb on my dick," he reminds me in a biting tone. "And you don't hate Ivy. You proved that when you showed concern for her when I had her locked up in the cellar here. She's supposed to be your enemy, yet you felt sorry for her. That doesn't make you strong, Mercedes. It makes you weak."

"You're the fucking weak one!" I shove at him again, but it gets me nowhere. He's like a brick wall, and I've never seen him as closed off as he is right now. "Who are you to talk, Lawson fucking Montgomery? You think you're special just because you've been granted some bullshit title by IVI? Well, I have news for you... everyone thinks you're an asshole! That must be why even your own family doesn't come around. I've seen the photos in your study. I know you have a brother, but it's funny nobody ever mentions him. I guess he can't stand you either. What did you do to drive him away? It must have been—"

My words are cut off abruptly when he swings me around, and his hand whips toward my throat, cutting off the very breath from my lungs. I know I've made a grave mistake when I look into his eyes and see a fury unlike any I've ever witnessed in him.

"Don't ever presume to know anything about my goddamn family." He squeezes my throat tighter in his grasp, and I claw at his hands. "Do you understand? If you mention them again, I will unleash on you a pain unlike any you've ever known."

For the first time since I've known him, real terror streaks through me. I don't recognize this monster standing before me. I don't recognize this pulsing, living rage within him. He looks like someone else. Someone I don't want to know.

I try to speak, but nothing comes out, so I'm forced to nod, which is all I can do. Even still, Judge doesn't release me right away. His eyes are so dark, I can't even look at him. And it's only when I shed a very real tear that he finally lets me go, and I cough and sputter, trying to drag air into my lungs.

If I expected any sort of an apology, he makes it clear I'm not getting one when he leads me to the stables and opens one of the stall doors.

"Get in."

When I don't move, he drags me in by force, turning me in his unyielding arms and unzipping my dress before he starts to remove it.

Against my better judgment, I try to resist, but it's futile. I'm still trying to catch my breath and make sense of what the hell just happened. And whatever fight I put up, it's not enough. Within a minute, Judge has me stripped bare, my dress tossed out onto the stable floor like garbage. My bra goes next, and then he rips my lace thong apart with his bare hands before tossing that aside too.

There is no heat left in his gaze as it moves over me, assessing me like he's looking for weaknesses. It scares me, but not as much as when he shuts me inside alone, and his boots echo off the floor.

I'm standing there naked in the straw, trying to understand what's happening when he returns with an armful of riding tack that he tosses onto the ground beside him.

"Kneel," he commands.

I shake my head and try to dart around him, but he grabs a handful of my hair and halts me.

"Do not fuck with me." He breathes the words

into my ear. "I'm all out of patience as far as you're concerned, and you don't want to know what I'm truly capable of."

His threat sends fear skittering down my spine, and despite my mind screaming at me to run, he easily lowers me to the ground and shoves my face into the straw. He straddles my back, reaching for straps of leather and a bit, and my chest starts to heave with the force of the emotion I'm trying desperately to hold back.

It's a pointless exercise because when he pushes the metal bar between my lips and teeth, the humiliation stains my cheeks with more tears I can't hide. Next, he fashions the leather straps into a makeshift bridle, which he secures with a lead. And for his final piece of cruelty, he secures my arms behind my back with more leather, wrapping it around my wrists so many times there's no question I'll ever be able to get it off.

He doesn't say a word as he rises to his feet, leaving me helpless on the floor, the straw chafing against my bare skin.

"You'll be sleeping in here tonight." He spits the words out unmercifully as he secures the lead to the hook on the wall. "Perhaps tomorrow morning, I'll find you in a more agreeable mood."

And with that final blow, he leaves me.

I wanted to believe Judge was bluffing. I had convinced myself of it. He wasn't going to leave me like this all night. But after an hour passed, and then two, I started to lose hope.

My arms were numb, and my whole body ached from being pinned in this position. The bridle and bit weighted my head down, and I couldn't get comfortable, no matter what I did. At first, I stood and tried to move around, but the lead kept me from going too far. I could stand in one place, or I could lie down, but neither of those options did anything to ease the ever-increasing pain.

My shoulders burned as I tried to wiggle even an inch of space into the restraints at my wrists, but nothing I tried worked. When I inevitably collapsed onto the floor, that wasn't any better because now my entire body was scratched from the straw.

Tears sprang to my eyes as I considered that he really did plan to leave me here like this for eight hours. Possibly even more. And there was no way I could endure it.

So out of desperation, I tried everything I could think of to loosen my restraints. I rubbed them against the wooden edge of the wall post, but that only resulted in raw skin. I tried to pull them up far enough behind me to use the metal hook as a tool to untether them, but I wasn't tall enough for that. After another two hours passed, I began to cry in earnest. And then I had an idea.

I might not be able to get the restraints off my wrists, but I had a much better chance at severing the lead. It took me what I estimated to be another two hours to saw it against the edge of the wall, nearly strangling myself in the process. But eventually, the last little bit of leather broke free, and relief breathed new life into me. That relief was quickly swallowed by the realization that it had taken me much longer just to accomplish that.

Now, peeking out through the bars of the stall door, I can see the sun will probably be rising soon. Which means all my efforts may have been in vain. And then something occurs to me. Paolo often comes down here in the early mornings to check on the horses before I even get to the stables. I know because I've seen him here at times when I arrive.

Regardless, my mind is made up. No matter who comes through that door this morning, I'm getting the fuck out of here.

I sit quietly by the wall and wait, listening as the birds began to chirp and sunlight gradually spills into the stables. It's the weekend, which means Judge will probably sleep later than usual, and Paolo might not show up as early as I hope either. But just as I'm about to nod off from exhaustion, I hear the sound of his voice as he greets Temperance in the stall closest to the entrance.

I breathe a sigh of relief and crouch down,

kicking my bare foot against the wood to draw attention to the stall.

There's a moment of silence before Paolo calls out, "Is someone there?"

I kick again, careful not to make it too consistent, and then I hear his boots drawing closer as he investigates each stall before he gets to mine. He pauses then, and I hold my breath, trying to stay as still as possible. I know there's no way he can see me from where he's at, as high as the barred windows are.

Then it happens. I hear the lock disengaging before he starts to slide open the door from the outside. I don't think I've ever heard a sweeter sound.

When I jump up, it startles him, and his eyes are wide as saucers when he sees my naked form shoot past him. There's nothing I can do about that. Judge either didn't take that into consideration last night, or he truly doesn't care who sees me this way. Regardless, I can't think about it as my feet hit the solid floor beneath them, and I take off, sprinting as fast and hard as I can.

I hear Paolo mutter a curse from behind me, but he doesn't give chase. He doesn't dare. There's a small sliver of guilt in my chest as I consider that he might get in trouble for this, but I don't care. I can't care. I have to think of myself now since Judge has made it clear he won't.

I know it will only be a matter of time before Judge is alerted to the incident, and he'll give chase.

With the dogs sniffing out my trail, it probably won't take him long at all. But I'm not about to give up. I'm going to do everything in my power to escape, even if the odds are stacked against me.

I veer into the wooded area beside the stables, knowing it might be a fatal mistake. But at least there's cover and places to hide. If I tried to go to the front gate, I know my chances will go down to zero.

My throat burns and so do my muscles as my feet pound against the terrain as pebbles and branches tear into my flesh. It fucking hurts, but I try not to think about it. Worse yet is the bit gnashing against my teeth with every step. It only gets harder to carry myself as the seconds pass, and I start to slip around in the unfamiliar area.

Still, I keep going. I don't have a choice. I'll find someone to help me as soon as I'm beyond the property line. It's what I have to believe. It's the hope I'm clinging to when I spot a small, unfamiliar cottage in the distance. I've never seen it before, and panic wells up in my chest when I realize it might belong to one of the staff. As I'm considering it, I see the face of a man I don't recognize in the window, and my heartbeat quickens as I dash to the right, hoping by some small miracle he didn't actually see me.

In my distraction, I lose sight of my footing, stumble over a gnarled root, and go tumbling forward, right down into the creek bed. My knees hit the rocks first, and instinct has me trying to flail my arms, but they're locked behind me, and there's nothing to soften the blow as my torso tips forward and my face bounces off a rock in the cold water.

A gurgling noise escapes my mouth as I try to suck in air, but I can't. And I can't pull myself up against the weight of the current without the use of my arms. Darkness seeps into my vision, and my chest feels like it's going to explode as the horrific reality of my situation sinks in.

I'm going to fucking drown in two feet of water. Because of Judge. Because of what he did to me.

I try and fail to flip over, but I can't. The current is pushing me along the creek bed, my body battering against the edges of the rocks. It's happening too fast. Dizziness clouds over my mind, and tears prick my eyes as my lips part wider instinctively, still trying to draw in air.

But it isn't air I breathe.

It's water.

26

MERCEDES

The large, muscular arm yanks me against him, my head lolling into his chest as he carries me away. I cough, the sound weak, my lips numb, and I wonder if I'm dreaming. Did Judge get to me in time? Or did I actually die?

I don't want to accept the latter, and the only thing I can do is try to make sense of what's happening as I listen to a door open, and then a woman's shocked voice fills the space around me.

"What happened?"

"I don't know." The male voice echoes from above me, but it doesn't sound right because it isn't Judge.

That can't be right. I'm curled into him, too weak to put up a fight. But it doesn't matter because a moment later, he's draping me across something soft. A bed?

"Jesus." The woman's voice draws closer. "She looks like she's been beat to hell and back."

"Let me get these off you," the man says, turning me onto my side.

I'm so numb I don't realize he's undoing the restraints around my wrists until the blood starts to flow back into my hands, pricking my nerves so painfully I can't help but cry out.

Soft fingers brush against my face. "Shh... it's okay."

I want to believe him. I want to cling to any small bit of comfort I can right now.

"Please." I try to speak, but it comes out garbled.

"I know." He removes the leathers around my head and finally the bit from between my chattering teeth. "I'm going to get you warmed up. Can you go turn on the shower?"

I hear the sound of footsteps disappearing somewhere else and then the sound of water in another room. I try and fail to open my eyes as dizziness returns and makes me want to vomit.

"Who are you?" I ask.

There's a moment of quiet before the man answers. "Well, today, it looks like I'm your hero."

Before I can respond, he scoops me up into his arms, and this time, I notice he's not wearing a shirt. We're skin to skin as he carries me into the bathroom and steps beneath the hot spray of the shower.

I cry out in pain as it pelts against my cold skin,

and he adjusts it to a lower temperature, pinning me to his body with one unyielding arm.

"Better?" he asks.

I nod. He holds me against him for a few minutes, allowing the water to warm me and bring me back from the brink of what I'm certain was almost death. When I finally manage to open my eyes, I'm surprised to see the same man from the family portrait in Judge's study. The man I know to be his brother. He has dark features too. The same type of brutish handsomeness that manages to make my stomach flutter every time I look at Judge. But there's something slightly different about him. Something more uncivilized. More charming, but also... more dangerous, I think.

"You like what you see?" he teases as he notices my eyes roaming over him.

I try to laugh at the awkwardness of the situation, but it hurts too much. My lungs are still burning, and I think I must have coughed up water. I think he must have resuscitated me.

"Do you think you can try to stand?" he asks. "I'll help you get cleaned up so we can dress your wounds."

"Yes." My voice is too faint when I speak, but he hears it, nonetheless, and gingerly lowers me to my feet.

He keeps a firm hold on me until I prove that I can actually stand, and then he reaches for the bottle of soap. It occurs to me then that I'm completely naked, and how inappropriate this is, but I can't muster an ounce of modesty to care at the moment. I'm too weak to clean myself, and there's blood streaking down my legs and my stomach from where the skin has split. Not to mention all the cuts on my feet. And from the feel of it, I'm guessing my face is pretty banged up too.

It's a strange sort of intimacy to have with a stranger, letting them wash you this way. And Judge's brother is as meticulous as he seems to be, paying attention to every inch of skin his hands move over. When he pauses on the cuts and bruises, taking extra care with those, I almost burst into tears. Not because it hurts, even though it does, but because he's being kind to me.

"I can do that—" I protest when his fingers skate lower and lower, delving toward my inner thighs.

"Don't worry." He flashes me a charming smile. "I'll be a proper gentleman, Scout's Honor. But you have a cut just there."

He's touching my inner thigh when the sound of a door crashing open in the cottage startles me, making me jump. And then comes the thunderous voice I'd recognize anywhere.

"Where the fuck is she?"

I don't hear the woman's reply, but I sure as hell hear the footsteps echoing off the floor as Judge stalks into the bathroom. Instinctively, I draw closer to his brother, seeking out protection even though I don't know him. But it's a grave mistake, one I only realize when Judge appears, and his fiery gaze alights on the scene before him.

I'm completely naked, pressed against his brother's bare chest in the shower, his palm sliding precariously higher between my thighs.

"Theron." His eyes move between us as he snarls the words like a demon. "What the fuck are you doing?"

27

JUDGE

My brother is back. My fucking brother is back.

And between us, drawing closer to him, stands a very naked Mercedes. I'm about to lose my fucking mind.

"Get your fucking hands off her!"

Theron's eyes narrow, and the right side of his mouth quirks upward in that way of his. That way I'd almost forgotten but fuck if it all doesn't just come crashing back as if I just saw him yesterday. As if he just stabbed me in the fucking back yesterday.

He switches off the shower and raises his hands in mock surrender, a grin fully on his lips now.

"I don't see your mark on her," he says, making a point of looking Mercedes over and fuck me. Because she's pressed against him, her back to his chest, her bare ass against his thigh. At least he's still wearing his jeans.

"As if that would stop you," I blurt out, reaching for Mercedes, who slaps my arm away.

"Don't touch me!" she says, her voice hoarse.

Theron is still grinning, enjoying this little show. And behind us, I feel my mother's presence like a dark shadow.

"For fuck's sake." I grab a towel, reach into the shower stall and physically take Mercedes out, wrapping the towel around her shoulders and looking her over. "Did you do this to her?" I ask Theron, shifting my gaze over her head to him. Her face is bruised, cut in places. Her body too.

"No, asshole. I don't get off beating women."

I grit my jaw at his insinuation.

"That's your area," he adds more quietly as if I may not have gotten it the first time around. He reaches for a towel, and I notice the tattoo on his chest that wasn't there the last time I saw him. A hand holding a sword, the scales of justice balanced on either side. Justice. Consequence. The Montgomery coat of arms. Although it's not exactly right.

"I'll deal with you later," I tell him and turn to Mercedes, who is staring up at me with her bruised face. It twists something inside me to see her hurt. I draw a deep breath in, wrap the towel tight around her, and lift her in my arms.

"Put me down, you asshole!"

I tighten my grip in warning while my brother grins. He drops the towel after scrubbing his hair with it and unbuttons his soaked jeans.

"You don't have to go with him, sweetheart," he tells Mercedes. "Give me the word, and I'll take care of it."

He'll take care of it. Fucking unbelievable. I don't see him charging me to do battle and save the damsel in distress.

"You just stay right here," I tell him, and against Mercedes's protests, I carry her through the cottage, making sure my mother sees my displeasure at her latest betrayal.

Paolo is waiting outside with Kentucky Lightning saddled and ready. I was on my way to the stable this morning when he alerted me to the naked Mercedes who ran past him. He takes care to avert his gaze as I hoist Mercedes onto the saddle and then climb up behind her. He's discreet and respectful. My brother? He's a whole other story.

I slip my jacket from my shoulders and wrap it around Mercedes's. She tries to shrug it off, but I wrap one arm around her middle and tug her to me, clicking my tongue for the horse to move.

"I don't want your jacket! I don't want anything from you!"

I can't speak just yet. I'm too angry. Blindsided

really. Although I knew he'd come when I cut off his money. He'll want what he thinks is his due.

Theron, my dear, blackmailing, back-stabbing brother, is back. And he was in the shower with Mercedes with his fucking hand between her legs.

"You're hurting me," Mercedes finally says, and I feel her nails digging into my arm.

I look down, loosen my hold a little. Force a deep breath in. "What the fuck were you thinking?"

"I was thinking I needed to get away from the asshole sadist who trussed me up like a horse and left me to sleep in the stable all night!"

I take it in. I'm still trying to figure out what the hell just happened. Still processing Theron's reappearance. The sight of them together. His fucking hands on her. It's making me crazy.

"Jesus Christ, Mercedes."

"Jesus Christ yourself, you fucking asshole."

"Grow your vocabulary."

She flips me off.

We reach the house, and Miriam steps out of the kitchen door. Mercedes makes a sound of disgust as I dismount. I grab her around the waist to take her inside. Again, she protests, and the jacket slides off her, exposing her nakedness. I don't miss Miriam's smirk.

"Stop fighting me," I tell Mercedes.

"I will never stop fighting you."

"Then you will never stop losing."

I haul her over my shoulder and tug the towel down to cover her ass as I march her through the house and up to my bedroom, which is still dark with the drawn curtains. I lock the door and toss her onto the bed.

She grips the towel, but I take one corner and tug it out from around her. I look at her, all her scratches, the red, raw skin. The bruise on her forehead, the cut on her cheekbone. I take one wrist, turn it over to see how the skin looks like she's been dragging her arm over sandpaper. I shake my head, drop it, and notice the bruised, cut-up knees. The bottoms of her ruined feet.

I draw back, raking my hands into my hair. This woman will literally have me pulling my hair out.

"Get a good enough look at what you did?" She sits up, her body uncovered from me, soft and so fucking fragile.

"Did he touch you?"

"What?"

I lean toward her, setting my hands on either side of her. "Did my brother touch you?"

She grins. She doesn't back away. Never does, this one. Most women would. So would most men. But not Mercedes De La Rosa.

"If by touch you mean did he resuscitate me when I almost drowned, then yes. So we're talking mouth-to-mouth."

She licks her lips.

I growl. My hands become fists on the bed.

Her grin widens. "And then there's our shower. I mean, I was so weak I couldn't even clean myself. So he, well, you remember how it was when you cleaned me, right? I mean, it's a very intimate moment between a man and—"

My hand is around her throat just like last night. And just like then, her hands close over my forearm trying to pry me off. It's clear that what she sees terrifies her. It's only happened a few times before, but it has happened. And I know what she's looking at. The beast.

I loosen my grip as much as I am able. "Did he fucking touch you?"

"I can't breathe," she croaks out.

I let her go and turn away, go to the window where in the far distance I can see the smoke coming out of the chimney of my mother's cottage.

"He found me naked, bound, and facedown drowning in a fucking creek. He saved my life. You owe him a debt of gratitude because if I'd died..."

I spin on her and find her standing. "Don't fucking say that."

"Which part?"

Her throat is raw. I hear it, and I see all her bruises again, all the scratches, and the animal inside me finally yields to the protector. The beast you feed is the one that grows. Theron chose his beast five years ago. Have I chosen mine?

I sigh.

"Come, Mercedes. You're hurt."

I'm not sure if it's my words or my tone that stop her, but for once, she doesn't argue. I walk around the bed to the bathroom and run the water in the tub. Rolling up my sleeve, I check the temperature to make sure it's not too hot for her cuts but not too cool so it's not uncomfortable. Once I'm satisfied, I plug it and stand, drying my hands on a towel.

She comes into view at the door, still suspicious.

"I will wash his touch off you before I take care of your cuts and bruises."

"You hate him."

I don't answer that. It's obvious enough. "What were you thinking to run? I wouldn't harm you. Don't you know that? I will punish you, but I will never take it too far."

"Last night was too far."

"Last night wounded your pride."

"You lost your temper, Judge."

I am mute for a long moment. I hang my head because she's right. It happened last night. And again just a few moments ago. What would she do if she ever saw that punishment room? She'd run for the hills.

No, she'd run right into my brother's waiting arms.

"I don't like when that happens," she admits in a voice I don't hear often. "It scares me."

I look at her, close the space between us to brush her cheek with the knuckles of one hand. "I won't lose control with you. I promise. Your scars... I'd never do that to you. Hurt you like that."

"But you already have."

Again, I'm struck mute. With a sigh, she brushes my arm off, then crosses to the tub and climbs in.

I will unpack that later. I can't right now. My head is still swimming, and she needs me. I strip off my shirt and toss it aside. What I mean to do is sit on the edge of the tub and clean her. It's my intention.

But she reaches to switch off the water and turns her gaze to me. The way she watches me, it's like she sees right through me. Her body is submerged, dark hair floating on the surface, her face so pretty, so overwhelmingly pretty, that I break my own rule again. I strip off my shoes and socks. My pants. She watches, holding her breath as I push my briefs off. Her eyes move to my cock, and I let her take it in before crossing to the tub and climbing in behind her.

She turns in my arms, water splashing onto the bathroom floor.

I hold her and push hair from her face. She straddles me, but I grip her hips.

"No."

She grunts her disapproval. "Yes."

I dig my fingers into her hips to halt her and force her to sit across from me.

"I don't care, Judge. I don't care if I'm pure."

"I do. And just to be very clear, my brother won't. You stay away from him. Now give me your foot."

She slides her foot provocatively along my thigh. I catch it and give her a look.

"Why do you hate him?"

"Sibling rivalry," I say, cleaning her, massaging her muscles as I do. She'd have been sore from the way I had her trussed up last night, but then adding what happened this morning, I'll take even more care.

"I'm sure he'll tell me if you don't."

I squeeze her ankle. She winces. "You won't ask him. You don't know what he's capable of. You will stay away from him. Am I clear?"

"I thought only sisters were jealous of each other."

"I'm not jealous of him."

"No, clearly."

I grit my teeth and concentrate on washing her, then drain the tub. I climb out to wrap a towel around my hips before helping her out, wrapping one around her shoulders to dry her. Even though my touch is light, I am aware of her every wince.

When I'm finished, I find the first-aid kit and a bottle of soothing arnica lotion, then guide her into the bedroom.

"Lie down on your stomach. I'll do your back first."

Mercedes makes a point of climbing onto the bed on all fours and looks over her shoulder at me.

I look. Of course I look. I'm a man. "If you know what's safe for you, you'll stop shaking your ass at me and behave."

"I've never wanted safe," she says and slowly lowers herself.

I adjust my cock. I should get dressed—at least put on a pair of pants—but I don't. And I don't want to think about why. Instead, I climb on the bed and straddle her thighs to massage lotion into her shoulders, her arms, and her back.

She moans as I make deep circles with my fingers all the way down over her ass before lifting off her to flip her onto her back. I settle on my knees between her legs and massage the lotion into her feet, bandaging the cuts as I go and bending each knee in turn to rub the ache out of her muscles. I'm very aware all along of how her pussy is right there, directly in my line of vision.

When I'm done with her legs, I lean over her to rub the arnica into her chest, her breasts. My dick dips between her thighs, and those moments it touches the wetness between her legs, I suck in a breath and grit my teeth. It takes all I have to hold back. She's wet, and I smell the sweet scent of her.

It's enough to kill me, never mind the dark heat in her eyes.

I cap the lotion set it aside, and watch her. She holds my gaze at first, but then hers falters, and she turns away.

"No, that won't do. Look at me," I tell her.

It takes her a minute, but she meets my eyes, her cheeks flushed.

"Good girl. Now put your hand between your legs."

"Judge—"

"Isn't this what you want?" When she doesn't answer, I continue. "Go on. Show me how you touch yourself."

She hesitates.

"Do it. And don't fucking look away from me when you do."

She swallows and does as she's told, her mouth opening, small white teeth biting her lower lip as she moves her fingers over herself. The sound of her wet pussy makes it hard for me to breathe.

"I want to watch you, too," she says.

"Have you ever watched a man?" I know the answer but seeing her shake her head somehow gets me even harder. "No one's ever touched you? Seen you like this?"

"Never."

"Good."

I lean over her, my cock in my fist, and kiss her

mouth. It's not a deep kiss. It's slow. She moans and closes her eyes when I take her lower lip between my teeth and suck before dipping my head to her chest, licking a path between her breasts, over her belly button to the slit of her sex, stopping there because I'm going to blow if I don't.

"Don't stop. Please. I need this so much."

I just want a taste. One taste.

I push her legs apart and take her hand away, then feast my eyes before bending her knees to lick her hole to hole. She moans, and when I take her clit into my mouth, she curls her fingers into my hair and arches her back.

"Oh, my God."

I remember she's never felt this before. Never had the tongue of a man on her. No one has tasted her but me, and fuck, is she sweet. Fuck if I don't want to devour her whole as my cock aches for release.

"I'm going to come," she says.

I lift my gaze to look at her as my mouth works over her clit. Mercedes arches her back, pulling handfuls of my hair as she moans my name and comes on my tongue, her orgasm drawn out, thighs tight around my neck. Her body collapses in exhaustion when it's over.

Her eyes grow dreamy and soft as she watches me wipe the back of my hand over my lips, then dip my fingers between her legs. She shudders, her body too sensitive after her orgasm, but I scoop up her wetness and rub it over myself, fisting my cock.

Mercedes climbs up onto her elbows, mouth open as if she's in awe as I pump. She looks up at me, then gets up on her knees and closes her hand over mine. I kiss her, and then with my hand around the back of her head, I guide her down and watch her as she takes me into her inexperienced mouth. Fuck, the sight of it, of her eyes looking up at me with her mouth full of me, it's enough to make me blow down her throat now.

I grip a handful of hair and guide her over me slowly, drawing it out because this will be the last time. I swear it. And I want to make it last. I pull her off, taking a moment to regain control of myself, then lay her onto her back and straddle her torso. She licks her lips and opens her mouth, and this woman, fuck, this woman. I am done for. She will ruin me.

She chokes when I push too deep, too fast and pushes against me.

"Relax," I tell her, giving her a moment to catch her breath but not pulling out fully because her tongue on my cock is doing things to me. "Just relax, little monster. Relax and take it. Because if you want to play this game with me, you'll need to learn to swallow my cock."

Her response is a deep moan.

I grip the footboard, and it takes all I have not to

fuck her face the way I want to, the way I would anyone else. But I have to go slow with her. As slow as any man can when she relaxes enough that I can guide myself down her throat, and I don't last long then. It feels too fucking good when we lock eyes, and she swallows me whole.

28

JUDGE

Guilt burns my gut.

One time has become two. And Mercedes is standing behind me now tracing the tattoo on my back, the broken sword with the elegantly drawn yet inelegant message *Crede Nemini*.

"Trust no one," she says, then finds the raised scar beneath.

I grab her wrist and turn to her.

"The sword is your coat of arms. Sword and scales."

"Finished?"

She looks down, gives me a half-grin, and runs her fingernails up along one thigh before cupping my dick, which is hard again.

I grip this wrist too, switch them into one hand. I turn off the water. "No."

Her forehead furrows. "Why not?"

I release her, then step out and grab a dry towel. I toss it to her. She catches it but looks affronted. I need to put distance between us. This is too fucking hard with her. I walk out of the bathroom and into my closet. She follows me, her towel wrapped around herself, and watches me pull on clothes.

"You know, you give a woman whiplash, Judge."

I exhale, slip my arms into my shirt, and turn to her. "This can't happen again. It shouldn't have happened this time."

"Well, it did. And who cares? We're adults. If we want to fuck, why can't we just fuck?"

"Mercedes." It comes out a groan. "You're a De La Rosa."

"And you're a fucking Montgomery. We're well matched."

That stops me. Takes me by surprise. I step toward her, and in a rare moment, she looks uncertain. "I won't marry, Mercedes. You know that, don't you?"

Blood rushes to her face, and she falters. "I'm not asking you to marry me. Just fuck me."

"No." I buckle my belt.

"Why won't you marry anyway?" she asks, following me when I leave the closet.

"That's personal."

"I just swallowed your come. I think we can get personal."

"Watch your mouth, all right? I don't think Santiago would appreciate you talking like that."

"I don't think Santiago would appreciate your dick down my throat."

"That's enough, sweetheart."

"That's what your brother called me."

"Fuck my brother."

"Besides, I thought I was your little monster."

I take her arms and lead her out of my room into the hallway, where the sun is almost too bright after the dark of my bedroom. As if out here, we're exposed. Our dirty little secret is out in the open.

There's movement at the end of the hall, and I spy Miriam disappearing into one of the empty guest rooms. I don't bother with her, though. Now isn't the time although given what I've learned, she'll need to be dealt with. Instead, I march Mercedes into her bedroom.

"Get dressed. Then go downstairs and have breakfast. And after that, return to this room and read or do yoga or whatever it is you do but do not leave this room until I come for you."

"Whatever it is I do? You're such a fucking jerk, you know that?"

"Do you hear me?"

"So I'm sent to my room again like an errant child? Why? What did I do?"

"Do I need to ask Miriam to lock the door after breakfast?"

She exhales. "Just go do whatever it is you do if you're so desperate to be away from me. Maybe Theron will appreciate my company—"

I back her into a corner and slam a hand against the wall. She jumps.

"I forbid you to seek out my brother."

"You forbid me?"

"I forbid you. Am I clear?"

"I haven't been forbidden to do something since my father passed away. I won't be forbidden by you."

"He's dangerous, Mercedes. Stay away from him."

"The only danger is you, Judge."

I blink, draw in too thin air. When Mercedes and I come together, it's like fire and ice. A battle of wills. Two beasts with our jaws on each other's jugulars. For one to win, the other must lose, but what will the cost be?

"You don't want me. Why do you care if I see him or not?"

"It's not that I don't want you. I can't have you, Mercedes."

"Because you don't allow yourself."

I sigh. She won't understand. She can't. "I don't want to see you hurt, and he will hurt you."

"You're impossible. Your demands are impossible!"

"Enough!" She winces as if physically struck.

"You'll do as I say, or you'll face the consequences. Am I clear?"

"Yeah, you're fucking clear as mud."

I open my mouth but close it again and walk out the door, leaving her staring after me. Being exactly the jerk she accused me of being.

29

MERCEDES

Even though I'm not hungry, I eat a quick breakfast with Lois and trudge back to my room. A part of me wants to disobey Judge just to spite him, but the other part of me is too exhausted to put up a fight right now. I didn't sleep at all last night, and after everything that happened this morning, I can barely keep my eyes open.

Everything hurts, and my throat is so scratchy I don't want to talk to anyone. I need to rest. And then I need to figure out what the hell is wrong with me.

I always do this. I always swear I'm not going to forgive the people who hurt me. I'm not going to give them the opportunity to keep hurting me. But that's all I know, isn't it? Chaos and pain are the closest thing to love I've ever felt. It's what my father taught me. It's what my brothers taught me. And now, here I am, hating myself for letting Judge do the same to me.

I shouldn't have wanted him to touch me this morning. I should have held on to my anger. But the second he showed even a sliver of regret, a will to comfort me for even a moment, I clung to it like the life raft I so desperately needed.

I'm lonely. So fucking lonely. My heart is fragile, and it pains me to admit I need those glimpses of comfort from him, however fleeting they may be. Because for all his showmanship, his insistence that this fire between us can't be stoked, he can't hide the truth in his eyes. He doesn't just want this. He needs it as much as I do.

But it doesn't change anything. The lines have been drawn. I've humiliated myself trying to get his attention. I've offered my body to him on a silver platter, and I've done everything short of begging. Enough is enough. After this morning, there can be no question in my mind about where he stands.

He will use me, and then he will leave me cold. I need to have more respect for myself than that. I'll show him I'm worth more than that, whether he believes it or not.

Those are the thoughts waging war in my mind as I fall into a fitful sleep. When I wake again, it's far too soon, but the sight of Miriam lurking at the end of my bed drags me back to an abrupt consciousness as any dark cloud would.

"What are you doing in here?" I glare at her.

"Just bringing your riding gear." She smiles far too sweetly as she sets the laundry on the tufted bench.

"Why?" I study her skeptically.

She shrugs. "Judge said you might want to get some fresh air this afternoon."

Two conflicting thoughts enter my mind. The first is that Judge is thinking about me while he's at work, and the second is, why the hell is Miriam still standing here? Can I trust that what she's telling me is even true? But then again, why would she lie about something so stupid?

"Okay, you can go now." I shoo her away with my hands. "I don't need you to supervise."

"I've been instructed to tell you to be back by five o'clock if you go."

"Duly noted." I drag myself upright and breathe a sigh of relief when she finally turns and leaves. That woman gives me the creeps.

I'm still painfully sore and not entirely certain riding is even a good idea, but after I splash some cold water on my face and brush my teeth, I figure some fresh air might help get me out of this funk. I can take Temperance out today and go slow.

Every muscle in my body aches as I dress and force my bandaged feet into the riding boots. But even so, I have to admit they are beautiful. Judge has good taste.

Downstairs, Lois catches me before I walk out the door and asks me if I'd like some lunch. I decline the offer but tell her I will take the hounds for some exercise too. She smiles at the idea and calls them to the entrance to meet me. After a few moments of eager greetings, they join me on my walk to the stables.

Paolo is nowhere to be seen, thank God, because I don't think I could even look him in the eyes after this morning. But as I retrieve Temperance from her stall and begin to dress her, the hounds alert me to someone's presence with their barks.

I turn around, dreading an encounter with Paolo, but to my relief, it's another familiar face. Theron is leaning down to greet the dogs, his smile wide and easy.

"Miss me, boys?" He chuckles.

"I'd say so." I laugh as they nearly knock him over in their excitement.

He looks up at me then, not bothering to hide the way his eyes move over my body. "Feeling better, I hope?"

"Much better, thanks to you."

"I was happy to be of service to a lady in distress," he muses. "Feel free to find yourself in peril often. I will gladly come to your aid as I'm certain most men do."

I laugh for what feels like the first time in months. "Does that line actually work for you?"

"You'd be surprised." His eyes sparkle with mischief.

It's so strange, seeing such a stark difference between him and Judge. They share some of the same features. Some of the same traits and mannerisms, even. But where Judge is always serious, always brooding, Theron is too charming for his own good.

"I'm sure you maintain a very busy schedule rescuing distressed maidens," I reply. "Or perhaps, on occasion, you even do a little more to encourage their fall from grace."

His eyes flare at my bold comment, but he doesn't deny it.

"Guilty as charged. I'd be happy to provide the same service to you, should you wish it. Just say the word."

"What makes you think I haven't fallen from grace already?" I tease.

"You're a De La Rosa." He smirks. "A fine Society daughter who will go on to marry a fine Society man and breed fine Society children. That's how this works, right?"

"In theory," I agree. "But it doesn't appear it's worked out that way for you, exhibit A, a fine Society man."

Something dark flashes in his eyes then, but it happens so fast that I can't even be certain I saw it.

"What can I say?" He shrugs. "We can't all be the Lawson Montgomerys of the world."

"Thank God for that. I don't think the world could handle more than one of him."

He smiles, but it doesn't quite reach his eyes. It only proves that there is definitely some lingering tension between the two brothers, but regardless, Theron has done nothing to me. So whatever feud Judge has with him won't be one I take on myself without proof it's actually warranted.

"Are you coming or going?" Theron asks, eyeing the saddle beside me.

"Going. Although it will be a slow ride today. I'm still pretty sore."

"It sounds like you need a gentleman at your side." He walks over to help me lift the saddle. "You know, in case of emergency."

"But of course." My eyes widen in false horror. "I wouldn't dream of going out there alone, being such a fine Society daughter. Imagine what could happen to me. I hear there are rogues about."

"Indeed." Theron winks at me as he secures the saddle in place. "I hear the same."

"In that case, you're welcome to join me." I extend the invitation, fully aware Judge will probably lose his shit when he finds out. But until he can learn to consider my feelings, I have no desire to consider his.

"Just give me a moment, and I'll happily be at your service." He walks to the closet to grab some tack and then heads straight for Kentucky Lightning's stall.

Clearly, he and his brother like to fight over their toys. I don't imagine it will go over well with Judge when he finds out Theron has been on his horse, but it sends a small thrill through me to know it.

True to his word, it only takes Theron a few moments to saddle up. He helps me onto Temperance before swinging his large, muscular body up onto the stallion. Then just like Judge, he clicks his tongue, and we're off.

We head out into the open field at an easy gait, and I'm surprised at how well Theron handles Kentucky Lightning, though I don't know why. I suppose he often rode, too, growing up.

We fall into an effortless conversation, and I find myself answering his questions about my interests and hobbies without being guarded. He seems to take an eager interest in me, but I'm not naïve enough to believe it's not just for sport. I think Theron very much enjoys my attention and company, knowing how much it will displease Judge. On that, we are both of the same mind.

"What brought you back here?" I ask him as we return to the stables. "You must have been gone for quite some time. I haven't seen you at any IVI functions since I've been of age to attend."

His back stiffens ever so slightly at my question,

and I want to know why. But just like Judge, he chooses to remain vague.

"I thought it was time," he says. "I want to settle down. Find a beautiful wife. Get married."

He's eyeing me as if I'm a possibility for that role, and I can't help but think he's really laying it on thick. Regardless, I appreciate the distraction, and I'll be glad to use his attentions to my benefit when I flaunt them in front of Judge.

"Well, you shouldn't have a problem with that." I dismount Temperance and stretch out my back. "I'm sure every eligible Society daughter will be lining up to offer their hands to you once they hear the news."

"Perhaps." He dismounts and helps me remove the saddle from Temperance. "But I don't want just any eligible Society woman. I want the best."

His fingers brush against mine as he says it, and I know it's not an accident. When I turn to look up at him, he's closer than I'd expect, the heat of his chest brushing against my arm. He is, admittedly, very handsome. And I suspect he's also very much used to getting his way.

For a moment, when I look into his eyes, I wish I could fall for it. But there's one glaring problem. He doesn't smell like warm spices and leather. He doesn't make my heart beat harder when he looks at me. He doesn't make me so goddamned angry I could scream. In a nutshell, he isn't Judge.

"Come to dinner tonight." He reaches down and

brushes a strand of hair off my cheek.

"What?"

"Dinner," he repeats. "Didn't Judge tell you? We're all having dinner together this evening."

"Oh." Of course Judge didn't tell me. Why would he? "I don't know that he'd even allow it."

Theron smiles, the mischief returning to his eyes. "You don't look like the type of woman who allows a man to permit her anything."

I never thought I was either. Until Judge told me what to do. But Theron is right. I need to remember who I am.

"Thank you for the invitation." I smile at him graciously. "I'd love to join you."

"Oh, Mercedes." Judge's mother, Margot, greets me in the hall as soon as we enter the house, fussing over me as if we are old friends.

I find it odd, considering that we've only ever seen each other in passing at Society events, and she's never taken it upon herself to speak to me. But I suspect her demeanor probably has more to do with the familiar face standing behind her. I recognize the man immediately as one of the Councillors from The Tribunal, The Society's own court system. Within IVI, the members are governed by our own sets of laws and rules, and when there are consequences to be meted out, they are done so by The Tribunal. But The Society doesn't stop there. We also have influence in the outside world. Members like Judge, who work within the boundaries of our communities, using their connections to benefit IVI when it's needed. It's safe to say that IVI has infiltrated every sector of government, politics, law enforcement, and any other industry or organization they find beneficial. These are the people I rub elbows with often as a Society daughter. Typically, I wouldn't even blink twice at being in the presence of such a high-ranking official. But that was before.

Before the murder. Before the very thought of The Tribunal sent fear skittering down my spine. I've witnessed Hildebrand up on his dais, large and indomitable as he presided over Ivy's initial appearance after my brother's poisoning. Truth be told, I couldn't tell if he would sentence her to death then and there. He is a terrifying man, and I suppose it's the way most people feel about Judge. The difference is that Judge might punish me and make life temporarily unpleasant, but Hildebrand has the power to destroy me completely should he ever find out what I've done.

I swallow, hoping my nerves don't betray me. It isn't logical, but a part of me still worries he could already know something. That maybe Santiago hadn't cleaned up the mess I left behind entirely. I want a moment to gather my senses, so I force myself to smile and charm him the way I always do when I see a high-ranking man.

"Hello, Councillor Hildebrand. It's so nice to see you. I must offer my apologies for the informal dress. We just returned from a ride. If you'll excuse me, I can go up and change—"

"Nonsense." He waves off the suggestion. "You aren't in court, Ms. De La Rosa. I'm here for a meal and the pleasure of company this evening. Margot invited me last minute as well, and as you can see, I'm no better dressed than you."

He's being far too gracious, considering he's wearing a bespoke black suit that certainly has a designer label. But I don't dare argue with him, accepting that I'll have no choice but to attend dinner in my current clothes.

"Why don't we all have a drink while we wait for Judge," Margot suggests as she gestures to the sitting room.

There are murmurs of agreement before we follow her into the room, and I can't help but wonder what this is about or why she invited Hildebrand in the first place. I know he's akin to a colleague to Judge, and I've seen them speak at Society events before, but even so, it seems odd to invite him for dinner.

Margot goes out of her way to ensure Hildebrand's comfort, taking his drink order and then scurrying off to the kitchen to relay it to Miriam. We all take our seats as she does—Hildebrand in a large wing-backed chair and Theron and I on the loveseat opposite. Hildebrand observes us keenly, his eyes bouncing back and forth between us before they settle on me and the obvious bruise on my face.

"Is Judge treating you well while you're in his care?" he asks.

I force a smile. "Of course. Although, I can't say the same for his horses. I took a spill yesterday, as you can see. Luckily, Theron came to my rescue. He was the perfect gentleman."

"Well, you let me know if that changes." Hildebrand's tone is teasing, but his eyes aren't. "I hope your stay here won't be too long. It's high time one of our Sovereign Sons takes you off the market and makes a proper wife out of you."

"I already told her I was up for the task," Theron answers boldly.

I stare at him in disbelief, but Hildebrand actually laughs, cutting through some of the tension. That is until a dark shadow enters the room in the form of Judge. His eyes move to his brother first, and then to me, and it's clear he heard that remark. I smile up at him sweetly, aware he can't say a goddamn thing in front of Hildebrand.

"Councillor." Judge moves into the room, his body stiff, the tension radiating from him palpable. "I had no idea we'd have the pleasure of your company this evening."

"Your mother's idea," Hildebrand informs him. "I couldn't turn down the offer when I heard beef Wellington was on the menu. And I thought perhaps we could have a word after dinner anyway. I have a business matter I'd like to get your thoughts on."

"Of course." Judge offers him a polite smile, but I can see he's not pleased. And now I think I understand Margot's reason for inviting Hildebrand. He's the buffer for tonight.

Judge can't be rude to any of us while in his company. It works to my benefit, but I don't doubt it's just as much for Theron's too. He does seem rather pleased with himself as he leans into me, whispering in my ear.

"Don't worry, we'll find a way to liven up this evening somehow. I suspect copious amounts of alcohol should help."

There's no earthly way Judge could have any idea what he's saying to me, but his eyes narrow in on us as if he can. And then they move over my riding gear before noticing that Theron is wearing his too. It's impossible to miss his nostrils flaring before Margot enters the room with a flourish, Miriam carrying a tray behind her.

"One martini with a twist." Margot hands the drink to Hildebrand herself. "And Judge, I took the liberty of having Miriam pour you a scotch. I'm sure you've had a long day."

Judge glares at her as he takes the drink from her

hand, and then Miriam approaches the loveseat, her lips twisted in indignation that she's being forced to serve me.

"Your Riesling, Ms. De La Rosa."

I take the wineglass from her with amusement. "Thank you, Miriam. That was so kind of you."

She ignores me and hands Theron another glass of scotch.

Once we all have our drinks in hand, Margot takes on the role of hostess, engaging Hildebrand and Judge in conversation, forcing him to participate. They discuss Society business, reminisce on old cases, and debate the merits of the current education practices for the younger generations.

Meanwhile, Theron takes every opportunity to move closer to me, never missing the way Judge's eyes move to us when I laugh at one of his brother's jokes or offer him a coy response. At one point, Hildebrand makes a casual observation that Judge will have to keep me under close watch, lest Theron steal me away to the altar. If that wasn't enough to send Judge's temperature to the boiling point, Theron's reply that he's already picturing a spring wedding does the trick.

He's goading him, and it's so obvious, but Judge is letting it get to him. I can see it by the way he keeps tugging at the tie around his neck as if it's choking him. As if he'd like to remove it and strangle the very life from Theron himself. It pleases me far too much to see we're getting under his skin, so I take it up a notch when we head for the dinner table, continuing with the joke that seems to amuse Hildebrand so much.

"I told him he'd have to get in line. I have my choice of Sovereign Sons. So many fine men vying for my attention. How can a lady ever choose?"

Hildebrand snorts. "I would have to agree. You do seem to be a favorite among the bachelors. In fact, I can recall one man being so flustered by your presence he walked right into a wall and knocked himself out because he couldn't seem to drag his eyes away from you."

"Ah, yes." I laugh at the memory. "Poor Mikael. The funny thing is he never said a word to me. Too nervous, I suppose."

"You have that effect on men," Hildebrand remarks. "But don't let it sway you. Find yourself a partner who doesn't shake like a leaf in your presence. I'm of the belief one can only ever be satisfied with a match their equal. And you, Ms. De La Rosa, need a strong man beside you."

"On that, we can all agree." My eyes intentionally move to Theron as I offer him a flirtatious smile.

I don't have to look at Judge to feel his gaze on me. It's burning right through me.

"Pardon the interruption." Miriam and Lois enter the dining room together, carrying trays of food. "Dinner is served."

30

MERCEDES

The conversation continues throughout dinner, and Judge grows increasingly quiet as Theron and I participate in a quiet game of who can piss him off more. Throughout the evening, Theron grows bolder, resting his arm on the back of my chair to play with strands of my hair. Kissing my hand before he helps me up from the table. Spinning me around to show off the dance moves his mother taught him as a boy.

I soak up his attention, intentionally avoiding any glances at Judge, though I can feel his eyes on me. It's a dangerous line I'm tiptoeing, and I know I'm probably going to pay for it later. But right now, I'm going to enjoy every second of torturing him.

"How about we have that word in private now?" Hildebrand asks after he's finished his third martini. "It's getting late, and I don't want to keep you."

Judge turns his focus to us, and I already know what he's going to say. He's about to issue his order to go to my room, but Margot cuts him off.

"I'll keep Mercedes and Theron company," she says. "You men go talk shop. We won't disturb you."

"It's getting late," Judge says. "Mercedes needs to get to bed."

"Oh, let her socialize for a bit longer," Hildebrand chides him. "It's good for her. And you won't do anything untoward, will you, Theron?"

"I wouldn't dream of it." He feigns dismay at the idea.

"See." Hildebrand pats Judge on the back, leaving him no choice but to follow.

Not five minutes after they've gone, Margot conjures up a fake yawn. "I am getting tired myself. Perhaps I should get back to the cottage."

"Do you need me to escort you?" Theron asks.

"No, no. You stay and enjoy the company of this lovely young lady." She smiles as she says it, but something about her tone is off. I can't tell exactly what it is, but the way she's looking at me seems to betray that she doesn't think I'm lovely at all.

It hasn't escaped my notice that she's only interacted with me tonight when someone was watching her do so. As if she needs an audience to speak to me. The whole situation feels strange, and I'm honestly glad when she leaves. But then it's just Theron with me, and I'm realizing this game we've been playing might not be a game to him when he reaches over and touches my face.

"You really are beautiful," he murmurs.

"Thank you," I choke out.

"It's not just that, though, is it?" he asks.

"What do you mean?"

"That's not the reason men fawn all over you. You're beautiful, of course. And that's always the first thing people notice. But you're intelligent too. Cunning, even, I'd dare to say."

"Sly as a fox," I tease. "You'd know something about that, I think."

"Perhaps," he muses. "Maybe that's why we get along so well."

For a moment, the room falls silent with a strange sort of tension that wasn't there before, and I'm thinking I should probably excuse myself unless I really want Judge to beat my ass red.

"I can't stop thinking about this morning." Theron's voice is thick when he speaks. "How I washed you in the shower. The way your body felt beneath my hands. Tell me you've thought about it too."

I stare at him, trying to formulate a response. But before I can, he's leaning in. He's going to kiss me. And it shocks me so much I can't seem to move. I thought we were just playing, but now, he's actually going for it.

Instinct tells me to pull away, and I want to, but

I'm frozen. That is until someone grabs me from behind and yanks me off the couch.

"What the fuck do you think you're doing?" Judge snarls.

I don't know if the question is directed at Theron or me, but I can feel his rage pulsing through his veins as he traps me against his chest. My legs wobble as his dark voice vibrates against my ear.

"Upstairs. Now."

He releases me, and I go, not daring to glance at Theron. I don't know what he's going to say to him, but I know I don't want to be present for it.

I hurry along the hall, my feet aching with every step I take. It's only once I'm a short distance from my door that I realize how stupid it was to follow Judge's order. He's going to come in here. He's going to find me, and he's going to punish me. But before I can consider any alternate escape routes, I hear his footsteps thundering down the hall behind me.

"Shit, shit, shit," I whisper in a panic as I dart inside my room and slam the door shut behind me.

I know that's not going to stop him, and I seriously consider if I were to jump off the balcony if it would break something. But then I eye the bathroom, and in a last-ditch effort, I run for it. My bedroom door slams open just as I'm flinging the bathroom door shut, and I catch a glimpse of Judge's fury. It sends a wave of panic through me, and my fingers tremble as I engage the lock on the bathroom door and scurry backward, seeking out a place to hide. Before I find any, he uses the weight of his body like a battering ram to bust the door in.

I scream. He comes for me.

"Judge, please!" My voice breaks as he grabs me by the arm and drags me back into the bedroom, tossing me onto the bed with a grunt.

"Please, what?" he snarls. "This is what you wanted, isn't it?"

I'm shaking my head in denial, but we both know it's a lie.

"You went riding with him." He grabs my boot and yanks it off, tossing it onto the floor. "You went fucking riding with him today after I explicitly told you not to go near him."

If I had an answer to that, it gets lost as he tosses my other boot and then starts to yank at my pants. I try to scurry across the bed, but he just grabs me by the ankle and tugs me back to him.

"Tell me, Mercedes," he growls. "Tell me what you did with him."

"Nothing!" I pant. "Nothing, I swear!"

"Did you let him kiss you?" He rips my pants off and then splits my thong in two pieces with his fists. "Did you let him touch you?"

"No! We didn't do anything, I swear it."

"You're a goddamned liar." He grabs both halves of my shirt and yanks, sending buttons scattering before he pulls the fabric off me and tosses that aside too.

When it comes to my bra, I stop resisting, understanding that it's futile. A moment later, he's got me naked and flipped over, facedown on the pillow as he starts to whale on my ass with his palm.

"Tell me," he demands. "Tell me what you let him do."

"Nothing!" I cry out. "I didn't let him do anything."

"You think this is a fucking game." *Whack.* "It's not." *Whack.* "I'm not fucking playing." *Whack.*

I bite down on my lip and bear his brutal spankings with as much dignity as I can muster. This is what I wanted, wasn't it? His attention, good or bad. And right now, I don't even know if I remember the difference between the two.

"Is this for him or for me?"

I squeak in surprise when he stuffs two of his fingers into my pussy, feeling the arousal I can't hide.

"You," I whine. "It's always for you."

"I'm going to ask you one more time." He curls his fingers into me, and I moan against the pillow. "Did you let him touch you?"

"No." I move my hips against him, desperate for more.

There's a long, quiet pause, and then he mutters, "I don't fucking believe you."

Tears sting my eyes, and I'm terrified he's going to go. But then I hear the sound of his zipper, the shuffle of his clothes as he removes them. Relief fills my chest as I try to turn, ready to make it up to him. Ready to suck his cock the same way I did this morning. Except, this time, he puts a hand in the center of my back and growls.

"I can't even look at you."

He shoves my face back into the pillow and yanks my legs apart. And then I feel him, the warmth of his body as he eases his weight over me. His scent surrounds me as he drags his cock through my arousal, coating himself while he squeezes my sore ass cheek with his other hand.

"There's only one way to find out," he says, almost as if to himself.

I don't know what he means by that. Not until he leans forward and thrusts his cock all the way into me in one powerful stroke.

I scream from the shock of the intrusion, and he freezes on top of me, clearly getting the answer he wanted. I was still a virgin, but now that virgin blood is smeared on his cock.

"Good girl." His fingers move to the nape of my neck, stroking me there. That same empty space he likes to touch, as if he could imagine his crest imprinted on my skin. "That's a good girl, Mercedes."

My lip trembles under his praise, and I can't tell

what it's for. Is it for telling him the truth? Or not giving myself to Theron like he thought I had?

He moves then, palming my ass as he drags his cock back out an inch, groaning at the sight of what he just took from me.

"That's good," he murmurs again. "That's mine, little monster. All. Fucking. Mine."

The last words are barely audible, but I feel it in the way he touches me now. The way he leans his body over mine, rocking into me slowly as he eases the discomfort with soothing words whispered low. He feels so huge inside me. So deep. And I like it. I like it very much.

"Please, Judge," I beg.

"Shhh, I know." He brings one of his palms around to my front, massaging my breast while the other slides down to my clit. "I'll take care of you."

"Yes, please," I whine.

I want to ask him if he means always. If he means that I belong to him now. But those thoughts get lost as he starts to rub his fingers over my body, playing me like a master of his craft. The pressure intensifies as he starts to thrust into me in earnest, his hips colliding against my ass. It feels so intense I want to scream his name over and over, and when I do, it stirs him into a frenzy.

"Nobody else touches you this way," he grunts. "Tell me you understand."

"I do," I pant. "Just you. Only you."

He groans into my ear, kissing his way down my neck before he drags his teeth over the delicate skin. And that's what sends me over the edge. I cry out as I begin to convulse around him, and he holds me up, riding me harder, faster, his own body on the verge of giving out. Then with a thunderous roar, he drags his cock out of me at the last second, fisting it as he milks out his release, shooting his come across my back.

When it's over, the sound of our ragged breaths is all that remains, and I turn to look up at him. I'm half hopeful, half terrified of what I might see. Confusion flickers across his face as he glances down at the scene before him, as if he doesn't understand how it just happened. And then his eyes move to mine, and any warmth I felt from him evaporates.

"You got what you wanted," he says coldly as he rises to his feet and stares down at me. "You're a ruined woman now. Nobody will want to marry you. Not even Theron."

31

JUDGE

What have I done?

I take one last look at her half twisted on the bed, hair in tangles, face flushed, forehead beaded with sweat. On her back, the evidence of the beast within tearing its way to the surface. Staining her thighs and the once-white sheets is the undeniable truth of what I took. The one thing forbidden to me. The one woman.

"Jesus Christ."

"Judge?" she starts when I can finally drag my gaze from the mess I've made to look at her. To see her confusion.

Without a word, I walk out of her room, still fully naked, and into mine. I go into the bathroom and switch on the shower. While water steams from the shower stall, I look at my reflection in the mirror. Rake my hands through my hair.

What the fuck have I done?

I glance down at myself. See the smear of red on my dick, my thighs, my stomach. Her virgin blood. I took it. It wasn't mine to take, but I took it all the same.

And I don't know what I'm thinking as I step into the shower. It's not as though washing it off will erase it from having happened. It doesn't matter how hot the water is. How it scalds.

The beast rattles inside me as my mind replays what just happened. As I remember how wet she was when I dipped my cock inside her. How tight when I took her, breaking her seal with a single punishing thrust. She deserved to be punished. That I won't deny. But fuck, I lost control tonight. Coming home to see them like that. See my brother in my house and them sitting so fucking close together on the loveseat. Flirting. Fucking flirting right under my nose. When he casually twirled her hair at dinner, it took all I had not to leap across the table, tackle him to the ground and beat the shit out of him.

I have to give it to my mother. She's clever. Inviting Hildebrand. Knowing I wouldn't be able to do a damn thing with him present.

Distaste curls my lip. My mother is a manipulative bitch. The way she talked to Mercedes with that fake sweetness. She hates her—hates the entire family but her specifically, if only because she was born into her status. Born a De La Rosa. She hated

Mercedes's mother too, before she passed. Did Mercedes see that, or is she fooled? She's clever, too, Mercedes. She'll see through her. For her sake, I hope she does.

Margot Montgomery is a conniving, greedy, jealous woman. She's a puppet master in her own right. Now that Grandfather is dead and Theron is back, she's gained some backbone. She wants back into the house. She wants to rule.

Those things, however, will not be allowed.

I know her game. She has been patient. They both have. They knew the old man wouldn't live forever. And my fist is not so much made of iron as his was. At least it hasn't been. But that changes now. This instant.

She wants me to reinstate Theron in his rightful place within the family. Within The Society. Except that he has no rightful place. There is not a drop of Montgomery blood in him. But a marriage with a De La Rosa would take care of that. It would put him so fucking high on the ladder it would be impossible to topple him. I wonder if she realizes once he gets what he wants, he'll drop her. Because like his mother, my brother is just as vicious, as conniving as she is.

Rage burns inside me. I switch off the shower and step out to dry off. I pull on a pair of jeans, a sweater, and my riding boots. I comb my hair back with my fingers as I stalk out of my bedroom, but I'm unable to simply pass hers without a pause. Without listening for any sound. What I hear is the shower. She's washing me off her. As if that will do anything. Prove anything. Change anything.

I have taken her virginity. A part of her will always belong to me. Always.

I swallow hard and force myself to walk on.

In taking her, I have betrayed my best friend. The man who trusted me with his sister. Will he demand I marry her? I've ruined her for any other man of rank. She will fail any virginity test. I have ruined her for marriage within The Society. Period.

My steps pound as I hurry down the stairs, only glimpsing Miriam picking up our discarded glasses in the living room as I pass through the kitchen and out the back door. The full moon's light is ghostly but bright, a spotlight on my guilt.

I don't bother saddling Kentucky Lightning. I've told Paolo Theron is not to ride him. I've ordered another horse for my brother. The thought should give me pleasure. A mare half the size of my beast. It's his welcome home present. Because one thing I do know is that old adage to keep your friends close but your enemies closer. And Theron is my enemy.

After bridling Kentucky Lightning, I mount and ride to the small cottage. The punishment room is a black hole in my periphery when I pass it. Always there. Always holding on to memories I wish had never been made.

The ripped skin of my mother's back comes to mind. Grandfather was brutal in his punishment. If she'd been his by blood, would he have done it? I don't want to consider the answer to that. Is that why she hates me? Because I sided with him? I was a child. Or is it that she only has the capacity to love one of us, and Theron wins? Because he, like she, was hated by that man. And I was loved.

I wonder if either of them realizes what that love cost me. What it made me. A man with a temper to match his. But perhaps that is simply my nature. Like it was his.

Cigarette smoke wafts through the air as I dismount while Kentucky Lightning slows his pace. My beast and I know one another well. When I ride, we move as one.

"I don't allow smoking on the property," I tell Theron as he sucks on the last of his cigarette and drops it to the patio floor.

He looks casually at me, then stubs it out with the toe of his boot.

"Is that because of the old man? He smoked his cigars like a fucking chimney if I recall."

"Don't give me another reason to kick your ass out."

"Well, I'll try to keep your rule in mind, your honor." He nudges the cigarette butt off the patio and onto the forest floor. He grins at me, then hops down the steps to meet me. "Twice in one night. To what do I owe the pleasure? Don't tell me. Do you carry the news that the lady will have me?"

I step toward him. "You stay away from her."

He smiles. I'm a fucking fool. He read me like a book the instant he saw me with Mercedes. And he'll use this weakness against me.

"Why don't you claim her then? You can. She's your match. A De La Rosa. Imagine our houses united. The power." I don't respond, and he studies me. "Or is it that you think you might do to her what grandfather did to our grandmother?"

"She wasn't your grandmother."

"Low fucking blow, brother."

It was.

"What he did to our mother, then?"

"My reasons not to marry don't concern you. What does concern you is my warning. Keep away from her. She's young."

"Twenty-five is not a child."

"Inexperienced."

"Is she?" Arrogance turns the corners of his mouth upward. My brother is handsome. Disarmingly so. He can feign innocence so easily. "Still? Are you sure?"

Heat burns inside me, and I fist my hands, force it down. He doesn't know what I did. He can't.

"I mean, just the way she is so at ease with men. The way she looks. I'm sure she's had her fair share of willing partners. I just assumed she'd, you know, have taken a taste."

I shove him against one of the porch columns and hold him there with the flat of one hand against his chest.

"Watch yourself. You won't ruin her reputation."

"It's just you and me, brother. We're just talking. No one is ruining anyone. Seriously though. Why not marry her? You like her, obviously."

"What are we, children? I don't *like* her. She is mine within the context of the Rite. She is my responsibility. And as such, I will not have you spoil her." God, I'm a fucking hypocrite.

When I release him, he adjusts his shirtsleeves. "No worries, brother. As long as she doesn't allow it, I won't lay a finger on her."

"I mean it, Theron. You find yourself another Society girl if that's what you really want. Stay away from Mercedes De La Rosa."

"They are so fucking boring, though." He sighs deeply as if truly bothered by this. "I suppose I'll have to manage. Don't want to anger big brother. Is my room ready yet?"

"Your room?" I raise an eyebrow.

"At the house. Mom's great and all, but it's cramped." He gestures to the cottage behind him.

I study him. He won't be staying at the house. No fucking way. But I will keep him within my sight. "I'll have Paolo get you a key to the South Cottage."

"South Cottage? In case you haven't noticed, Judge, I'm not a cottage kind of man."

I shrug a shoulder and turn to walk away. "You can always get your own place off my land. Of course, you may need to get a job first." I mount the horse and look down at him. "You'll stay in the South Cottage. You will swear to keep away from Mercedes. You'll do as I say, and I'll reinstate your allowance."

"You'll reinstate my allowance. We're not children, remember. And fuck you."

"If it's beneath you to accept it, of course—"

"It's my due."

"I decide what is your due."

"For now."

"What the hell does that mean?"

He stares up at me, and it looks like he has something to say. But he bites it back, which is worrying in and of itself. Instead, he offers me his most charming smile. "South Cottage then. I'll send you an invite for my housewarming once it's inhabitable."

"I can't wait."

I click my tongue and turn to ride away, then pause and glance back at him. "Oh, and you won't ride Kentucky Lightning again. I've ordered you your own horse. My welcome home present. She'll be here bright and early tomorrow."

I don't bother waiting for his reply before I ride

back to the stable, where I take time tending to the horses. I'm hoping Mercedes will be asleep by the time I'm back, but as I near the house I see her light is on, and she's standing at the window. She can't see me, though. So I study her as she looks off into the distance while brushing out her long hair. And I swear I see a tear roll down her cheek.

But no, she wouldn't be crying. She got what she wanted tonight. She wouldn't be crying. She'd be celebrating.

32

JUDGE

I instruct Paolo to keep an eye on Theron as he moves out of my mother's cottage and into his own. Mercedes is on strict watch as well. Her freedom has been curbed, and I know she's pissed about it, but I don't trust Theron. She's left word with Lois that she needs to speak with me, but I haven't seen her in four weeks. I go to work early. Get home late. Long after everyone has gone to bed. Because I can't trust myself around her.

Paolo is one of the few people who knows what happened five years ago. He was here. Carried me to the car to drive me to the private clinic where my grandfather paid god knows what amount of money for my injuries to be treated. My life saved. Discreetly, of course.

I could have died in the back of the car. I wonder how he'd have covered that up.

His Rule

My secretary left a few hours ago, and although I should be home, I'm still here, holed up in my office. I drink a long sip of scotch as I remember how it happened. It was Theron's twenty-fifth birthday. The day he would have gained access to a large portion of his inheritance. My mother was at the house. That itself was rare. By then, my father was long gone. My grandfather had gone out of his way to prepare for the celebration.

Theron had sensed grandfather's distance, his dislike of him, for years by then. I'm sure of it. I'd known the truth since I was sixteen. Ten years. I hadn't realized what my grandfather was planning. I should have, maybe, but I didn't. Maybe I'd stupidly thought he wouldn't hold Theron responsible for his mother's actions. Or naïvely thought he'd loved him.

I'd been away at school a lot those years, and when not at school, I traveled quite a bit. Perhaps I'd have known how far things had deteriorated if I'd been home.

Lois had prepared a special meal, and the four of us ate it in near silence, the tension almost a tangible thing. The papers would be signed after dinner. The funds released by morning. I still remembered when it had been me the year before. I remember the exhilaration of it. Independence, true independence, for the first time.

After dinner was cleared, the cake was set in the center of the table, the papers laid out, a fountain pen purchased for the occasion that Theron would keep laid on top, uncapped. I still had mine.

My mother may have suspected. I remember how anxious she'd looked.

My grandfather was overly jovial. Not himself.

And then he did it. He gave his speech about family, about duty, about blood, and handed Theron the pen.

I still remember Theron's face before I couldn't look at it any longer. It makes me sick to this day to think of the extent of my grandfather's cruelty. Makes me sick to know he had a hand in creating the beast my brother has become.

Because as he read the words, as he saw the birth certificate naming his true biological father, as he saw the amount of money he would receive and the condition on which he'd receive it, I watched something snap in him. And as we stood there, a darkness surfaced from inside him. It expanded, touched the very edges of him.

Theron's eyes landed on me while my grandfather explained that his inheritance, since he wasn't truly blood, had been transferred to me. That he would receive a small portion of those funds with the agreement that he go away. That he leave the family. The grounds. The Society. That he'd be allowed to keep the name for the sake of appearances. And that he'd never show his face to my grandfather again.

But my grandfather miscalculated. He thought Theron weaker than he is. Thought he'd be easily bought. Manipulated. Cowed.

And before my eyes, my brother changed. As he watched me, he funneled his hate, and he became something different.

He never did sign anything. He came to me instead. He trusted me before that. We were supposed to be close.

I swallow the scotch in my glass as I force myself to remember what followed. As I remember when he asked me if I had known the truth. If I had known that he was a bastard.

I didn't have to say a word for him to see the answer on my face. And he just stared at me for such a long time before smiling that smile that I saw again last night. He hugged me. And he buried the knife that would have sliced his cake in my back.

A knock on my door startles me. I am jarred from my reverie, grateful and shaken at once.

"Judge."

Fuck.

I clear my throat and stand. "Enter."

Santiago opens the door, and for a moment, we remain facing one another in uneasy silence. I think of Mercedes. Of her beneath me. Of what I did.

"You're working late," he says. "I stopped by the house, but they told me you were here."

"I had to finish some things. Come in."

He does, closes the door behind him, and glances over the surface of my desk. "My sister's friends." He picks up the paper where Solana Lavigne and Georgie fucking Beaumont have taken out a full-page ad in a local paper asking if anyone's seen her. They know her as Mercedes Rosa at least. A slight difference from her real name. Enough to keep out of IVI? We'll see.

I hand him a scotch and take my seat behind my desk. "I'll take care of it."

"How?"

"Leave it to me."

"That's the thing, Judge." He swirls his scotch in his glass. "Something's gotten back to me, and I know the fucking rumor mill those Society ladies can be. But I need to make sure it's not true."

I clear my throat. Wait.

"You were seen kissing my sister the night of the party."

"Ah. Well, it wasn't quite like that. Mercedes was upset when I dragged her out of there. And her friends were watching."

"Go on." He drinks a sip of his scotch.

"She is impulsive."

He snorts. "Always has been. Too emotional for her own good. The kiss?" His posture is casual, but his gaze intense, and he doesn't take his eyes off me.

"She kissed me just as we reached the vehicle. I wasn't expecting it, so there was a moment when I can see how it may have been perceived as us kissing, but I can assure you it wasn't that. Those women were clearly relishing Mercedes's... predicament, and she decided to show them up."

He nods.

"So she kissed me in an effort to do exactly what's happened. Stir up the rumor mill to her advantage."

"So you didn't kiss her back?"

"No."

"And you explained it would not happen again."

"Yes."

He studies me. "Is there anything between you two? You need to tell me now if there is."

"I know my duty, Santiago." Fuck. God. I'm a piece of shit. "Mercedes is a beautiful, alluring woman, no doubt, but I know the rules."

"Good. She cannot be compromised."

"I know that."

"I've heard you haven't been to the Cat House."

"Well, not sure if you've also heard that Theron is back."

"Ah."

"Babysitting him has taken up much of my time."

"Why did he leave in the first place? Your brother? I never heard that story."

"Bad blood between him and Grandfather." It's true at least partially.

"And now that the old man is dead, he's back to take what he thinks is his due, am I right?"

"You are right."

"My sister will not become a part of that due, will she?"

"I've warned him to stay away from her, or he'll be cut off for good. Men like Theron answer to money. He'll do as he's told."

"Good." I'm not sure if my guilt has me imagining his gaze lingers overlong. "I will match Mercedes to a man deserving of her rank. A man who can handle her. Perhaps even tame her," he says, and I feel my gut clench. "But Theron is not that man. He cannot ruin her. As you said, she's impulsive."

"He will not touch her." Because I, the friend you trusted, already have.

"Good." He stands. "I need to get back to my wife. Good night, Judge."

"Good night."

33

JUDGE

It's three in the morning when I get home. I'm exhausted. I haven't slept much in the past two weeks what with trying to avoid Mercedes. The house is dark, and my footfalls quiet as I make my way down the hall to my bedroom. I glance at Mercedes's door like I do every time I walk past it, then open my own, wondering how she is doing. What she's thinking. How hurt she is by my refusal of her. Especially after what I did. What I took.

I close the door and switch on the light only to hear a gasp from my bed. I'm not sure who is more surprised, her or me, because Mercedes sits up, squinting into the sudden light, her hair a dark waterfall over her shoulders and her naked breasts.

"What the hell are you doing in here?" I set my briefcase down and stalk across the room to her.

She scratches her head and rubs her eyes. "I fell asleep. What time is it?"

"Time for you to go to your own room." I jerk the blanket off her, very aware that I'm taking my anger at myself out on her. But then I see she's naked, and it takes me a minute because fuck, I want her. I want to be inside her again. Hear her breathe my name. I want to hold her. Feel her warmth when I kiss her.

These weeks of avoiding her have done nothing to lessen my desire. And this is exactly why I can't be near her.

She stretches her arms over her head, back arcing, making her breasts jut out toward me. It's feline, the movement, and sensual as hell.

I take her arm and haul her up. She resists. "How did you get out of your room, Mercedes? And into mine?" Lois knows to lock it after she cleans, and Miriam should be locking Mercedes's bedroom door every night.

"Stop. Jesus. You're hurting me."

With a sigh, I let her go. She rubs her arm but doesn't cover herself, and my gaze sweeps over her, taking in the dark, hard nipples and her shaved sex. I scrub the scruff on my jaw, which needs shaving, and try to look away.

"What time is it?" she asks, glancing at the clock. She yawns, appearing at home. She clearly isn't having the same struggle I am.

I strip off my jacket and set it over the back of the chair, then unbutton my vest.

"Your brother paid me a visit tonight."

Her forehead furrows. "He came here? I didn't see him. Didn't he want to see me?"

"Not here," I lie, leaving out the part about him stopping by here first. "The office." I busy myself taking off the vest, undoing the buttons of my shirt, then remove the links from my cuffs and set them on the tabletop before taking off my shirt.

"Oh." I don't have to see her to know she's still hurt by the fact.

"He asked me about our kiss at the compound the night of the party."

She clenches her jaw, raises her chin, ever stubborn. "What did you tell him?"

"That you did it to skew the conversation from something embarrassing for you to something that would make all your little girlfriends jealous."

"They're not my friends."

"Not the point."

"Was he angry?"

"He was concerned."

"Well, he shouldn't be. I'm an adult. He gets to have his own life on his terms, and I want my own." She gets up out of the bed and comes to stand a few inches from me. "And I don't deserve how you're treating me. You've been punishing me for weeks because you're angry with yourself, and it's not fair."

"Life isn't fair."

"You think I don't know that. Me?"

I grit my jaw.

"You're supposed to be different, Judge."

"I'm a man, Mercedes. And you're fucking hard to resist, but I need to do just that. For both our sakes."

"No, you don't. Not for my sake."

She puts her hands on my chest, and I physically move her out of the way to walk into the bathroom, where I switch on the shower. Ice cold. I expect her to follow me in. She does but instead of coming into the stall, she just leans against the doorframe, watching me as I stand under the spray. When it's clear she won't go away, I switch off the water, step out, and dry off. She follows me into the bedroom, where I pull on a pair of pajama pants.

"What do you want out of this, Mercedes? You know I won't marry."

"Which is stupid."

"You don't know my reasons."

"Then tell them to me. Trust me with your secret. I won't hurt you with it."

I grit my teeth. I know that. I believe she has honest feelings for me. And she's right. I'm punishing her for my own shortcoming because I have feelings for her. And therein lies the crux of the problem.

I tilt my head to the side and narrow my gaze. I

need to end this. Now. And I'm going to have to hurt her to do it for her own sake. But before I get a chance to speak, she does.

"I'll even go first." She takes a deep breath in, clenches her hands, and steels herself. When she looks up at me, I see the child she was in her eyes. One who once trusted the world. "My father," she says, her chin trembling, voice a quiet breath.

"Your father what?" I ask tightly, seeing how the emotion of what she's trying to tell me is taking a physical toll on her.

She swallows hard. It's a long minute before she continues. "The scars. You wanted to know who did it. And I've never told anyone in the world. Only Antonia knows because she found me that night in the chapel. She's kept my secret even from Santi."

A lump forms in my throat. Something familiar. But for Mercedes to have endured something as brutal as the beating that left her scarred, it's just wrong. I have the urge to draw her to me and hold her. It takes all I have to keep my arms at my sides.

"How old were you?"

"Ten."

"Jesus."

"I wanted to stop playing the piano, and he basically told me I wasn't stopping. It's why I haven't played since he died. It's why playing here has meant so much."

I drop into the seat behind me and rake my hand through my hair. "Jesus fucking Christ."

Kneeling between my legs, she puts her hands on my knees and looks up at me. Fuck. She's so hopeful. So vulnerable.

"Now you tell me why you won't marry." I watch her little face and brush hair back from her forehead. How could he have done it? But isn't that what my grandfather did to my mother? She wasn't ten, though. Still. What he was capable of. What I know I'm capable of. Violence runs in our family. "That's how trust works, Judge. It's how it grows."

"I don't want to hurt you." She won't understand the meaning of these words and how deeply I mean them.

Mistrust hardens her eyes. Wipes away any trace of the vulnerable girl.

I get up, grab the pajama set she must have taken off and left on the foot of the bed, and drop it on the chair I just vacated.

"Get dressed and go to your room, Mercedes."

"What?"

I can't look at her. Jesus. I won't be able to do this if I have to see her.

"Judge." She's behind me and puts her hand on my shoulder. "No one has ever seen me the way you do. And I trusted you. Trust you. Shit. I don't know what tense that should be. Just please don't make that be a mistake. Don't make telling you a mistake."

Fuck. Fuck. Fuck.

I turn to face her, taking my shirt from the back of the chair and draping it over her shoulders since she won't put on her pajamas.

"Do you want to know why I'm so late, Mercedes?" My voice sounds foreign to me. The lie so clear. The wound I'm about to deal so final. So vile.

She shakes her head, and I'm not sure I've ever seen her as sad as I do at this moment.

I draw in a deep breath. "I was at the Cat House. It's where I've been practically every night since you got here."

For a moment, she looks like I've slapped her. "That's not true." She backs away a step. "You told me it wasn't true." Her voice sounds different too. Broken.

"I lied to you. You're very sweet. And lovely. And so very inexperienced." I go to her, touching her cheek.

She slaps my hand away. "I don't believe you!"

"It's true."

"I don't fucking believe you, you asshole!"

"I'm sorry, but I don't want you."

Hurt turns to something else. Something dark. Her lips curl in disgust, and the way she looks at me then is with pure hatred. She pushes my shirt off her shoulders as if she can't stand having it touch her, having any part of me touch her, and stalks toward me. She raises her arm and slaps me so hard my head snaps to the right. My cheek stings, and the sound of it is still reverberating in my head when I slowly turn back to her. The vulnerable girl is gone, and a broken thing in her place.

"I hate you. I hate you so much. And I will make you pay for humiliating me. Mark my fucking words. I. Will. Make. You. Pay."

With that, she spins on her heel and leaves my room, exactly like I wanted. Exactly.

34

MERCEDES

People like to say time heals all wounds, but it's a lie. Wounds don't heal. They fester inside you, turning everything rotten. I should know. Because I must be pretty fucking rotten to deserve the never-ending parade of betrayal that colors the landscape of my life.

It's been two weeks since Judge uttered his confession so callously and opened my eyes to the truth. I was foolish before. Naïve enough to believe we could have something. Stupid enough to believe I actually meant something to him. I clung to that desperate want in a hopeless situation. But I'm not the same woman now that I was then.

I'm completely and utterly broken. Empty. Emotionally bankrupt. Yet I'm wiser for the pain. Because I know now that Judge was right about one thing. You can't trust anyone. Especially him.

Tarring him with the same brush as the rest of The Society men would be too gracious. He's worse. His lies have shattered every ounce of trust I had in him. His betrayal and complete rejection of me have made me feel worthless, but that's what they want, isn't it? That's how these powerful men keep women in the tidy little cages they have designed for us.

Don't be too outspoken. Don't think for yourself. Don't dare have a sexual appetite before you're married. And if you do any of those things, then be prepared to face a reality you never wanted to see. You're disposable. If you break the mold, if you step outside of your tidy little cage, you'll no longer be granted a sugar-coated existence. It doesn't matter what your status is. It doesn't make a goddamned difference what your last name might be. If you break their rules, they'll find a way to break you.

I see it now. I can't unsee it. This is what my life will be like in The Society, no matter who I marry. Love and loyalty are the bullshit they spoon-feed us to keep us tame, but every woman knows there's no such thing. Men will be men, and women are expected to turn a blind eye. This is the false sense of security Society daughters cling to in their marriages. They busy their days with activities designed to make them feel as if they're important. As if they matter. All the while, their men disappear and only come home to sleep in their beds at night or grace them with the occasional appearance at an event.

I'm never going to be able to do that. I'll never feel okay with drowning in silence while my husband inevitably disgraces me behind my back at every opportunity. This might be the life I was born into, but it isn't the life I signed up for. And right now, more than anything, I want out.

Yet I know Judge will never let me go freely. This choice is not mine to make. He's imprisoned me in my room, not even allowing me out to clean the stables. Once a day, Lois comes to get me for lunch, but that's the extent of my freedom. I eat the rest of my meals alone. I sleep alone. I stare out the window... alone.

At times, I wonder if I brought this on myself. Because Judge warned me. Over and over, he warned me. He told me he wouldn't marry. He told me I didn't want to know him this way, and now I understand why. His words were clear, but it doesn't change what I feel. And I do feel... *too much*.

I wanted to believe I was simply seeking comfort from him. But the truth is, I wanted something that could never be. I didn't care about his warnings. I felt something with Judge I've never felt with anyone else in my life. There has always been a yearning there. One I've tried to ignore, tried to stifle. But it lived on, and he breathed life into it with every look, every touch, every moment of connection he offered, as rare as they may have been.

I can't put a label on what these feelings are. Not now. Maybe not ever. Because it doesn't matter how I feel. He's proven that, and it's time I grow the fuck up and start listening. He's shown me who he is, and now I have to accept it.

My heart is heavy with sadness as I sit by the window and contemplate what I have to do. The prospect of leaving everything I've ever known behind is terrifying, but the alternative is slowly dying inside if I don't.

It won't be easy. There's no doubt in my mind they'll try to drag me back. But Georgie and Solana will help me. They will harbor me until I can figure out how I'm going to survive in a world I've never really been a part of.

I spend a week putting the pieces together. Admittedly, a part of me still thinks Judge will come to me. He will knock on my door and tell me it's all a lie. He will find a way to prove he didn't willingly take a butcher knife to my heart. But I would die holding my breath if I was waiting for that to happen.

It's a Tuesday evening when the opportunity I've been waiting for finally arrives. I've thought of all my options, exhausting them completely, and the one I settled on is the one that hurts the most. Because it means I have to manipulate my only friend in this house to get what I need.

When Lois comes to deliver my dinner, I lie and tell her I'm not feeling well, complaining that I'm hot and nauseous. She takes pity on me, as I knew she would, and unlocks the smallest window, cracking it open to let some fresh air in. I thank her and pretend to go back to sleep, guilt eating at me as I consider that she might get in trouble for this too. But all I can hope is that Judge won't blame her.

I wait for a few minutes until the sound of her footsteps in the hall disappears entirely, and then I get to work, stripping my bedsheets and tying them together to fashion a makeshift aerial silk out of them. In my closet, I find an additional set of sheets that I use to supplement the length, and then I secure the knots with pillowcases, praying to the gods it will hold up.

As I tie one end to the foot of the armoire, I'm very aware of all the ways this could go wrong. But I don't care. If I die trying, then at least I can say I did something.

I wrap the sheet around my leg and pull my body through the narrow gap in the window, which is a challenge in itself. Lois probably assumed I'd be crazy to try to fit through there, but that's the benefit of being flexible. The fabric dangles beneath me as I pull it through my fingers and inch it closer to the ground below. Once

I've done that, I use it the same way I'd use my silks at class to shimmy down. I'm not afraid of heights, and I'm accustomed to being suspended in precarious positions. But the silks I use in class are more reliable than the knotted sheets I'm currently relying on.

The first knot begins to stretch under my weight, the fabric slowly giving way. I pick up my pace, moving faster, trying to narrow the distance between myself and the ground. The second knot starts to groan too, and then abruptly the whole design gives way, dropping me in a tangled mess of sheets before my body jars against the ground. The fall knocks the wind out of me, and when I stand, my ankle hurts like hell. But I don't care. I'm one step closer to freedom. And this time, I'm determined to get the hell out of here.

I dart across the lawn, hissing in pain as I head for the wooded area behind the house. I know where the property line is now, and I feel like I have a better idea of the areas to avoid. Unlike last time, I have no intention of going near the cottages, so I take the alternative route, the one that passes through the old outbuildings Judge warned me to stay away from.

I walk for about fifteen minutes, checking over my shoulder often to be sure I'm in the clear. My heart is pounding, and I can't help feeling like I'm being watched, though I'm sure it's just paranoia. That is until I hear a twig break somewhere in the distance.

"Shit," I mutter, glancing around frantically.

I don't see anyone else out here, but the hairs on the back of my neck are alerting me to impending danger, and I can't trust my vision. It's too dark to see much of anything other than the one familiar outbuilding up ahead.

Unwilling to risk being caught, I run toward it as quietly as I can manage, slipping into the darkness of the open space inside before I feel my way blindly to the locked door. The door that Judge made a point to block off.

I couldn't understand why at the time, and I'm surprised to find that when I jiggle the lock now, the jagged edges of the metal come apart, and it falls onto the floor.

It's been cut, I think. But why?

I freeze again when I hear something else. Then it goes silent, and I wonder if my mind is playing tricks on me. My fingers curl around the door handle, and uncertainty makes me pause. This could either be the worst place to hide or the best. The sound of another twig snapping makes the decision for me, and I tug the door open and slip inside.

It's pitch black and admittedly terrifying. I don't know where I am. I don't know what's in here. But I can smell the musty odor of dust and something else. Rust, maybe. Old metal and leather too.

It's an odd combination, and curiosity has me feeling my way around the room. I bump into a table, fingers moving over the splintered edges and then over the metal instruments on top. At first, I think maybe it's a gardening shed. These feel about the right size for garden tools. That is until my hand freezes on the unmistakable shape of a cane. I'd recognize that shape anywhere.

I'm trying to make sense of it when the door creaks open quietly, and I suck in a sharp breath, silently cursing my luck. I know it can't be Judge because he's not even home yet. But there's a good chance it's Paolo or possibly even Raul.

I stand completely still, hoping whoever it is can't hear me breathing. For a moment, I'm even convinced I pulled it off. Then a light flicks on overhead, blinding me.

I blink rapidly as my eyes adjust to the light, and my gaze locks on to a familiar face.

"Oh, my God, Theron," I murmur in relief. "You scared me."

"Did I?" There's a strange undercurrent of tension in his voice, and the amusement I'd expect to see is absent from his features.

"What are you doing here?" I glance over his shoulder, wondering how he even knew I was out here.

"You know, I've been asking myself that very same question since I returned." He slowly shuts the door behind him and seals us into the room together. "I thought I had a way back in with you, but

Judge ruined that for me. The same way he ruins everything."

There's a darkness in his eyes that makes my skin break out in a sweat, and for the first time since I've met him, I'm wondering if I can really trust him. He seems different tonight. More amped up. His pupils huge. Something's not right, and I don't like it.

"I'm sorry about Judge." I attempt to pacify him. "If he took it out on you—"

"Don't be sorry." Theron smiles, but it doesn't reach his eyes. "You can still help me. It just has to be a different way."

"I don't understand."

"No, I suppose you wouldn't." He sighs. "Truth be told, I would have gladly taken you for a wife. That could have solved both our problems. But Judge has never been one to let me have nice things. After all of his posturing, I suspect he's found a way to ruin that for me too."

"What are you talking about?" I try to back up a little, but I bump into the table.

"He fucked you, didn't he?" Theron spits the words out.

When my face blanches, it's obvious I don't have to answer. I already gave it away.

"I thought so." His eyes drift to the wall beside him, where there is a selection of leather whips and chains I didn't notice before.

My stomach lurches as he drags a finger over the length of one of the whips.

"No offense, Mercedes." He stares at the collection absently. "You're a very beautiful woman, but I'd never be able to enjoy my brother's leftovers as a wife. So now he's forced my hand, and I realize I'll have to use you in a different way."

"Theron, please," I choke on the words as I eye the door behind him. "I don't know what's going on with you and Judge, but it has nothing to do with me."

"That's where you're wrong." He looks at me, eyes shifting over me rapidly. "It has everything to do with you. It occurred to me during his display of barking and growling that he actually cares about you. And I have to say, it surprised me because Judge hasn't ever cared about anyone but himself."

"He doesn't," I protest. "I promise you he doesn't. He's proven that over and over again."

Theron simply shakes his head as if my argument is too weak to consider. "You don't know how long I've waited for an opportunity like this. I never even thought it possible, truly. But here you are. The one weakness Judge can't deny. What better way to destroy him than to aim where it will hurt the most."

"Theron, please..." My words die off as he pulls the whip from the wall and turns his attention to me.

Fear streaks through me as I shake my head violently, recalling the pain. The open flesh, the scars. I can't go through that again. I won't survive it. I'd rather die than feel that level of agony again.

"It could always be worse," he tells me. "You think I'm the monster, but you don't have any idea what he's truly capable of." Theron steps forward then, cracking the whip against his hand before he raises it into the air and lasers in on me. "I'm only sorry that it has to be you."

Instinct has me reaching for a weapon from the table. I don't even know what it is until I raise my arm and catch a glimpse of the long wooden paddle. It's heavy and awkward, and it brings back the memory of that fucking lamp. The lamp I smashed over the courtesan's head.

She died. And I don't want to go through that again. I don't want to kill Theron, but I know I'm past the point of pleading with him. Something in him has snapped. His darkness has taken over, a darkness I didn't even know lived in him.

"I don't want to hurt you." My lip trembles as I try to skirt around him, moving toward the wall. "Don't make me."

He snorts as if the thought is so amusing. As if I ever could.

"Look, if you want to get back at Judge, I can help you," I lie. "We can figure something—"

Crack.

The whip lashes out at me so fast I don't even

have time to react before it cuts into my wrist and the heavy paddle clatters to the floor.

A silent scream heaves from my lips as I try to run, but Theron captures me by the hair and yanks me back against him. I thrash and fight, trying to twist in his arms and get away, but he's not having it. He's not going to let me go, and he's so strong, I know I can't really hurt him. That's why he laughed at the very idea of it.

Hope is a dying ember, but I can't give up. I throw my head back into his chin, and he grunts before wrapping his hand around my throat and squeezing.

"Behave," he growls. "Don't make this harder than it has to be."

I claw at his hands, trying to drag air into my lungs as my vision darkens and real fear soaks into my veins, slowing everything. Gradually, I become too weak to fight. My slaps are sluggish, my body boneless, and I know when I start to collapse, I'm screwed.

Theron releases his hold on my throat, and I gasp for air, but my muscles have stopped cooperating. I fall into a useless heap on the floor, my need for oxygen greater than anything else. I can't even fight him as he drags me over to a leather bench and starts to rip at my clothes.

A solitary tear slides down my cheek as I shake

my head violently, but as I do, the room spins, and I nearly pass out again.

"You don't have to do this," I croak.

Theron discards my shirt, and then moves onto my pants, dragging them down over my hips along with my thong, leaving me completely bare. His knuckle caresses the length of my back as I try to get up again, and then he slams me back down with the weight of his palm. It knocks the wind out of me, and again, blackness threatens the edges of my vision.

"I know I don't have to, Mercedes." He leans down, his voice dark silk against my ear. "But I want to. And I'm going to enjoy every second of it."

THANK YOU

Thanks for reading *His Rule*. We hope you love Mercedes and Judge.

Their story continues in Her Rebellion available in all stores.

ALSO BY A. ZAVARELLI

Kingdom Fall

A Sovereign Sons Novel

The Society Trilogy

Requiem of the Soul

Reparation of Sin

Resurrection of the Heart

Ties that Bind Duet

Mine

His

Boston Underworld Series

Crow

Reaper

Ghost

Saint

Thief

Conor

Sin City Salvation Series

Confess

Convict

Bleeding Hearts Series

Echo

Stutter

Standalones

Stealing Cinderella

Beast

Pretty When She Cries

Tap Left

Hate Crush

For a complete list of books and audios, visit http://www.azavarelli.com/books

ALSO BY NATASHA KNIGHT

The Rite Trilogy

His Rule

Her Rebellion

Their Reign

The Devil's Pawn Duet

Devil's Pawn

Devil's Redemption

To Have and To Hold

With This Ring

I Thee Take

Stolen: Dante's Vow

The Society Trilogy

Requiem of the Soul

Reparation of Sin

Resurrection of the Heart

Dark Legacy Trilogy

Taken (Dark Legacy, Book 1)

Torn (Dark Legacy, Book 2)

Twisted (Dark Legacy, Book 3)

Unholy Union Duet

Unholy Union

Unholy Intent

Collateral Damage Duet

Collateral: an Arranged Marriage Mafia Romance

Damage: an Arranged Marriage Mafia Romance

Ties that Bind Duet

Mine

His

MacLeod Brothers

Devil's Bargain

Benedetti Mafia World

Salvatore: a Dark Mafia Romance

Dominic: a Dark Mafia Romance

Sergio: a Dark Mafia Romance

The Benedetti Brothers Box Set (Contains Salvatore, Dominic and Sergio)

Killian: a Dark Mafia Romance

Giovanni: a Dark Mafia Romance

The Amado Brothers

Dishonorable

Disgraced

Unhinged

Standalone Dark Romance

Descent

Deviant

Beautiful Liar

Retribution

Theirs To Take

Captive, Mine

Alpha

Given to the Savage

Taken by the Beast

Claimed by the Beast

Captive's Desire

Protective Custody

Amy's Strict Doctor

Taming Emma

Taming Megan

Taming Naia

Reclaiming Sophie

The Firefighter's Girl

Dangerous Defiance

Her Rogue Knight

Taught To Kneel

Tamed: the Roark Brothers Trilogy

ABOUT NATASHA KNIGHT

Natasha Knight is the *USA Today* Bestselling author of Romantic Suspense and Dark Romance Novels. She has sold over a million books and is translated into six languages. She currently lives in The Netherlands with her husband and two daughters and when she's not writing, she's walking in the woods listening to a book, sitting in a corner reading or off exploring the world as often as she can get away.

Write Natasha here: natasha@natasha-knight.com

NATASHA KNIGHT
sexy dark romance with heart

www.natasha-knight.com

ABOUT A. ZAVARELLI

A. Zavarelli is a USA Today and Amazon bestselling author of dark and contemporary romance.

When she's not putting her characters through hell, she can usually be found watching bizarre and twisted documentaries in the name of research.

She currently lives in the Northwest with her lumberjack and an entire brood of fur babies.

Want to stay up to date on Ashleigh and Natasha's releases? Sign up for our newsletters here: https://landing.mailerlite.com/webforms/landing/x3s0k6

Printed in Great Britain
by Amazon